We hope you enjoy this book. Please return or renew it by the due date.

11/22

You can renew it at www.norfolk.gov.uk/libraries or by using our free library app.

Otherwise you can phone 0344 800 8020 - please have your library card and PIN ready.

You can sign up for email reminders too.

NORFOLK ITEM

30129 087 732 880

NORFOLK COUNTY COUNCIL
LIBRARY AND INFORMATION SERVICE

About the Author

Born in 1956, Lorraine Fouchet has published over 20 novels, several of which are prizewinning international bestsellers. After a successful career in A&E in Paris, Lorraine now works for a division of the French Ministry of Culture that dedicates itself to the book trade.

LORRAINE FOUCHET

A Letter to Remember

Translated from the French by
Deniz Gulan

HODDER

First published in the French language as *Poste Restante à Locmaria* by Editions
Héloïse d'Ormesson in 2018

First published in Great Britain in 2022 by Hodder & Stoughton
An Hachette UK company

1

A CIP catalogue record for this title is available from the British Library

Paperback ISBN 978 1 399 70618 6
eBook ISBN 978 1 399 70619 3

Typeset in Plantin Light by Manipal Technologies Limited

Printed and bound in Great Britain by Clays Ltd, Elcograf S.p.A.

Hodder & Stoughton policy is to use papers that are natural, renewable
and recyclable products and made from wood grown in sustainable
forests. The logging and manufacturing processes are expected to
conform to the environmental regulations of the country of origin.

Hodder & Stoughton Ltd
Carmelite House
50 Victoria Embankment
London EC4Y 0DZ

www.hodder.co.uk

But now I know. Now I really know. Of one thing I am sure.
Love is a gift. Love is a gift.
("But Now I Know", performed by Jean Gabin, lyrics by
Philip Green)

For postmen and postwomen everywhere.

For those books which change your life; I hope you find yours.

*For the members of the Tonnerre (Thunder) family who live on
Groix Island and elsewhere. You have such a wonderful name
that I borrowed it for my characters.*

For you, Papa.

Rome, Piazza del Popolo, twenty-six years earlier

He glimpses her on the terrace of Caffe Rosati in the fierce summer-like April sun, sat there with just an espresso to keep her company. Since they got together, he can't bear to fall asleep, can't bear to be separated from her even when he dreams. She literally stole his heart. Today, she is wearing an orange dress, her favourite colour. He now sees life through an orange filter. Her hands are wrapped around her cup so sensually that he almost envies it.

The terrace is crowded; the other customers blur into insignificance alongside her beauty. Her legs are crossed, and her hair is tousled. He is the luckiest guy on earth: she loves him! He was brave enough to ask her to marry him, to dare to be happy together. They got married just last week and haven't yet had a chance to open their wedding gifts. They still haven't thanked Uncle Peppe for the ghastly lamp and Aunt Maria for that hideous picture they'll have to hang up when she visits. From now on, he'll wake up beside her every morning. How will he find the strength to tear himself away from her to go to work?

He is standing in front of the Chiesa degli Artisti, the artists' church. She looks up, sees him and flashes him a big warm smile. He has butterflies in his stomach and feels like he's lying on the beach basking in the glorious Mediterranean sun. Their life together promises to be just that, sunny and joyful. He can hardly believe his luck; she is his wife now; their initials are engraved on their wedding bands uniting them forever.

She waves to him, and her ring catches the light. Just a few more steps before he can take her in his arms. It's too early for Prosecco, they'll have some later on. It's her birthday, he hopes she'll like the surprise he has prepared for her. They are dining with friends tonight though he would rather spend the evening alone with her, between the sheets.

A song by Paolo Conte goes round and round in his head: "Via con me". *Come away with me*. He can already feel the softness of her body. He craves her perfume; he is just crazy about her. He hums the lyrics, *It's wonderful, it's wonderful, it's wonderful, I dream of you*. And doesn't see the yellow Vespa coming . . .

Suddenly, his beloved's face twists in sheer horror. She knocks over her cup as she jumps up. The coffee spills all over the table and onto the ground. In a fraction of a second, every detail flashes before his eyes. Just before the Vespa hits him and sends him flying. And he crashes to the ground of the eternal city.

He's not in pain, he's not scared, he's not cold. He can't feel a thing. He can't hear the scream of the driver as he falls, nor the crash of the Vespa as it smashes into a car, nor the screams of his young wife. He is unaware that she is rushing towards him, cupping his face in her hands, her wedding band gleaming in the sun. He can't smell or taste her tears. He has forgotten about her birthday present. The last words of the song spin round and round in his crushed brain, *It's wonderful, I dream of you* . . .

Then there is silence. The silence ignores the young woman weeping in the street in the April sun, a young woman for whom it will now always be winter.

Rome, on the banks of the Tiber river

My name is Chiara Ferrari, I am twenty-five years old. My family is comprised of four people, two of whom are still alive. My mother, whom I call by her first name, Livia; my father, who stupidly got himself killed before I was born; my grandmother, *nonna* Ornella, who was reunited with her son in heaven just last year; and my godmother, Viola, who is my mother's childhood friend. We never laugh at home; it would be disrespectful to my father who popped his clogs before I even came out of the womb.

What purpose does a father serve anyway? I didn't lose mine, I just never found him. I grew up in Rome, surrounded by framed photos of a young, sporty, funny, charming dad with a gleaming white smile. Every September when the schools went back and I had to fill out the emergency contact form, I would invent a new job for him. Policeman, fireman, lawyer, frogman, and even Swiss Guard at the Vatican, which was foolish of me as they only take unmarried men! When parents had to sign my homework, I only ever had my mother's initials. One year, I got sick of having a ghost for a father and wrote that my father raised me alone and that my mother was dead, which wasn't a complete lie. It caused a ruckus, and my mother was summoned to the school by the headmaster. For me I had just wanted to give my father credit where credit was due, and show everyone how much he meant to me.

I was saved by my best friend. Alessio is warm and protective, and has a loving mother. He too lost his father, so we've always had a lot in common.

Frankly, I would have preferred to have been put in an orphanage. Livia was so cold, and never hugged me because she couldn't hug her husband anymore. The only time she ever touched me was when she held my hand to cross the street. This was the only time we had any physical contact, though she immediately let go as soon as we got to the other side. She would back away if someone tried to kiss her. We were more like housemates than mother and daughter. She would drink grappa before going to bed alone. With a heavy heart and a twinge of guilt, I waited to grow up, leave home and console myself with grappa too.

Livia blamed me for not being sad about my father's death. But how could I be sad? I only ever knew him dead. "You're a wicked girl," she once said to me when I lit a candle on Dad's birthday and joyfully sang, *Happy Birthday to you!* It came from the heart. I had never heard him speak, never seen him move, all I knew of him was his silent, pearly white smile on glossy paper.

I can best describe his death as a blurred and melancholy presence, rather than an absence. Livia once told me she would have preferred to have him, rather than me. I don't blame her. After all, a husband takes you on holidays, he parks the car, he brings you flowers after work. He is of more use than a little girl, who has to be taken to school, the doctor, the dentist, and helped with her homework. Deep down, I knew what she meant. Me too, I would rather have had him than her. He was amazing. A guy who made it all the way to heaven a week after his wedding, run over by a Vespa while crossing the Piazza del Popolo. Now that's quite a feat. A record breaker; something to be proud of.

Being born in the country of close-knit, happy, loving families to a mother who won't touch you, is an affliction worse than not liking pasta or tomato sauce; it's simply unforgivable. Apart from my school photos, there isn't a single picture of me as a child. Her husband's portraits are the only ones that Livia lets us put up. I am surplus to requirements, no more no less.

This evening, twenty-six years and one day after the death of my father, we are celebrating Livia's fiftieth birthday on the edge of the Tiber river, in my godmother Viola's favourite restaurant. The magnificent absent one will be there too of course, between the glasses and plates, the *anti pasti* and the *torta* with the five candles.

In actual fact, Livia's birthday was yesterday, but as her husband died on her birthday, she erased that date from the calendar. Every year on this fateful day, we keep our heads down, sulk, look miserable and avoid her. The next day, life resumes its normal course.

We start the evening with a Spritz and move on to Prosecco. Livia blows out her candles, Viola claps. Mattia, Viola's married-lover-with-kids, calls to wish Livia happy birthday. My mother and godmother's eyes take on a glazed look, they are drunk. Only a quarter of an hour to go, then I'll be able to go home with a clear conscience.

Suddenly, Viola raises her glass and looks my mother in the eye. "It's better for everyone."

No one knows what she is talking about. So she goes in for the kill.

"It's better for everyone, that's what you decided twenty-six years ago, Livia. Don't you remember?"

My mother frowns. She looks daggers at her friend.

Viola turns to me. "Livia has been lying to you since you were born. She is not the perfect grieving widow that everyone thinks. She doesn't know who your father is."

Feeling very uncomfortable, I grin stupidly.

"Don't listen to her, Chiara," my mother says sharply.

But Viola is relentless. "No, you must listen to me. You may be the daughter of a Frenchie. Livia decided at the time that it was better to pretend your father was her dead husband. In fact, there's a one in two chance he is."

After dropping her bombshell, my loving godmother smiles maliciously. Livia is reeling from the shock, and I am trembling. At that very second, our whole world comes tumbling down.

My father is French? Paralyzed with shock, I repeat Viola's words over and over to myself. The waiter gets his timing wrong. He comes up to our table and asks if we want another bottle. No one answers him. Livia glares at her childhood friend. Viola has a spiteful look on her face, I don't recognize her anymore. Their mutual hatred is palpable.

"You're drunk!" shouts Livia.

"Like *you* were, the night you met your French friend!" screeches Viola. "A bit less limoncello and Chiara might never have been born!"

"How dare you say such a thing in front of her, have you no shame?"

"And you, you're not ashamed about lying to your own daughter?"

"Why today of all days?" asks Livia.

Her voice trembles. My mother looks like a betrayed and wounded child. For the first time ever, she drops her guard.

"Revenge," says Viola. "You told Mattia to dump me. He told me what you said, I didn't believe him at first. When he called earlier, I could see from your face it was true."

I hold my breath. Maybe I'll wake up from this nightmare and find my father grinning in his photo frame, Livia and Viola thick as thieves, and Alessio calling for a chat. Everyone back in their rightful place.

"Mattia will never leave his wife," croaks Livia.

"You're a witch," hisses Viola. "*Strega! Puttana!*"

"He makes you suffer! He doesn't deserve you! I just want what's best for you. And you crucify me? I trusted you! Chiara, I can explain . . ."

"No," I say bluntly.

In a stupor, I witness these two women tearing each other apart. The same two that raised me, both battered by life's harsh realities.

"Viola is lying," screams Livia as she grips my wrist. "Don't believe what she says. Your father was wonderful, besides you're the spitting image of him!"

My mother just deliberately touched me. For the first time in years. This shocks me as much as discovering that my mythical father may not be my real father.

"Livia is lying!" screeches Viola yet again, grabbing my other wrist. "I kept the letter she wrote to me saying that it was better for everyone. The Frenchman was from an island in Brittany. I think his surname had something to do with the weather."

"I'll never forgive you!" roars Livia.

She looks me straight in the eye to convince me.

"Your father was killed crossing Piazza del Popolo," she pleads. "It was my fault because he was looking at me instead of watching where he was going. He died because of me. And I have to bear this cross for the rest of my life."

She closes her eyes, she doesn't see me anymore, she's elsewhere; in that dark place she wakes up in every morning.

"Mattia is dumping me because of you!" shouts Viola with fury. "*Ti odio!* You are hateful! Believe me, Chiara, there's a one in two chance your father is alive."

Livia jumps up with a start and runs out of the restaurant in hysterics.

I'm too upset to go after her.

I look at my godmother. My whole life is in tatters.

"Why today, on her birthday of all days?" I ask.

"Her birthday was actually yesterday, not today. And I'm fifty years old too, you know. Your mother lost her husband, but in return she gained the esteem of the idiots who think that a woman has to be a wife and a mother to have made something of herself. I've got nothing, no husband, no *bambini*, all I had was Mattia a couple of afternoons a week. And she's snatched that tiny crumb of happiness from me. All I did was give her a dose of her own medicine."

"Yet I'm the one paying for it."

"You're what they call collateral damage. She should have told you the truth a long time ago. She ended up believing her own lies by blotting out the past."

"What actually happened? Did the Frenchman rape her?" I ask, raising my voice in my distress.

At a nearby table, my words startle two priests about to tuck into a mountain of *risotto alla parmigiana*.

"Her husband had just died, she was sinking lower and lower," says Viola. "I forced her to come away with me for a weekend to the island of Elba in Tuscany, to stay with my cousin. Your mother was very beautiful, you know, she had all the men at her feet. They never noticed me, they only had eyes for her . . ."

I think of that picture at home of the two friends on the beach in Ostia. They were the same age I am today. Livia was bewitching, Viola had a pleasant face, but they weren't in the same league.

"Your mother couldn't dance; she was in mourning. She was the only one dressed in black, and she sat watching us, sipping her limoncello. The previous day, some French fishermen returning from the port helped my cousin change her flat tyre. She had driven her Panda over a nail in the countryside, so she bought them a round of drinks to thank them.

One of them came over and spoke to your mother, who burst into tears. I thought that was a good thing, as she needed to let go, cry, let it all out, instead of being holed up at home as if she was dead."

"Did he console her?" I ask angrily.

"I danced the night away without giving her a second thought. I saw her again the next morning, as we were flying back to Rome. She didn't tell me a thing. She had got drunk and was ashamed. The grieving widow who betrays her husband's memory, just imagine what people would say! When she discovered that she was pregnant, she told only me, not even the gynaecologist. The Frenchman looked a lot like your father. You were a premature baby, the doubt persisted, you could have been the daughter of either of them."

Livia, the model widow, went off the rails after his death with a passing stranger. I can hardly believe what I'm hearing.

"I'm the only one who knew, for twenty-six years," concludes Viola.

"And you just decided to spit it out now," I say in disgust.

"You'll notice that I waited until your grandmother had passed!"

Nonna Ornella always looked for her son in my every word and gesture. But if my father is not my father, does that mean she's not my grandmother? Yet I loved her more than Livia. I sigh.

"Revenge is clearly a dish best served cold. Do you feel better now?" I ask her.

Viola shakes her head, she doesn't dare look me in the eye anymore. I get up and head towards the door. I came to this dinner full of good intentions and I'm leaving with my whole life in tatters, feeling even more unwanted than before. The crack has now become a chasm. Questions go round and round in my head. Outside, I take deep breaths to calm my nerves. But something is bothering me. I rewind. Viola is settling the bill. I go back inside.

"His name had something to do with the weather, but which island was it?"

Fiumicino Airport, red postbox

The Red Postbox has two distinct slots, one marked "Rome and district" and the other one marked "All other destinations". A young woman slides three envelopes into the left slot. The Postbox must be immune to sorrow in view of all the sad words it sees, be it letters announcing bad news, heartbreak or suicide. Airports exacerbate emotions. This Postbox prefers receiving love letters. It can tell what emotion the letter contains—rage, affection, despair, desire— by the way the addresses are written.

In the fourteenth century, in Rome, Venice and Genoa, the first public postboxes were actually a means for the people to denounce their fellow citizens; anonymous accusations were dropped into the postboxes to be sent to the state. Monogrammed writing paper was the preserve of the aristocracy at the time—nothing like the emails, texts and social media used today. The young woman who just posted three letters for Rome knows that they will take two days to reach their recipients: two women and a man.

If the Red Postbox had arms, it would hold the envelopes up to the light and read their contents or steam them open and unfold the paper. This is impossible, of course, but it doesn't stop the Postbox from letting its imagination run riot.

The young woman is called Chiara Ferrari, her name is on the back of the envelopes. She has written to Livia, Viola and Marco. Her handwriting slopes to the right and is so nervous and violent that it has punctured the paper in several places.

Beauvais Airport

As the plane touches down on French soil, the Italian passengers clap. I'm exhausted, I only slept three hours last night.

The island is called "Groix", Viola pronounced it phonetically. "Gro" and then "ix" in her Italian accent. As soon as I got home, I bought a one-way plane ticket to Paris, not knowing how long I would stay. I told Alessio everything, he was very supportive and reassured me I was doing the right thing.

I'll take a bus to Porte Maillot in Paris, then the metro to Montparnasse station, and then a train headed for Brittany. I'll get off in Lorient, in the Morbihan region. Then all I'll have to do is board the boat.

I've switched roles. I've gone from the heroine of a tragedy, daughter of a grieving widow, to the protagonist of a vaudeville comedy.

Crossing from Lorient to Groix

I learned French at a French convent school in Rome where Livia insisted on sending me. Now I finally understand why . . . But I don't speak Breton, which is spoken exclusively in Brittany. All the signs here are in both languages. I board the boat at Lorient and get off on Groix Island. This is the first time I have set foot in France.

The map of France is the shape of a hexagon. It also resembles a man in profile, and his big, hooked nose is Brittany. I've heard that the Breton people are gutsy, assertive, and down to earth. I'm searching for an islander. I just hope he is still alive, that he hasn't sailed off to some far away land and that I won't disappoint him. You've never disappointed me, Alessio, and I hope you can say the same about me. I bet I'm the only passenger on this boat who has no one waiting for them and nowhere to stay.

You can always spot an Italian speaking French because of the way they pronounce the "u" and the "oi". We don't say "u" but "ou". We don't say "oi" but "o-i". At the ferry terminal, I approach the ticket office.

"A ticket for *Gro-ix*, please."

"Where?"

I refer to the flyer with the timetables and prices of the ferry connections. The young woman smiles.

"One way or a Two-Island Pass with two round trips?"

My stomach rumbles, I haven't eaten anything since my *panino* at five o'clock this morning.

"One way please."

The boat is heaving with passengers, groups of overjoyed families and couples brimming with vitality. It's a spring bank holiday weekend. I miss you, Alessio. You know how the sight of a happy family always tugs at my heartstrings. Livia raised me on *pizze* and *pasta*, and I was a chubby kid. I lost weight and my illusions the day I heard her confiding in Viola. *If it weren't for Chiara I would have remarried and lived happily ever after!* Our little cocoon, *papa, mama, bambina*, was like prison for her. In Italian, we put the accent on the second "a" of "*papà*". The word "*papa*" without an accent, means the Pope. To be frank, the Pope is more real to me than my father. At least he is alive and he always looks welcoming.

"Dad, look!"

I love other people's dads. I love them all: tall, small, chubby, lean, bald, hairy, moustached, bearded, sophisticated or rustic. I would have settled for any dad, whatever he looked like, even ugly or toothless. And I would have been a daddy's girl.

The upper deck of the boat is packed, there are people with suitcases, sandwiches, dogs, cats, guitars, smiling faces, sunglasses, headphones, you name it. I sit down with my duffel bag in front of what can only be described as the model family, beaming with happiness, like something out of a breakfast cereal ad. The father is a tall, muscular, sporty-looking blond with a surfer's jaw, blond curls and pale eyes, dressed in blue jeans, a cable knit sweater and red New Balance trainers. The mother is a sexy brunette in a light green puffer jacket, jeans and black boots. I envy this couple for a second; they are good looking, carefree, and parents to a pair of boisterous twins in dungarees, one red, the other blue, who are playing in between their legs. I can imagine all four of them cuddling up in bed on Sunday mornings, sat around the kitchen table on dark winter nights or opening presents around the Christmas tree. The parents are wearing the same round-beaded bracelet, probably from some far-flung destination they visited before the twins arrived. We're the same age, but we clearly haven't experienced the same solitude. I've tried my hand at several trades, I've been a market stall holder at Porta Portese flea market, a waitress at Caffe delle Arti, and a sales assistant in one of the boutiques on the exclusive via Veneto. I'm currently working in a large bookshop. In fact, I left Rome this morning without telling Livia, Viola, my boyfriend Marco, or even my employer. After last night's drama, I quit everything on a whim. We were celebrating my mother's life, yet it was my life that changed forever.

I don't live with Marco, I'm a commitment-phobe, scared of getting hurt, and suffering because of a man. This way, I'm not responsible for anything or anyone. I don't have kids or a goldfish, I don't even own a coffee machine. I drink my espressos at the Nuclear Bar next door. I don't have a car, I get around on a Piaggio Scarabeo moped—I avoid Vespas. I'm not a homeowner either, I rent a one-bedroom flat in Monte Mario.

"Nolan, stop rolling around on the floor. Evan, get up!" The twins in dungarees are not listening to their mother.

Their father is busy typing away on his laptop. The mother's phone rings, she turns around to answer it. Her attention is elsewhere for a second. At that very moment, a woman walks past with a wrinkled Shar-Pei puppy. The little boys stare, their eyes like saucers, then run after the puppy, waddling and staggering on their little legs as the boat rolls. It all happens so fast. The puppy's owner picks the dog up and walks down the iron staircase leading to the lower deck. Confused, the twins stop short. Red dungarees begins to climb clumsily down the iron steps, nearly breaking his neck in the process.

Blue dungarees approaches the handrail that separates the passengers from the ocean and slips underneath. Their parents haven't noticed a thing.

I instinctively kick their father, who is sat opposite me. Startled, he eyes me warily as if I'm mad. There isn't time to speak, so I point at both children and we dive towards the twins. I grasp hold of blue dungarees by one foot as he squirms under the railing on the edge of the abyss. Fear gives me hidden strength. He resists but I manage to pull him back onto the deck, away from the big black waves crashing against the hull. I turn around breathless. The father has red dungarees clasped against him tightly, the child struggles but he is out of danger.

"He missed a step, I grabbed him by his dungaree strap. I had the fright of my life," he said.

"*MUMMMMMYYY!*" screams Nolan, trying to escape his father.

"*MUMMMMMYYY!*" echoes Evan, pulling at my arm. Their mother turns around, frowning.

"What *are* you doing? Let go of my children!"

I nearly choke in rage.

"If I hadn't been there, one would have drowned and the other would have broken his neck falling down those stairs. You should thank me, rather than yelling at me!"

She goes pale, pockets her phone, rushes to the toddlers and flings her arms around them, squeezing them against her. They nestle up to her. They had a near miss. Their father goes to shake my hand.

"My name is Gabin, like the actor."

"My name is Chiara, like my mother's middle name. Which actor?"

"*When I was young, love was my right, A passing cloud, a pleasant night, Love was my right, and love was my delight . . . But now I know, but now I really know!*"

"Excuse me?"

"You must know Jean Gabin! You're not a cinema goer?"

"I am, but I know Italian cinema, not French."

"You idiots!" shouts the mother of the dungareed twins, giving them a shake. "Do you have any idea?"

"Everything is fine, they're safe and sound," Gabin just says rather than hugging his wife to calm her down.

"No, everything is not fine!" she wails. "If I had arrived without them, I would have died of remorse *and* my parents would have killed me!"

"They're alright now," I add, before turning to Gabin.

"You can't take your eyes off that pair for a second, can you!"

"I don't know, I don't have children," he answers. I stare at him astonished.

"You're not their father?"

"No, this is the first time I've ever seen them. By the way, you've got a mighty kick on you . . . my poor shin, I'll be limping for days! When I saw those kids in danger, I just sprang into action."

"Their father cleared off to Nepal," whispers their mother. "The bastard dumped me to get high in the Himalayas."

"But you're both wearing the same bracelet!" I say, pointing to their wrists. Gabin's beads are black with a purple sheen, those of the twins' mother are a beautiful deep crimson.

"Sheer coincidence," she says. "My ex gave me mine when I was pregnant, apparently they're meant to protect newborns. I hung onto it out of superstition."

"The garnet is the sacred stone of Native Americans, it was a gift," says Gabin-like-the-actor.

I smile. Firstly, because no one died, and the twins have their whole life ahead of them to screw up. Secondly, because the model family is *not* a model family after all.

We always think the grass is greener on the other side. And lastly, because you, Alessio, would have known that Gabin wasn't their father. You would have pointed out that they were looking at their mother, not the man sitting next to them. I feel so alone right now, and this emptiness weighs heavily on me as we enter the port and the ferry solemnly sounds its horn. Families, friends and dogs are waiting for their loved ones, delighted to see them again. I, on the other hand, am looking for a man whose name is weather-related in some way. It's getting dark. I don't know where I'll be sleeping tonight. The island is tiny, just five miles long and two and a half miles wide. If the hotels are full, what will I do?

The boat manoeuvres and docks. The mother of the dungareed twins takes a pair of toddler reins out of her bag that she hooks to both her sons' trouser straps, and holds her hand out to us, pale with fright.

"The word 'thank you' can't begin to convey my gratitude," she says, overwhelmed by emotion. "My name is Urielle. It's the name of a Celtic archangel. I'm *Grèke*."

"That's where the Athenians landed," replies Gabin to raise her spirits.

She manages a weak smile, holding the reins tightly.

"Not Greek from Greece, but *Grèke* from Groix. The Groix islanders are known as *Greks*, which is the Breton word for the special coffee pots traditionally used by the fishermen on the tuna boats. We also say the *Groisillons*. I was born here, but I live in Paris, right next to the Bataclan. I've come to stay with my parents for the weekend."

The Parisian concert venue and its tragic past seem to have become a landmark like the Eiffel Tower or the Louvre. She points at us and asks if we're together. I laugh, despite my anxiety. I had been convinced that she was married to Gabin, and she thinks Gabin and *me* are an item!

"In fact, we don't even know each other. My name is Chiara Ferrari, no connection with the car. I live in Rome."

"My name is Gabin Aragon, no connection with the poet. I'm Corsican. And a novelist. I'm here to research a book I'm writing about the island."

The passengers gather their belongings, children stare, dogs bark, it's time to get off.

"Do you have friends here or are you staying in a hotel?" asks Urielle.

"I haven't booked anywhere," I say. "I'll go to the tourist office for some ideas."

"My parents have a big house; I wouldn't dream of you staying in a hotel!"

"Do they rent out rooms?"

"It'll be their way of thanking the person who saved their grandson's life. I'll be offended if you refuse. How about you?" she asks Gabin.

"I'm like a snail, got my house on my back," he jokes, pointing at his backpack. "I've rented a bungalow at the Red Sands campsite. That'll do nicely while I scout around and interview anyone willing to talk to me."

"Come for dinner tonight in Port-Lay, we can help you. I'll pick you up around eight? If it wasn't for you, Nolan could have been killed."

She bites her lower lip. Her hands tremble.

"I'll rent a bike," says Gabin.

"I'm warning you now that the downhill stretch along the coast to our house will be tough to climb back up after my mother's dinner. You should accept my offer."

He gives in. They agree to meet in front of a guesthouse called the Sémaphore de la Croix.

Groix Island, Port-Tudy

We get off the boat and Gabin heads to a bike rental shop called Coconuts. Urielle hands the children's reins to a woman who looks just like her, only thirty years older, and kisses a man in a faded pink jacket. I stand back. The person I'm looking for may well be on this busy dock right now to welcome his family and not have the foggiest that I exist.

"Welcome to our little rock, my *korrigans*," says Urielle's mother beaming at her grandchildren. "*Korrigans*" I later find out are goblin or sprite-like creatures from Breton folklore.

"I took the reins off during the crossing, and I got a call from the studio. I should never have taken it! The boys escaped, and things nearly ended badly," gasps Urielle, still in shock. "Chiara saved Evan. So I said she's welcome to stay with us."

"Oh no, how dreadful! Thank you my dear!" exclaims the woman as she hugs the twins who are squirming to get away from her. "I'm Rozenn, Roz for short. And this is my husband Didier."

"I only took my eye off them for a second!" says Urielle.

"A second is all it takes, as we know only too well," says Roz, suddenly serious. "We'll stop off in the village and light a candle to thank the good Lord."

Nonna Ornella also lit altar candles in Rome until they replaced them with electric ones. She was so angry with the parish priest that she decided that she would no longer give anything to the collection. But every month, she would still discreetly slip an envelope into the rectory letterbox.

We all pile into a small French car that smells of wet dog. The parents sit in the front, I have my bag and Evan on my knees, Urielle has Nolan and her laptop on hers. While the car struggles to climb the hill, Urielle leans in towards me.

"You're going to meet my big sister Danielle," she whispers. "One day when she was three years old, before I was born, my mother was working in the garden and my father was doing odd jobs when Danielle leaned out of the upstairs window and fell out. We lived in the village of Le Méné at the time. She smashed her head on the patio that day and her future along with it. Since then, she is neither happy nor unhappy, she is emotionless, obedient, dependent, infantile. She no longer speaks only sings, and can imitate any voice to perfection. She can't read a score, but she has a perfect ear. She can only express herself through song lyrics. Stop wiggling around, Nolan, you're hurting me!"

The little boy bursts into laughter while unbalancing his brother who is squirming around on my thighs. The car arrives in the square, and halts in front of a war memorial. Nearby there is a merry-go-round, a gift shop called Bleu Thé and a bookshop, L'Écume.

Urielle points out the church bell tower, crowned by a life-size tuna fish, because, she explains, the island was the main French fishing port for albacore tuna until 1940. Inside the church the twins trot towards the nave and the lit candles.

"Don't touch!" roars Roz.

The boys obey her silently. She gives them each a coin, which they slip into the box, and she lights the candles.

"Thank you, dear God, for protecting my little rascals," she says fervently.

Above us swings an ex-voto of a boat. I realize the man I am searching for most likely knows this place, has probably been here for a christening, a wedding, or a funeral. It then hits me that if he has left the island, I've come for nothing.

"I forgot to post my letter," says Roz to Urielle. "Could you do it for me darling? I'll take care of the little ones."

I walk down the village with Urielle. The large yellow post-box has two slots: On the left it says "Morbihan 56", and on the right "Other districts and abroad".

"In Rome, our postboxes are red," I say, surprised.

"In France they've been yellow since the 1960s, before that they were blue," replies Urielle. "They are manufactured in Brittany, in Nantes. I know that because my mother works at the post office. In fact, each country has its own colour, yellow in Germany, green in China, blue in the United States, red in England—and Italy of course."

I watch the letter slide into the postbox.

Groix Island, Port-Lay

Urielle's father parks in front of a house that overlooks a small harbour where fishing boats are bobbing up and down. I get out of the car, relieved to have found somewhere to sleep. I got to bed late after the bombshell my godmother dropped last night; I can hardly keep my eyes open.

"Danielle, we're back!" hollers Roz.

A graceful young woman with a frozen expression opens the door. Urielle introduces us, telling her I'm from Rome. Danielle turns around and disappears into the house. A male voice can be heard from the living room. *It's me, the Italian, I have returned from afar, The road was long ... Let me in, open the door, Io non ne posso proprio più.*

"It's Danielle," whispers Urielle. "She is imitating Serge Reggiani for you, it is her way of welcoming you in our home. My parents were fans, they would take the boat to the mainland every time he gave a concert, and they always took her along."

The pale young woman continues to sing. *I'm coming back home, I've tried many professions, Thief, tightrope walker, Army sergeant, Actor, poacher, Emperor and pianist.*

I think back to the jobs that I used to invent for the pearly-toothed father in the photo frames. I don't look like him, he was handsome, I'm rather plain. He was blond, I'm brunette. He was tall and well-built, I'm slight. His eyes were light brown like caramel, mine are a darker chocolate brown with a weird blue spot in the middle of the right one. At school, they used to tease me because of it. Urielle on the other hand looks a lot like her father. They have the same almond eyes, the same mouth, the same smile. Danielle is more like Roz. If I had been the spitting image of her husband, would Livia have loved me? Or do I look like the Groix seafarer?

I suddenly notice the red and blue letterbox in front of the house; it's shaped like a boat with a small round door closed by a catch. There is a label indicating the family's name: *Thunder.* My heart misses a beat then races to catch up. Thunder. That's weather! I look at Didier who is carrying his daughter's luggage. My head spins. What would you deduce from this, Alessio? Is it just coincidence? Have I fallen into the lion's den? I can't get Viola's words out of my head. *It's better for everyone.* My heart crumples under the weight of her words. It would have been better for everyone if I'd never been born.

Groix Island, Port-Lay,
red and blue letterbox

Unfazed, the letterbox observes the occupants of the house as they go past. Didier, the head of the household, receives bills, taxes and his pension payments, as he retired very recently. He used to receive letters from his mistress, back before the advent of texts and email, until the day Roz opened one. The girls were very small. The house shook with screams and shouts until slowly but surely peace was restored. The letterbox played its role in calming things down. It withheld a letter which was stuck in its upper corner for ages, out of sight, sent by the woman trying to patch things up with Didier. When it finally released the letter, Didier had already moved on, so it was of no consequence.

The red and blue letterbox is devoted to its maker, the carpenter William le Rouquin Marteau. It grew up in Port-Tudy, in his workshop, near the new restaurant Les Fumaisons, which is supplied by local fishermen. The letterbox is also devoted to Anne, the carpenter's wife, and their children, as well as the boats, houses, and objects that William builds or repairs. It has a particular preference for its twins, the other letterboxes, who are all wooden boats of different colours scattered around the villages. They may not conform to official standards, but this island doesn't conform in a lot of ways. The box doesn't lock, it just has a wooden latch. Not that there are any thieves here anyway, you can trust people here.

Everyone has their own way of dealing with their post. Since he broke up with his mistress, Didier lets his wife handle it. Roz opens everything, she throws away the advertising, reads the cards, sets aside the bills. Danielle leaves her envelopes half opened as if she's worried about a mountain of pages spilling out, though all she ever gets is her disability allowance. Urielle doesn't receive any post here since she moved to Paris.

The day Didier's first pension payment arrived making him feel a hundred years old, the letterbox softened the blow by putting a birth announcement on top of it. If the box receives a black-edged death notice, it closes its latch and refuses to open its door to give the recipients time to prepare for the bad news. It knows that grief is to follow.

Tonight, however, it has an uneasy sense of foreboding when the family's new guest smiles at it and then instantly shudders on noticing the name "Thunder". It's as if they share an invisible bond, as if a strange force has pushed them until they collide and smash into each other.

Chatou, thirteen years earlier

Your name is Charles. You've never been to Italy or Brittany. You don't know Chiara Ferrari. Statistically there is little chance that your paths will ever cross. You're about to celebrate your thirteenth birthday.

The doorbell rings.

"Can you get it, boys?" shouts your mother, Alice.

You groan. "I'm reading!"

"I've got my exams in two months, I'm revising!" protests your brother Paul, who has just turned eighteen.

You live with your mother in an old ramshackle house in the lower part of town, the kind that an estate agent would describe as "in need of renovation". Everything needs to be redone: the electricity, plumbing, heating, insulation and roof. You bicker a lot with your brother, but it's not for real. He has got your mother's dark eyes, but yours are pale like your father's, the man you never knew. You grew up without a television in the house and you never go on holiday. You've been raised by a bohemian, whimsical mother who constantly has her head in a book. You walk along the banks of the river Seine, you go to the market on Wednesdays and Saturdays, the cinema, the swimming pool, and, in September and March, to the antiques fair on the Ile des Impressionnistes, just across the street. Your mother teaches French at the local Steiner-Waldorf school. The lessons are comprised of arts and crafts activities, and the pupils learn foreign languages from primary school age. The food at the canteen is organic. Paul, who is in his final year, is mad about photography. But you want to be a writer.

Alice named you both after her favourite poets, Paul Éluard and Charles Baudelaire. She also gave you both a bottle of Mercier champagne from the year you were born, to drink on your twenty-first birthdays. For his tenth birthday, Paul received the complete works of Éluard. When you turned ten, you received both volumes of Baudelaire's *Correspondences*, printed on the same fine Bible paper. The booksellers at the Chatou flea market always offer Alice a preview of their best second-hand copies from the prestigious *Bibliothèque de la Pléiade* collection. She is a wonderful teacher; she gives each of her pupils a book that will change their life, be it a novel, poetry, a religious work, a comic book, a manga or a technical manual. She has faith in words, music, and her quirky little house overlooking the river, which she has rented since Paul was born. You all walk to school and take care of the garden together, and you're happy. Each year, you plant a new flower or shrub and watch it grow. This year, it is a pale blue wisteria.

"You're always using your exams as an excuse," you moan at your brother.

You go to see who is at the garden gate in your orange Converse trainers. Everyone wears bright coloured footwear in your family. Alice's are yellow, and Paul's are a fashionable peacock blue. You greet the postman and hand the registered letter to your mother. Alice calmly unseals the envelope. Your new landlord announces that he will not be renewing the lease. His mother, who rented the house to you, has died, and he has inherited it.

This comes as a terrible shock. Distraught, Alice rushes to the telephone. And gets the answering machine. She leaves a message in a quivery desperate voice.

"Hello, I have just received your letter. Listen, I'm sure we can work something out. If it's a question of money, I'll see what I can do. I teach in the next street, my sons go to my school, and last year your mother let me repaint the whole house entirely at my own expense, you can't throw us out now! We had an agreement, we trusted each other. Call me back please. I'm sure we can come to some arrangement."

She trembles as she hangs up.

"He is a reasonable man," she says unconvincingly.

The new landlord turns up one night without warning, he wants his house back. Alice pleads with him, but he won't listen and insists you must leave. According to the rota, it is your turn to clean the house. Distracted by the visitor, you plug the vacuum cleaner into the wrong socket, the power fuse blows, and you plunge the whole downstairs into darkness. You're used to it, it happens all the time, there are a few torches scattered around the house. Alice calmly looks for the nearest one.

"There's a lighter on the fireplace to your right, can you pass it to me?" she asks the landlord.

"Light," he mumbles.

"A fuse has blown, I already informed your mother about this, the electrical system is not up to standard."

"Light," he repeats.

He is gasping in the dark. You find a torch and direct the beam towards him. Ashen-faced, the landlord is fighting for breath and starts hyperventilating. Alice yells at you to locate the offending fuse and turn the meter back on while she watches over the listless man.

"Do you have a heart problem?" she asks. "What's going on?"

Petrified, he doesn't respond.

The second the lights come back on, the man regains his composure and reverts to his arrogant and vindictive self. He accuses you all of not taking care of his property, yells that being in pitch blackness is dangerous, and then walks out the door, repeating his threats. He sends an email and a second registered letter of formal notice. He is within his rights, the law is on his side, and he sets a deadline.

You overhear a neighbour tell Alice that the guy is a slum-lord who owns several blocks of flats in Paris. You don't understand the word "slumlord". She explains that he rents out expensive, filthy, tiny, substandard rooms to families in need or undocumented immigrants. He's a trafficker, a crim-inal. Your home belongs to him.

Alice panics. Paul has been an adult for three months so you are the only one dependent on her now, but she still wants both of you to go to university. She refuses to leave, your life is here. Disorientated and lost at the idea of being thrown out of your home, she buries herself in her work and becomes an insomniac. This house is her everything, she can't survive without these four walls that have seen centuries past. She starts chain smoking, drinking too much coffee, neglects her beloved books, and spends her nights doing research on legal forums and blogs. An unscrupulous lawyer demands a sub-stantial advance and then drops the case when she can't pay. She suffers from heartburn that subsides as soon as she eats, only to flare up again afterwards. To relieve her migraines, she takes strong doses of aspirin, which aggravate her stomach pain. She loses her energy and strength in the battle.

You wish you could console her, she loves dancing, she taught you how to dance the waltz and the rock and some-times after dinner you dance with her and she laughs like before. Not for long, but it's better than nothing.

One evening you are curled up on a giant pouf daydream-ing, while Paul sits in the rocking chair and your mother is nestled in an old, scratched leather armchair; your furniture is second-hand and comes from the flea market. Alice is reading aloud a poem by Paul Éluard, "The Earth Is Blue Like An Orange", which is the latest treasure rescued from the bottom of a box of old books from your last expedition to the flea market. Suddenly, she doubles over in pain, and droplets of blood fall from her mouth onto the pages.

The emergency doctor arrives and diagnoses a perforated ulcer. She must be taken to hospital immediately. You and your brother watch terrified as the ambulance pulls away. Paul goes online and reads some articles which say frightening things like "a ruptured stomach ulcer is life-threatening" or "with a digestive haemorrhage, the patient bleeds to death". You read the screen over his shoulder, but you don't ask any questions, you're too afraid of the answers. You close the book and hide the dried blood. The last four lines of the poem are spattered with red dots and are now illegible.

Alice spends a week in the intensive care unit. You don't have the right to visit her as you are under fifteen. You repaint her room in blue and orange because of the poem, as a surprise for her. You hope she will be back for your birthday. The silence in the little house in Chatou gets thicker by the day, like the buttercream icing Alice used to make for you as a special treat.

Rome, today

Livia parks her Fiat 500 in the middle of the pavement and aggressively jabs the intercom with her finger. Up on the third floor, Viola leans out of her window then quickly steps back. Too late, Livia has seen her.

"LET ME IN!" she shouts. "You're not answering your phone, but you're going to let me in, otherwise I'll camp right here on the doorstep!"

The window closes.

Livia lights a cigarette and sits down in front of the entrance to the apartment building. She has all the time in the world. Upset by the tragedy of the day before, she didn't go to the office this morning. She tried in vain to reach her daughter Chiara and left her umpteen messages. She recalls that night on the island of Elba twenty-six years ago, the limoncello that betrayed her, and the yellow Vespa that robbed her of her youth. She thinks about the Piazza del Popolo, which she avoids at all costs, preferring to make long detours. The main doors finally open. It's Giacinto, the former policeman, with his white hair and impeccable shirt. He is taking lunch to his daughters who work down the street. Every day he delivers them a meal lovingly prepared by their mother Maria. Livia knows everyone who lives in the building. She grew up there and only moved out when she got married. Whereas Viola still lives there with her mother, a domineering old bat who still makes the rules and scares men away.

Giacinto gallantly holds the door open for Livia. She goes in, races up the stairs and hammers on Viola's door, which eventually opens.

"Why?" says Livia.

Viola shrugs. She purses her lips and clenches her fists. She makes her way to her bedroom, Livia at her heels, as her mother has taken over the living room. The old friends enter the room where Viola still sleeps in the small bed she had as a child. Posters from her adolescence have left white traces on the pink wall.

"I hate this room," she says miserably. "I hate my life, my mother, you and Mattia."

"Group will never leave his wife," repeats Livia.

"I forbid you to call him that!"

When Viola goes out with her lover, who is married and a father of four, she always tells her mother that she is seeing a "group of friends" to cover her tracks.

"I will never forgive you for betraying me in front of Chiara," says Livia.

"I did it on purpose," admits Viola. "And it worked."

"But I chose you as godmother; I trusted you."

"It was just your way of buying my silence."

Livia no longer recognizes her friend.

"But why, Viola? We've known each other since kindergarten, we've always been inseparable. We looked out for each other at school. You even slept at our house the night your father committed suicide. You were a witness at my wedding. You sobbed even louder than me at the funeral. You held my hand when I gave birth. We're like sisters!"

"No, *I've* been like a sister to *you*, not the other way around!" hisses Viola angrily. "You were popular at school, while I was only ever your shadow, your stooge. I helped you revise, I explained what you didn't understand, and on the day of the exam I blew it and you got a higher mark than me. I was always second best, less beautiful, less funny, less interesting. And I hated you for that! My own father preferred you to me, he smiled when you came to our house, he became a different man. He committed suicide abandoning me and mum. If you had been his daughter, I bet that he wouldn't have done it. And then you went and married the man I was in love with, and you had the nerve to ask me to be your witness!"

"What?"

Viola glares at her.

"You were so busy snogging that you didn't even notice. It was me who introduced you, remember?! I liked him, he asked me to dinner. As I was an uptight idiot, I asked you to come along too and you stole him from right under my nose! You walked in and he forgot I was there. You bewitched him. We were sat together in the pizzeria in Piazza San Cosimato and I became invisible. If I had dropped down dead at the table, you wouldn't even have noticed!"

Livia is stunned.

"You never told me!"

"What good would it have done? He only had eyes for you! He proposed to you two weeks later. He even got run over staring at you. *You* killed him!"

Livia is shaken by the violence of Viola's words.

"I wanted to have children with him. But because of you, I never will. You've got Chiara, but you've always neglected her. If I hadn't been there to take her to the cinema, the circus, or the Villa Borghese gardens, she would have grown up staring at the silver photo frame on your sideboard, under the gaze of your perfect husband who is now probably cavorting around in heaven with some sexy cherubs!"

"That's blasphemy!"

"I saw right through your game yesterday. You stole the man I loved. You stopped me from having a family. And now you have the nerve to tell Mattia to dump me!"

Livia shakes her head. "I didn't want you to get hurt. Group is lying to you!"

"Don't call him that!" screams Viola.

"I ran into him in Piazza Navona with a very pretty young woman. He was kissing her."

Viola catches her breath.

"On the mouth, and passionately," adds Livia, her anger making her ruthless. "I went up to him and he was as startled as a rabbit caught in the headlights of an Alfa Romeo. He begged me not to tell you. He will never leave his wife, and you are not the only 'other woman'. He's cheating on you both."

"I don't believe you!" barks Viola, enraged. "Mattia loves me, his wife is sick, he can't leave her in that state! You are to blame for the death of your husband. You're a bad mother to Chiara. You're a terrible friend. Did you think I was going to keep your dirty little secret all my life? I have kept quiet way too long."

"Did you really keep my letter?" asks Livia with icy composure.

"I don't throw anything away. It's all there in black and white: *'It's better for everyone.'* Your daughter will love it."

"Give it to me!" roars Livia.

She dives towards the desk and ransacks all the drawers.

"I've hidden it," sneers Viola. "Turn the house upside down if you like, you won't find it."

"I have always been there for you," says Livia. "When your father sank into depression after losing his job, when he blew his brains out, when you were a total wreck."

"Welcome to the land of the wretched!" spits Viola. "It's a little overcrowded, there's a lot of us, but the more the merrier!"

The two childhood friends size each other up. Just then Viola's mother opens the door and immediately senses something is not right. Just like when she used to burst in and catch them red handed when they were teenagers wearing make-up or smoking.

"Are you fighting? At your age? Come on, kiss and make up."

Livia storms out of the room without a word and slams the front door behind her.

Groix Island, Port-Lay

Urielle's parents have a dog, a black and white cocker spaniel. He's a male but his name is Belle, after the neighbouring island of Belle-Ile. When I was a child, I begged my mother to let me have a dog, but she doesn't like animals any more than she likes humans. The pearly-toothed absent one had a labrador. In one picture, you can see him running along the beach with him. He named him Paolo, after his favourite singer, Paolo Conte. Livia gave the poor thing away to friends after the accident. One day, we ran into each other in the street, and the dog, who had never seen me before, rushed towards me. They told me that it was my father's dog.

Belle jumps up at Urielle and the twins, but he senses my reluctance and sniffs me, wagging his tail instead.

"He's waiting for you to stroke him."

I reach out cautiously. His fur is soft to the touch. He lies down in front of me.

"He likes you," says Urielle. "This dog is clever you know. When I introduced my ex to my parents, he growled and peed on his shoes. I should have taken the hint."

I help Roz prepare the dinner, we set the table for eight: Didier and Roz, Urielle and Danielle, the twins, Gabin and me. Having so many people at the table doesn't faze them, they must do it regularly. Roz is one of ten apparently, and today she has cooked enough for a whole regiment. I grew up with Livia, who only ever gave me readymade meals. And every Sunday I had lunch with *nonna* Ornella who would prepare me her deceased son's favourite meal: *penne all'arrabbiata* and *osso-buco*. I never dared tell her that I didn't like either.

Urielle goes to pick up Gabin at the campsite, and he arrives with a bottle of Corsican red wine.

"We stopped off at the village to go to The 50, it's a restaurant with a wine cellar."

I blush, I should have brought something.

"I'm sorry, I've come empty handed."

"Nonsense, you are our gift, heaven sent," says Roz kindly. "I love Italian cuisine. Do you know how to make *osso-buco?*"

There's clearly no getting away from my least favourite delicacy . . .

"Do you know Italy?" I ask Didier.

"We spent our honeymoon in Venice."

"Have you visited the island of Elba? Where Napoleon was exiled?" I ask next.

"No. We're so happy here on our little island, that we don't see the need to go away."

His surname is Thunder, he's around sixty and older than Livia. Is this the man I'm looking for?

I quit everything back home to find out the truth. Normally at this time I would be in my bookshop in Rome advising customers which novels to purchase. I'll be fired, but never mind. The only person I'll miss is Valérie Lübeck, the blonde Parisian who always leaves with her two-wheeled shopping trolley full of books. As I never stay long in the same job, I don't get too attached to it. The same goes for men.

I have been sharing a bed with Marco for a year now, but we don't actually know each other. We don't talk because we don't really have much to say. The physical contact is what we seek, it's enough. He'll find someone else. I didn't let Marco introduce me to his parents. I don't want to get married or live with him. I don't cook for myself, so why would I cook for him? Who needs to cook when you've got the *tavola calda* next door selling such delicious food? I don't want children either, it didn't make Livia happy. Where I come from, mothers don't touch their children, fathers only exist in photos, and being happy is a sin. I hoped that a knight in shining armour would rescue me from the sadness and loneliness. Marco didn't succeed.

I miss you, Alessio. You are the only one I confided in and you encouraged me to leave. I left Rome, let down my boss and his wandering hands, and forgot that I was having dinner tonight with Marco at Alberto and Lori's restaurant, Losteriacarina. I left behind my little basil plant. It will wait for me faithfully, imbuing the kitchen with its scent. Then its earth will crack, its leaves will dry out, its stem will wither, and it will perish. No one has a spare key, no one will water it. Sorry, basil. This is why I don't have children. I would be a bad mother, it must run in the family.

Roz places a steaming dish in the middle of the table. Urielle gets up and puts her arms around her to say thank you. The Thunder family do like hugging each other.

"This is a Groix Island specialty," explains Roz. "It's hake, wrasse, pollack, gurnard, conger eel and potatoes. Then I added white wine. Take some dressing."

Danielle, poker faced, passes her plate. At Livia's, you only eat to ward off hunger, you don't enjoy your food. For her, eating is another of life's inescapable constraints, like brushing your teeth, sleeping or getting dressed. And we don't talk at the table. Marco, on the contrary, talks for Italy when he eats. He is football mad; he supports AS Roma and hates any fan of Lazio, the rival club. He has never read a book and is proud of it. He only uses newspapers for one thing: to wrap up the fish that he catches with his buddies from the office on Bracciano lake in the summer. He is a decent, stable sort. If he had stopped wanting to marry me, we could have enjoyed each other's company for another few years. I'm not the easiest person, I admit. It is better for him that it ends this way. Rome is full of pretty girls who will lovingly iron his football club's yellow and red shirts and prepare him a gigantic pizza before snuggling up next to him to watch the game.

"Chiara, give me your plate. I hope you like fish?"

"I like everything," I say. I'm lying out of politeness. I don't like fish; I rarely eat it. Fish is a luxury in Rome.

Didier scans the table.

"Can you pass me the bread?" he asks, putting his hand on my arm.

His gesture startles me. Urielle's father touched me. My skin burns where his fingers made contact. No one finds his gesture inappropriate. He waits for the bread with a smile. I picture him, rolling around on top of Roz, conceiving Urielle, who in turn conceived Nolan and Evan. Is Didier my father?

"You're an angel, Mum!" cries Urielle, serving herself a large helping.

"Delicious smells have been wafting out of the kitchen since yesterday," says Didier, squeezing his daughter's shoulder with his big hand. "This is more than fish, this is love."

Urielle is obviously used to her father being tactile. Danielle starts singing, imitating a man's voice and rolling her r's: "*The pleasurrrrre of love lasts only a moment, The grief of love lasts a lifetime.*"

Then she carries on eating, as if nothing has happened. The fish is steaming in its tureen. The twins get down from the table and run outside to play. The dog places his paw on my leg.

"So, you're a writer?" says Didier to Gabin. "Maybe I've read something of yours. What's your pen name?"

"I actually don't publish under my own name; I'm a ghost writer. I write for famous novelists. You'd be surprised! But I'm under contract not to disclose their names."

"Why such a choice?" asks Roz. "Wouldn't you like to see your name on the cover?"

"I prefer to earn a decent living rather than live hand to mouth."

"How do you mean?" I ask, not fully understanding.

"It means struggling to make ends meet, to earn enough money to get by," explains Gabin.

"You have a noble profession. I couldn't live without books," says Didier, pointing to his bookshelves.

Gabin stands up, examines the rows of novels and sits back down again, smiling.

"You have three of mine there. Don't ask me which ones. So you *have* read my work after all!"

Everyone laughs, except Danielle.

"I raise my glass to our beautiful language, to Breton hospitality and to this excellent fish stew," announces Gabin.

Chatou, thirteen years earlier

Your name is Charles, and you are thirteen years old today. Perhaps you'll go to Italy or Brittany one day, you have your whole life ahead of you.

You are waiting for your brother to come back from the hospital. Paul took Alice a note you wrote saying that you had tidied up your room, mowed the lawn, arranged your paperbacks in alphabetical order, and that your life is empty without her. The house feels dead.

You bought two cream puffs as a birthday cake. Visiting time is over, your brother is late. You have already set the table. You've lived on nothing but Frankfurter sausages for a week. They are easy to heat up and are filling. It strangely reminds you of the school holidays. When you all go to the flea market together, your mother always orders a foie gras sandwich with a glass of Sauternes, while you and your brother have a hot dog and a Nutella waffle.

You hear the gate open. You light the gas under the saucepan and empty the tin of sausages into it. You go outside to meet your brother.

"Will Mum be back soon?"

Then you see Paul's face. You go weak at the knees. Your older brother doesn't speak, he just shakes his head in dismay. You start hiccupping and your eyes fill with tears. Paul clenches his fists in rage. You run to your room. You tip over the shelf containing your well-organized books that your mother will never see.

Paul comes and finds you. You forget all about your birthday; your existence shatters into a million pieces, it truly is the end of the world. You throw yourself on your bed and bury your face in the pillow. Paul sits down beside you. You remain there, without speaking, without crying, completely numb. Then, you have an uncontrollable bout of hiccups again. You drink a glass of water upside down and repeat ten times in a row without breathing, "Hiccups, hiccups, go away, come again another day". But nothing helps.

"Am I imagining it or can I smell burning?" Paul says suddenly, wrinkling his nose.

"The sausages!"

You rush to the kitchen. The water has evaporated and the bottom of the pan is burned. The room is full of smoke and the smell gets caught in your throat. You open the windows. You have no appetite, but your growing bodies are crying out for food, so you both gobble down the charred, shrunken sausages. To cheer you up, Paul dips one in the cream puff and pretends it's delicious. You do the same. It's disgusting. Paul throws up that night. You go to his bed; you are unable to sleep alone. You lie down, back-to-back, shoulder to shoulder.

"Your feet stink," moans Paul.

"You've got dog breath," you retort.

"They told me to bring a dress for Mum in the morning," whispers Paul.

You're wide-eyed in the dark, seized by eager hope. "A dress? So, she isn't . . ."

"For the coffin," interrupts Paul.

That word devastates you. Victor Hugo comes to mind: *The eye was in the tomb and watched Cain.*

"I'll take the black one with lace on the shoulders," mumbles Paul in the dark.

"Why not the red one with the three-quarter length sleeves?"

"They want black."

"She prefers red."

A few days later, at the Notre-Dame de Chatou church, just off the bridge, Paul steps up to the microphone and reads the words of his namesake in a husky voice: "*I love you for all the women I have not known, I love you for all the time I have not lived, for the smell of the open sea and the smell of warm bread, for the melting snow, for the first flowers.*"

Then you mumble some lines by Charles Baudelaire, swallowing half the words: "*What then, extraordinary stranger, do you love? I love the clouds—the clouds that pass—yonder—the marvellous clouds.*"

The church is packed with colleagues, parents, students and neighbours. But since Alice had no family other than you, no one thought of organizing a get-together after the service. People were expecting your father to have it all in hand, not realizing that you don't even know his name.

Alice, in her red dress with three-quarter length sleeves, her feet in her yellow Converse, now lies next to her parents in the cemetery where she used to take you to recite poetry on All Saints' Day. The two of you stand there alone in front of her grave—the family with the brightly coloured feet. The other members of the congregation didn't want to intrude out of respect. "*Never again shall we see one another, Odour of time sprig of heather, Remember I await our life together,*" whispers Paul to your mother.

He turns to you, and repeats the questions Alice always used to ask you:

"Do you remember Apollinaire's real name?"

"Wilhelm Albert Włodzimierz Apollinaris de Kostrowitzki," you say proudly, under the astonished gaze of the master of ceremonies hired by Paul.

"And now Éluard?"

"Eugène Grindel."

"Rimbaud's first name?"

"Arthur."

"And Aragon's?"

"Louis, unacknowledged biological son of Louis Andrieux."

"Verlaine's?"

"Paul."

"I'm proud of you."

When you get home, you find the eviction notice in the letter-box. The landlord who is terrified of the dark is kicking you out. You no longer have a mother or a home.

The next morning, you sit at the breakfast table silently, frozen to the spot, not eating your cereal or drinking your hot chocolate. You stare blankly into space like a stuffed animal. A concerned Paul shakes you.

"You're scaring the hell out of me!"

You then spit out the question that has been obsessing you since your birthday. "Were you there?"

"When?"

"You know . . . when she . . . when she um . . ."

Paul shrugs. "I'd gone down the corridor to look for a drinks machine. When I got back, her room was full of doctors. They asked me to wait outside."

Your hackles rise. "You left her? So, she was all alone?"

"I couldn't stay there all day," Paul grunts. "I had to eat, drink, and pee."

"You should have stopped her!" you yell, crimson with rage. "She promised me she would get better and come home!"

"Do you think that's how it works?" says Paul, annoyed now. "That she was flying up to heaven, flapping her wings, and that I could grab her ankles and pull her back down? The doctor explained everything to me: she had two ulcers, two perforations in her stomach, because she was so worried about that scumbag landlord. The surgeon repaired one of the perforations, but there was a big blood vessel next to it, a big tube full of blood that started gushing out everywhere."

"I would have stayed with her and told them right away."

"You weren't there," says Paul, coldly. "Because you're just a child."

Alice had said to you just the other day: "I'm sick of telling you to tidy your room, it's a real pigsty!" You grunted like a little pig, and you both laughed about it. Now you put two and two together and conclude that it's all your fault: you actually made her sick. Paul awkwardly places his arm around your shoulders, but you pull away.

"We've been kicked out of here," sighs Paul. "We're going to move in with Patty."

"Your girlfriend? Mum didn't like her and neither do I!" you protest, furiously. "Go if you want. I'm staying here."

Paul ruffles your hair. "We have to leave, kid. Don't make things harder than they are."

"Mum used to call the landlord 'the slimy rat', remember? We should lie to him, pretend that Mum is on the mend and will be home soon. I can get a job to help you out, deliver letters or carry shopping, I'm not a baby anymore. We'll manage it, just the two of us. We can't leave, it smells of Mum's perfume here. And what about her room, and all her clothes in the wardrobe, and her bag on the chair?"

Paul takes you in his arms, something he has never done before. "But this house belongs to the slimy rat, Charles. We can't sleep in the street. Patty has said she'll take us in, we're very lucky. She's fond of you."

He is lying. He almost had to beg her to agree to take you too. She wanted to pack you off to boarding school.

Groix Island, Port-Lay

The twins are asleep. They went out like a light at exactly the same time, to the split second, like two toys whose batteries have been taken out. Belle is lying across their door to protect them. Calm reigns in the house once more. Didier retires to his room early. He rises at dawn to walk with Danielle. He suggested we accompany them.

"We walk twice a week with friends, it does us a world of good. Tomorrow we're doing a short circuit of just over four miles: Quelhuit, Pointe du Grognon, Pen-Men, Kervedan, Moustero, and back. It will take less than three hours. Would you like to come with us?"

"I'm here to work," apologizes Gabin.

"I'm not very sporty," I say.

Roz, her daughters, and me and Gabin go out to sit in front of the ocean, which sparkles in the moonlight.

"When there are storms, the foam from the waves flies into our garden and lands on all the bushes. It looks like snow. Belle goes mad, running around, jumping up trying to catch it, it's magical!" says Urielle enthusiastically.

She pauses for a moment, then continues: "Granny used to say: 'when you can see the mainland it means it's going to rain, when you can't see it, it means it's raining.'"

"Thank you both for saving my little *korrigans*," repeats Roz, tearing up. "Urielle will leave after the weekend but you are very welcome to stay in our house as long as you like. Really, it's no trouble."

I can tell she means it, so I accept. Yesterday, I didn't even realize that "Gro-Ix" existed. France had never been on my bucket list. I had dreamt of New York, Berlin, Barcelona, Amsterdam, Vienna or London. And now I've washed up on this small Breton island. I deliberately left my phone in Rome. I'm free, nothing to connect me to my previous life. Livia, Viola and Marco will receive my letter soon. I wrote the same message to all three of them: "I'm going on a trip, I'm not taking my mobile and I won't be getting in touch. Don't worry about me, I need some time alone to think." Marco won't forgive me for standing him up tonight or for not being at his brother's wedding in a few days' time. But we were hardly a match made in heaven. What about Livia? Who was *her* match made in heaven? Her husband or the Frenchman? Alessio, do you think I have a living, breathing father waiting for me here? Do you think that Urielle and Danielle are my sisters and that fate has guided me to them? When Didier touched my arm, should my skin have recognized his? What will happen now?

"Is your surname really Thunder?" I ask Roz in the dark.

"It's my husband's name. It's a very common name on the island."

That's just my luck!

"Are there many of you?"

"In almost every village. Altogether, there are about two thousand inhabitants on Groix in winter, and more than twenty thousand in summer. Thunder is the most common surname here."

I feel the blood drain from my face, hands and feet, only to flow back up to my heart, which starts racing. A boat passes in the distance, its lights dancing on the black water.

"Do you all know each other?"

"The ones the same age as us and the ones in Didier's branch of the family, yes. I know less about the others."

"The island isn't big; were you all in the same class together at school?"

"There are two schools, one public and one private; one secular and one Catholic. Our forefathers used to say that one was blessed by God, and the other was run by the Devil. In those days, we only mixed with the youngsters from our village after school. Nowadays everyone is friends with everyone. There is no longer a divide between the two halves of the island, east and west; and nowadays you can marry whoever you want."

"Did you fall in love at first sight with Mr Thunder?" asks Gabin boldly; I can sense the big grin on his face.

"Fortunately, he's not as stormy as his name suggests! The name comes from a warrior who appeared in the cartulary of the town of Quimperlé; it's an eleventh century manuscript that lists old Breton names."

"Has he ever worked in Italy?" I ask.

"Didier is the only Groix islander I know who hates travelling. The *Greks* are adventurers, they sailed the distant seas, returning with fantastic stories. But my husband prefers his pipe and slippers to piracy."

"Do you remember my tattoo?" asks Urielle. "When I was eighteen, in the summer after my exams, I came back home with a pretty blue mermaid on my foot, and Dad refused to let me in the house. I slept at my cousins for a week. Mum begged him; he wouldn't budge. It was a fake tattoo, I wanted to test the water before getting the real thing. I didn't get it done in the end. Dad was born old and staid, he's always liked staying at home and being sensible."

"In Corsica young people get tattoos too," adds Gabin. "I prefer not to have distinctive marks on my body though."

"What distinguishes me is being a Groix islander," says Urielle. "I'm so glad I wasn't born on the mainland."

"The mainland?" I ask.

"The other side of the water," explains Roz.

"In Corsica, the other side of the water is called the continent," says Gabin.

"A shooting star! Quick, make a wish!" cries Urielle.

In Italy, we call them falling stars. *Nonna* Ornella said that after losing her son, she made a wish to join him. This used to upset me. *But you've got me!* But she would just shake her head. *You've got your mother. I miss your father. You'll understand when you're older.* The shooting stars finally granted her wish, and she went up to join the magnificent absent one in heaven. The whole neighbourhood showed up for her. The crowd couldn't fit in the church: the women and children went in, and the men stood outside, smoking and talking, but refrained from going to the café out of respect. When the hearse arrived, people clapped.

I wish the shooting star would help me find Mr Thunder. Even though the island is small, it's going to be like looking for a needle in a haystack.

Someone is playing the harp in the darkness. Gabin beckons me to look to the left. Danielle's extra-terrestrial vocal cords imitate both the human voice and a musical instrument to perfection.

"The Breton twins of the Triskell band play the Celtic harp," says Urielle. "Perhaps Nolan and Evan will sing together one day, rather than fighting?"

"It's great to have a brother," says Gabin.

I find Gabin strange, as well as handsome and kind of nice. I like his black beaded bracelet, his red trainers and his big sweater, but I can't work out if his eyes are blue or green. When he boasted that he had written several of the books on Didier's bookshelves, I found him a bit conceited. He might be a suitable match for Urielle.

Marco must hate me for dumping him with no explanation. The guys I've been with have enormous amounts of patience, I'll give them that. My first boyfriend was called Sandro, a so-called expert in love, according to a classmate. We had some good laughs together. When I lost my virginity, the earth didn't move; instead it felt like I had passed an exam of some kind. After Sandro, came Fabio, then Marco. I'm normal like other girls. Unlike Livia, I don't live in horror of being touched. She was my age when she got married.

"What does your husband do for a living?" I ask.

"He was a maths teacher but he recently retired."

"On the island?"

"Yes, we have never left it."

"Was he ever a fisherman in his youth?"

"Hey look!" interrupts Urielle.

A dolphin is playing with a buoy in front of the harbour entrance. Its dorsal fin dances on the waves. It capers and falls back splashing the dark waters with silver glimmers.

"What's the most common surname in Italy?" asks Gabin.

"Rossi. Bianchi. And Ferrari," I reply, after a pause.

"So you have a common name too?"

I nod. Whether my father is Italian or French, whether his name roars like a Ferrari or crashes like Thunder, I clearly share my name with many others. The dolphin is still frolicking in the moonlight, joyful and free.

Danielle pays tribute to its dance with an Elvis impersonation: "*Blue moon, You saw me standing alone, Without a dream in my heart, Without a love of my own.*"

Groix Island

Gabin pedals furiously in the dark towards the Red Sands campsite. Apparently his bungalow has a view of Belle-Île-en-Mer. He doesn't care. What matters is being where he is, not looking elsewhere. This is the first time he has set foot on an island. He plans to stay a few months, get settled in and make friends. Chiara seems very sad, yet there is poetry in her shy smile. She has a minute piece of blue sky in the warm brown of her right eye. When Danielle sang this evening, he almost asked the Italian girl to dance, but changed his mind. Maybe best just to speak to her instead. This girl is a tourist, she'll have a quick look around, buy some postcards, and take a few selfies standing in front of the port and the creperies. Then she'll return to Rome with a lucky *triskell*; a Celtic symbol with three spirals, meant to bring you good luck when it turns clockwise. You can't get attached to a smile, thinks Gabin to himself. This Italian girl is a *triskell* too, but one which spirals the wrong way. She'll only bring you trouble. He pedals fiercely in the night. Two eyes appear on the side of the road, he swerves and almost skids, the cat meows with fright. Roz had advised him not to stop if he spotted children playing on the moor. She said these were likely to be the real *korrigans*, who dance in circles at night and entice lost travellers into their midst. Gabin had laughed, thinking it was a joke, but Roz had been deadly serious. As a final warning she had told him that mortals who enter the *korrigans'* circles never make it out alive.

Small rabbits leap along the roadside. The elegant guest house, the Sémaphore de la Croix, now appears at the end of the road. The campsite is further along on the right, towards the Pointe des Chats.

Gabin is relieved to get back to his little bungalow. He has nothing with him except the contents of his bag; he likes to sail alone with nothing weighing him down, no mooring ropes or anchor. He will relax for a few days before getting down to work.

Groix Island, village centre

Urielle parks in the carpark behind the covered market and the pharmacy. She says the island looks completely different in the summer. In high season, the town is packed with pedestrians by early morning, and all the parking spaces are full. You have to queue for hours to do your shopping, as the tourists are in a hurry to get to the beach. Those who say it always rains here don't know Brittany—the island enjoys as many days of sunshine as the town of Cannes all the way down in the south of France. In the summer the ocean is a playground for children, pleasure boats, catamarans, windsurfers and swimmers. Out of season you can take your time and park where you want. And the ocean reigns supreme.

We have only come to buy bread, meat and newspapers, but it has taken us two hours. Every five seconds, Urielle runs into someone she knows. She introduces me, I shake hands and listen to their names. She knows more people on this island than I do in the whole of Rome. She tells me stories about them. Her parents regularly meet up with a group of their friends called the 7 Gang, on the seventh day of each month. Françoise used to run the café Chez Soaz on the harbour. Brigitte feeds homeless cats. Véronique is Lucette's daughter. Loïc the handsome butcher has just retired.

We go into the Boutique de la Mer, run by Pat and Mimi, to choose a children's book about *korrigans* for the twins.

We get them both a copy. One looks at the pictures quicker than the other, but they both want to read the same books; this is about the only time they don't fight.

"I understand now why your mother calls your sons the *korrigans!*" I say.

Urielle laughs. "That's how grandparents consider their grandchildren here. Little darlings when they arrive, and little rascals by the time they leave."

On the other side of the street, she chooses an old pulley for her father from Jo and Marie-Aimée. Their surname is Thunder too.

"It's dad's birthday in a month, he'll be sixty-five years old. How old's your father?"

"Twenty-five."

Urielle raises her eyebrows. "What?"

"He died twenty-six years ago; at the age I am now."

"Oh! I'm so sorry."

"I don't really miss him; I didn't get the chance to love him. Unlike my mother who misses him dreadfully. She takes it out on me, in a roundabout sort of way."

"How come?"

"Your mother cooks, your father smiles, your sister sings, you all love each other. I didn't know families like that existed in real life."

"I thought Italian families were really close knit."

"Not mine. My mother can't stand physical contact, she backs away if you get near her."

"What about you, does she kiss you?" asks Urielle, sounding concerned.

I shake my head.

"We say hello. That's it."

"When you were little, did you ever sit on her lap? Did she take you in her arms?"

"No."

I look into her eyes and imagine her laughing crazily with her parents, clambering over them, cuddles, hugs galore, sitting on Didier's shoulders or snuggling up against Roz. I don't know how it feels. You were close to your mother, Alessio, you said that mine needed time, but we're way past that now.

I stop dead in front of the bakery, struck by the obvious. It has taken me twenty-five years to realize. Livia loved her husband. I have a one in two chance that he is my father. It's as if I've drawn a line through the middle of the picture frame on the sideboard. On the left, is the blue eye of *nonna* Ornella's son. On the right, is the blurred eye of a stranger. If Livia couldn't bear to touch me, it was because I reminded her that she had betrayed her dead husband. I am a constant living reproach. And you don't embrace a nasty reproach, you avoid it . . .

"Chiara, this is Guy Thunder," says Urielle. "He has written a book about the local lifeguards. His father, Pierre, ran the Groix station."

Guy is older than the man I am looking for. His son Erwan, who rears abalone and fine oysters, is too young.

"Do you know the island of Elba?" I ask anyway.

He shakes his head.

"You asked my father the same question. Why are you so interested in Elba?" asks Urielle, intrigued.

I shrug with calculated indifference that could earn me an acting award at the Venice Film Festival.

"My godmother met a man with the surname Thunder there a while ago."

"I can research it online. There are three sites about Groix, two private ones and Anita's news blog. Do you want me to ask?"

I prefer to stay under the radar. "No, it's okay. We still have to pick up the newspaper, right?"

We cross the town and pick up *Ouest-France* and *Le Télé-gramme*. We don't pay for them as Didier has an account with the store. I say hello to Marie-Christine and Celine, and won-der if my father gets his newspaper there every morning.

The post office is just opposite, we go up the steps. As soon as Roz sees her daughter, her smile lights up the whole room. She kisses her even though they already kissed this morning. When Livia's husband was laid to rest at the Roman cemetery in Verano, she still let bereaved family and friends hug and kiss her. It was after my birth that she became allergic to any form of physical contact and affection. Now I know why.

"What time shall I put the chicken in Mum?" asks Urielle.

"Midday should be fine."

"How many of us will there be tonight?"

"Twelve," replies Roz cheerfully.

Twelve people around the table? Livia had the perfect excuse to escape any festivities: we were in mourning. I wasn't allowed to invite anyone for my birthday, and I was hardly ever invited to other people's houses. Fortunately, I had Alessio.

"How can your mother cook for twelve people when she's working all day?" I ask, in surprise.

"Oh, she's used to it. Danielle will help her. We'll take Nolan and Evan to the beach so they're not under her feet."

"Hello, ladies!"

Gabin heads towards us, looking pleased with himself.

"I've been chatting with Anne, the bookseller at L'Écume. I told her about my project."

"Does she sell your books?" teases Urielle.

"Of course! Can I get you girls a coffee?"

We take a seat outside the Bleu Thé café. Urielle decides that we must try Gwenola's Far Breton, a French cake filled with custard and prunes. I'm intrigued by the name; when it arrives, it turns out to be a triangular-shaped piece of tart.

"We always beg her for the recipe, but she promised her father before he died that she would never give it away," says Urielle.

I take a mouthful. It's delicious. It's like a fluffy cloud bursting with joy.

"It was their main dish in Brittany in the nineteenth century."

She turns to Gabin. "Are you having dinner with us tonight?"

"No!" I cry out instinctively.

Urielle stares at me in surprise and Gabin bursts out laughing. I quickly explain myself.

"There are twelve of us at the table and with you it would make thirteen which is bad luck. My grandmother was superstitious, and it rubbed off on me. It goes back to the Last Supper, with the Twelve Apostles and Jesus, when Judas betrayed him."

"Then why don't we invite a fourteenth person?" suggests Urielle.

A woman at the next table is reading a newspaper with a front-page story about Salvador Dalí and Yves Montand, whose real name was Ivo Livi. They have both been exhumed for a paternity case. I shudder. In the past, there were blood groups to determine kinship. Now they use DNA analysis. My grandmother rests in peace beside her son in Rome, there is no question of digging them up. When we studied blood groups at school, I asked *nonna* Ornella what my father's blood group was. She told me he was A positive. Like me. Nothing prevents him from being my father. But nothing proves it either.

"Do you know what blood groups you guys are?" I ask.

"AB," says Gabin.

"O negative. I can give my blood to everyone, but I can only receive mine," says Urielle. "It's a rare group; my parents and sister have the same. When Danielle fell off the balcony, my parents gave their blood as there wasn't any in reserve."

I can't be Didier's daughter then. So I'm not Urielle's sister. I need to find the Frenchman from Elba and do a DNA test. If it's negative, then I really am the daughter of my official father.

Back at Urielle's, we put on some music. My heart feels full as I listen to Michel Tonnerre's husky voice. *I will love you until the end, and when the journey is over, and it is she who takes my hand . . .* Danielle sneaks in and finishes the verse: *I will give her your face . . .*

Nanterre, thirteen years earlier

Your name is Charles, your brother Paul is now the only family you've got left. Your life has been turned upside down. Your brother has become your official guardian. You leave your home in Chatou to go and live with Patty in a neighbouring town on the other side of the bridge.

You carry on going to school at Perceval. Everyone is worried about you, teachers and students alike. You stiffen up to stop yourself from collapsing. You refuse to talk about Alice to the therapist and the headmistress. You act as if everything were normal, even though you are broken inside.

Patty is in charge in Nanterre and once Paul's back is turned, she makes sure you know it. When he is there, she is warm and kind. But when he's not, she turns into a witch. She is older than Paul who is flattered to have a real woman interested in him. She hates reading, and when she's not at work she spends her time in front of the TV channel-surfing. Sometimes Paul reads her poetry. *You are like the sea, you cradle the stars, you are the field of love, you bind and separate lovers and madmen, You are the hunger the bread the thirst the highest euphoria.* But she doesn't give a damn about Éluard, and interrupts, dragging him into the bedroom before giggling with pleasure, which does your head in. So you leave the flat and go and sit in the stairwell to read, but the light goes off automatically and you have to get up each time to turn it back on.

Paul now has to provide for you. His dream of becoming a photographer has gone out of the window. He has decided not to sit his exams next month either. You plead with him saying that Mum would be furious, but he doesn't listen. Now that he has to work for a living, studying is well and truly off the cards. Patty's brother, a baker in Rueil-Malmaison, has just fired his apprentice after yet another quarrel. Paul proposes to take his place. Eighteen isn't that young to start vocational training. He works nights, weekends and public holidays. He is never there when you wake up. No more breakfasts together. A new chapter has begun. Or rather, has been forced on you. Patty, who works as a sales assistant in a shopping centre, gets up later. She is a very light sleeper so she bans you from using the kitchen or bathroom before going to school. You're not even allowed to turn on the tap or use the toilet. She claims that the sound of the cistern would wake her up.

Embarrassed, you hold it in and dive into the school toilets as soon as you arrive. You brush your teeth in the school toilets too. Every morning, you go to school with a tummy ache and an empty stomach. You don't dare tell Paul, you're too ashamed. He works both Saturdays and Sundays. On those days, Patty acts like you're not there. She walks around naked in front of you and doesn't answer when you speak to her. One day you stand in front of her and block her path.

"Hey oh, I'm here! Why don't you want to talk to me? What have I ever done to you?"

She looks at you like you're an ugly little nobody.

"I love your brother," she finally says reluctantly. "You're just some extra baggage. You don't exist."

"I'm not baggage, I'm a boy! I don't have a handle or wheels, I've got arms and legs, see!"

You spin around and flap your arms.

"I didn't want you here, but Paul forced me. You're a burden to him."

"I'm not a burden, I'm his family!"

"*Used* to be. Now *I'm* his family. Can't you see three's a crowd?"

You close yourself off. You bury yourself in your mother's beloved poetry. You have kept her La Pléiade collection, you sniff the bible paper, hoping for a whiff of her perfume. You haven't removed the stars of dried blood from the page your mother was reading when she collapsed. You hold onto that book like a precious relic. You read the poems over and over again. Every evening you go to the pool in Chatou, near your old house, and swim length after length until you drop. You become a ghost in Patty's flat. You keep out of their way. You're not even sure you exist anymore.

The school year ends. Paul's friends all pass their final exams. He drinks himself stupid the evening the results come out and gets morose. You fall asleep wearing earplugs to avoid hearing his sobs.

The nightmare continues throughout the school holidays. Paul works nights, Patty gets up late. You are still banned from using the bathroom and toilet. But the school is closed now so you can't go there, plus you have no money to go to a café. Patty triumphantly comes home one day with a plastic chamber pot, which she holds out to you.

"You'll use this in your room from now on."

You are thirteen years old. You give in. You promise yourself you won't tell a soul, you're too proud. You try not to use the damn thing.

Paul informs you that you will no longer be able to continue your education at Perceval. As your mother taught there, the headmistress made you a very generous offer, but it's still more expensive than the state school, and makes no sense now that you have changed catchment areas.

"I'm sorry, mate," says Paul. He has dark circles under his eyes and his cheeks are hollow. "We have no choice. But you do get delicious fresh bread to eat!"

"Your bread is disgusting," you say, teasing him.

"Your feet stink!"

"You've got dog breath! And what are those ugly things on your feet?"

Paul is no longer wearing his blue Converse trainers.

"Patty threw away my old shoes and gave me these. She'd be upset if I didn't wear them."

How dare he betray Mum's brightly coloured shoe tradition, just when you were about to pour your heart out to him? You decide to drown your sorrows in the Chatou swimming pool.

The last thread that linked you to your old life has just been severed. At Perceval, everyone knew you as Alice's son. In Nanterre you're just another anonymous pupil, whose elder brother signs his school reports. A boy with a head full of poetry and a broken heart.

Groix Island, Red Sands beach

Groix is nicknamed the "garnet island", because here in this cove the sand glimmers with the same dark red reflections as Urielle's bracelet. I am sitting with her in front of the sea. Gabin is off doing research, Roz is working at the post office and Didier has gone out with Danielle to help a friend repair his boat.

"When I was a kid, my mother wouldn't allow herself to be happy after her husband's death. So, to be polite, I would ask other people if they were unhappy too. They thought I was nuts. Life on your island is no easier than anywhere else, but you seem to be at peace here," I say.

"It's no longer my island," sighs Urielle.

The *korrigans* collect shells and fill their pockets with purple sand and seaweed. Urielle lets them play. She will change their clothes when she gets home. She grew up on this tiny island in the middle of the ocean. She spent her secondary school years as a boarder in Lorient. But she dreamt of leaving, seeing the world, longed to live near traffic lights, underground stations, nightclubs, multiplex cinemas, concert venues, and entertainment. She left Groix at eighteen. But since the twins' father left and the Bataclan terrorist attack, she finds the Parisian traffic suffocating, the pollution worrying, the droves of people infuriating, and the metro anxiety inducing. She is constantly racing against the clock and is a permanent bundle of nerves. She has turned into one of the many tourists who take over Groix Island in August: a highly-strung, high-performing, stressed-out city dweller.

"Do you know why I fell in love with my ex? Because he was a cataphile."

"Excuse me?"

She smiles but the smile doesn't reach her eyes.

"He was fascinated by the catacombs. He loved going down there with his friends, they would access the tunnels through manhole covers in the street or via the Petite Ceinture, a former railway line that circles Paris and was abandoned in the 1930s. It's illegal though. The catacombs are monitored by the "catapolice" who patrol the tunnels and dole out fines to those who dare to go down there. Imagine a lawless underground world, where parties, exhibitions and concerts take place. I wasn't claustrophobic at the time; it was rather exciting."

She sighs. "My parents don't dare ask me why I've turned up this weekend without warning. Actually, something weird happened to me last week. I had a panic attack on the metro."

She was rushing home to relieve the babysitter, when suddenly she felt the sides of the train drawing closer. She shook her head in surprise and took some deep breaths. But it started all over again. The walls were shaking and sliding down, bending in towards each other and crushing the passengers who seemed oblivious to it all. Urielle tried to tell them. She then jumped up and ran to the door, but the train was in a tunnel, and she couldn't get out. She thought she was going to die like that, trapped between two sheets of metal. She was gasping for air, trembling, shaking the door handle, shouting to the other passengers. *Can't you see that we're all going to die?* People panicked, thinking it was a terrorist attack. Fortunately, the train came out of the tunnel and stopped.

Urielle sprang out onto the platform and ran down the passageway. Finally, she emerged from the underground labyrinth into the street. It took her an hour to calm down and regain composure. When she got home, the babysitter was furious at how late she was and quit on the spot. That was when Urielle decided to take refuge at her parents' home on Groix.

"I work in events management; we organize trade fairs and shows. It's exciting, but very stressful. You're on the go all day long. Plus, it's just me and the *korrigans* now."

"Does their father not help you?" I ask.

"He went to Nepal just after their birth, asking me to go with him. I left Groix to discover Parisian life, not to smoke weed in the Himalayas! But I'm drowning in the big city. My life on Groix feels so effortless it's like floating in comparison . . ."

She sinks her bare feet into the wet sand and curls up her toes.

"I grew up knowing that one day I would have to take care of Danielle. I'm actually responsible for three people: my children and my big sister."

"Your parents aren't old," I say. "And Nolan and Evan will help you when the time comes."

"I won't ask anything of them!" she exclaims fiercely. "I'm not putting that burden on their shoulders."

Alessio, I tell Urielle about how you took care of your mother after your father's terminal cancer when you were just eighteen years old. Freedom may not have a price, but it has a cost. You refused to let his death drag either of you down. You quit your architectural studies and dumped your girlfriend to travel with your mother. You were a shoulder for her to cry on in Istanbul, Syracuse, Munich and Bruges. When she was strong enough, you returned to Rome and got your independence back.

"No, Evan, in your pocket, not your mouth!" shouts Urielle. "You can't eat shells. Spit it out now!"

The child obeys and spits it out onto his trousers. His delighted brother sticks a handful of sand in his mouth before happily dribbling it onto his pirate T-shirt.

"I'm just as crazy as Danielle, you just can't see it," says Urielle. "The walls of that train carriage really had closed in on those people, in a manner of speaking. I mean, Parisians are trapped in the metro morning and evening, all year round. In Groix, the starry sky makes your imagination run away with you. Did you know that from the coastline you can glimpse America? In Paris, you can't even see the next metro station. I want to come back, but it's impossible, I'm too proud."

"It would be a decision, not a failure. Your pride would be saved."

"I was wrong, Chiara. I have to hold on in there. I won't use the metro; I'll walk everywhere or get a bike. I'm not going to let a bunch of stressed out commuters ruin my life. I'm Breton for God's sake, my ancestors survived storms and shipwrecks and thunder!"

That reminds me of my mission to find Mr Thunder from Groix. We gather up the spades, buckets, soaking wet laughing *korrigans* and all pile into the car.

"Besides, I don't believe you're only here for sightseeing," says Urielle as she gets behind the wheel. "There's something you're not telling me."

Taken aback, I look away.

"You don't just turn up on an island by accident," she continues, starting the engine. "You're on a mission. It's not the beach, the seagulls or the crêpes that lured you here. Here, everything is symbolic. This island was created by the collision of two tectonic plates four hundred thousand years ago. It's known as the Witches Island, *Enez Ar C'hoaz'h*. It's a crucible, an athanor, a cauldron of white magic. Are you looking for a Mr Thunder who once went to Elba?"

I nod as the twins kick us from the back seat.

"Stop it boys! Is it important that you find this guy?"

I nod again. But I can't explain why it's so important; the words remain stuck at the bottom of my throat like an anchor.

"I'm going to help you; I owe you that. Tomorrow morning, we'll go and see Perig in Kermarec. He's a press correspondent here, he knows everyone. Vicars and doctors may have come and gone, the town hall may have switched political sides, but Perig is still here.

Nanterre, ten years earlier

You are now a broad-shouldered sixteen-year-old, thanks to the lengths of crawl and butterfly that you force yourself to do every evening at the Chatou pool. At school, you excel in French at the expense of all other subjects.

One Saturday, you're on your way back from a party with friends, when your old moped breaks down. You don't want to wake up Paul and Patty. You know Paul leaves early in the morning ready to put the first batch of bread in the oven, and won't check if you're back. Patty won't even notice you're gone. You spend the night in a classmate's basement, you got in through a broken window. You stay there for a whole week. No one even realizes. You are finally kicked out by the cleaning lady who almost has a heart attack when she discovers you. Your friend's father calls home. Patty picks up, and whines on about the weird orphan boy she took in out of pity. She is a good actress. The father forbids his daughter from seeing you. In revenge, Patty opens the window of your bedroom to let the rain in. In the evening, when you come back from school, you cry out in horror: your exercise books, your binder and your La Pléiade collection are soaked. With trembling hands and a racing heart, you open your mother's book. Phew, the red stars are intact. You storm into the living room, where she is slumped in front of the TV.

"You're a bitch and a miserable old hag!"

"And you're just a little shit!" she shouts back. "This is just the beginning. Your brother will believe me, not you!"

Patty is good at playing the innocent. When Paul returns, covered in flour and exhausted, she looks him in the eye and swears that it was you who left your window open.

At the end of the year, you come first in the national French composition test. Paul will not be able to attend the award ceremony at the Sorbonne; he has taken over Patty's brother's bakery in Rueil-Malmaison and is now self-employed. You have no one to tell the good news to. You will be the only winner there alone.

The awards secretary wants to know the names of your guests. "Your loved ones wouldn't want to miss such an important moment, would they?"

You utter the first words that come into your head: "My parents live in the United States, they work at NASA, they've got their heads in the clouds."

"It can't be easy to live so far away from your family," the secretary sympathizes.

She's fallen for it. And you discover the power of your imagination. Writers do this all day long, they invent characters and invent situations to put them in.

You stand beaming, sad and alone in the huge amphitheatre at the Sorbonne. You think about your mother, you think about the baby Patty is expecting. That little girl will have a great father and a lousy mother. She would have had a fantastic grandmother. Paul wants to call her Alice, Patty insists on Luna. Alice will be her middle name. You'll call her Luna-Alice. Patty will never forgive you.

Groix Island, Kermarec

The village faces the sea, positioned on the rugged coastline at the other end of the island.

"*La donna é mobile, qual piuma al vento!*"

I recognize Verdi's *Rigoletto* that *nonna* Ornella absolutely adored. Perig and his wife belong to "La Kleienn", the local choir. We wait for the tenor to stop singing before knocking on the door. There's a doorbell, but it's not connected to anything, apparently that's quite usual on the island.

The man inside is imposing. He has hands like carpet beaters, feet like flippers, round, dark eyes, and a deep, articulate voice. His wife, Aziliz, is a miniature doll in comparison, a delicate soprano.

"Urielle, it's a great pleasure to see you! Didn't you bring those rascals, your *poulpiquets*?"

"No, they're with Mum. We need to pick your brains."

"Come along in! There's a little bit of *tchumpôt* left over from last night."

Urielle tells them that I'm from Rome. Aziliz slips a small slice of *tchumpôt* onto my plate from the pan where it has been frying in butter. Tiramisu has the calories of a lettuce compared to this scrumptious dessert. You would have loved it, Alessio. Five bites of this culinary delight would satisfy the whole of the AS Roma football team.

"Chiara is looking for a Mr Thunder who went to the island of Elba precisely twenty-six years ago," explains Urielle.

"Do you know how many Thunders are alive today?" I ask.

Perig thinks while Aziliz clears the table, singing. Then he rummages in his bookcase and takes out a file that he flips through.

"It's difficult to determine precisely. I once looked into it for an article. Some of them live here, while others have travelled, moved away, or become city dwellers. There were five initial families, which produced three unrelated branches."

He points to the file on the table. "The branches were descended from Bonnaventure Donnerch who married around 1603, Jan Tonnerch who married around 1628, and Jacob Thonnerch who married around 1629. They still exist today. Urielle's father is a descendant of Bonnaventure. Guy and Erwan are Jacob's descendants. Alain, Marielle's husband, is a descendant of Jan. I'll find out. Nicknames were given to each family to differentiate between those having the same name. Between 1627 and 1900, there were 1700 Thunder births."

The sheer number amazes me.

"I met a writer on the boat over who is here to research a novel, can I send him to you?" asks Urielle.

Perig nods, then stares at me.

"Why are you looking for this Mr Thunder?"

"My godmother met him back in the day, she would like to know what became of him."

"I'll do my best. I don't rely on those social networks you lot use. Twitter is no match for café gossip, Facebook is not a patch on queuing at the newsagent's or the post office, and Instagram is not anything as helpful as photo albums. *A galon vat*, it will be my pleasure!"

"We were supposed to do our choir practice this afternoon," Aziliz reminds him.

"We'll do it tomorrow."

Perig is like a bloodhound who has just picked up a scent. Urielle was spot on, we came to the right place.

"History fascinates me," he continues. "During the winter of 1835, a woman abandoned her baby at the turnstile designed for that purpose at the Lorient hospice. The little girl was five or six months old, and had two sets of undergarments, two sets of flannelette clothes, and a bonnet with her. It was Saint Sabine's day, so they called her Sabine. The child grew up and came to work at the sardine press in Port-Mélite. She married on the island in August 1860 and produced one of the branches of the Thunder family."

"The turnstile?" I ask, not understanding.

"Mothers who couldn't keep their children would leave them there at the hospice just as you post a letter today. Every family has a story, every house and every boat too. I'm writing an article about shipwrecks. Have you heard about the *Coranna* that was wrecked on Groix at the end of the nineteenth century, Urielle?"

"Vaguely."

"It was a Danish three-master that set sail from Bordeaux bound for Cardiff, loaded with wooden support beams for the mines. She lost her rudder and ran aground on the Terrible Rock between Locqueltas and the Storan, in 1894. The Groix islanders managed to save the crew's fifteen sailors. The sea destroyed the boat, but several families were able to keep warm by using the timber as firewood. Another boat laden with boots and shoes had sunk fifty years earlier in the same spot."

"We found the remains of a drakkar near the beach at Locmaria," adds Urielle. "It was the tomb of a Viking chief, and it's now kept at the castle in Saint-Germain-en-Laye."

"A Greek cargo ship, the *Sanaga*, ran aground in March 1971 near Les Chats lighthouse while en route to Saint-Nazaire," continues Perig. "Divers like to swim around the wreck. I do the same out of the water, without mask, fins or wetsuit. I search for clues and anecdotes. Does your friend know the story of the postman that got eaten?"

Urielle shakes her head.

"Wounded soldiers had jobs reserved for them. One day, a postmaster who had lost an arm in battle died on his rounds between two villages on the island. When he was found on the road, someone shouted: 'They've already eaten his arm!' The rumour spread like wildfire and, like a game of Chinese whispers, soon became: 'The villagers ate the postman!'"

I smile. "You have enough there to write a book."

"I published one in my youth, but it didn't sell. Now I prefer to write my articles."

As he walks us to the gate, a huge ginger tomcat runs between his legs and into the house.

"Standfirst, you're late!" he calls to the cat.

"Standfirst, the cat?" I say, amused.

"The standfirst is the introductory paragraph in an article," explains Perig. "It's formatted in larger and bolder type than the rest. And this animal certainly is larger and bolder than the other cats! He lives his own life and has no master. We're honoured that he wants to pay us a visit today."

"Perig is an amazing man," says Urielle as we walk to the car. "He's highly cultured and down to earth, a rare combination. He's not a fisherman, but Dad says he must have caught wisdom and strength in his nets. He and Aziliz lost their teenage son, he was a windsurfing champion and he drowned. After that tragedy, he buried himself in his work, and became an expert on the island. Do you still not want me to put out a message on the websites and blog I spoke to you about?"

I shake my head. Too many people would know about it. I prefer to keep my investigation discreet.

"By the way, he didn't call the twins the *korrigans*. He used another word, didn't he?"

"Yes, '*poulpiquets*', but it means the same as *korrigans*, it's from Breton legend. They are the gnomes of the *Petit Peuple*, the Little People. In Breton fairy tales, they hide their treasure at the foot of rainbows. They are blacksmiths, alchemists, and magicians. Perig would have made a wonderful grandfather."

Groix Island, Port-Lay

After dinner, I help Danielle and Urielle clear the table. I now know where the cutlery drawer is and how Roz stacks the plates in her dishwasher. Is this what they mean by a real family, Alessio? Shopping, cooking, eating, laughing and doing stuff together?

"Cory told us this morning that she has to stop work for a week for a minor but urgent operation. I don't know how we're going to manage for the Locmaria round," Roz sighs.

"Can't you recruit someone temporarily?" suggests Didier.

"It's not easy this time of year. The young people we hire in the summer are on the mainland. And the hours are demanding. Those who already have a job can't do both."

"Can I help?" he asks.

"The bicycle is heavy with the mail, even if it is electric. Your knee wouldn't hold up."

"Dad refuses to have the operation," Urielle tells me.

"I've got the twins," she adds. "Besides, I have to go back to Paris for work."

Roz shrugs. "Let's sleep on it. We'll see tomorrow."

She explains to me that the collection office is in Lanester for the Greater Lorient area. In Groix, there is the post office counter, the post office bank, the branch offering general postal services and a postwoman.

The Italian film *Il Postino* comes to mind: on the island of Salina in the 1950s, Mario is the exiled poet Pablo

Neruda's postman. Neruda teaches Mario the power of words to seduce the beautiful Beatrice. Viola took me to see it because my father adored Neruda. She gave me a poem by him that I hung above my bed. It starts with the lines: *He who does not travel, who does not read, who does not listen to music . . . dies slowly.* And ends with: *You start dying slowly If you do not risk what is safe for the uncertain, If you do not go after a dream, If you do not allow yourself, At least once in your lifetime, To run away from sensible advice . . .* I imagine that I am the postman who ends up befriending the poet while delivering his mail to him. I would love to deliver mail to the father I don't know. I have never travelled. I read, but hardly ever listen to music. Since I was born, I have been dying a slow death. It is time I took risks. I pluck up the courage and take the plunge.

"I can pedal at lightning speed. If it's just for one week, maybe I could help out?"

My offer is met with amazement and silence.

"You're not from here," says Urielle eventually.

"You're not French," says Roz. "So our insurance wouldn't cover you."

"I won't be driving a car on the main roads, I'll be riding a bike on a quiet little island and slipping envelopes into letterboxes," I protest.

Danielle sings: "A *bicycleeeeeettttteeeeeee.*"

"I don't know, Chiara," says Roz, hesitantly.

"It's just to help you out."

If Perig finds the man I'm looking for, I'll have a brilliant excuse to approach him if I'm the replacement postwoman. Roz simply has to agree. I appeal to Urielle, catching her eye.

"I'll talk to the collection office about it," says Roz dubiously.

"Can't you say that Chiara is your goddaughter and that you can vouch for her?" suggests Urielle.

Roz, an honest and law-abiding civil servant, frowns. "I don't like lying."

"She saved Evan remember," says Urielle. "For me that beats anything! If he had fallen overboard . . ."

Roz pictures Danielle falling from her bedroom window all those years ago. Then she imagines Evan drowning in the ocean.

"I'm only trying to help," I say.

Roz weighs up the pros and cons. She really does need someone.

"It's kind of you to offer, Chiara, it would certainly solve the problem. I'll recommend you. If they agree, you'll spend a week with Cory so she can show you the ropes."

"Will you give her the folder you used for last summer's replacement, with the plans and pointers?" asks Urielle.

"The records and names have just been updated."

Urielle has figured out why I'm doing this.

"Did your godmother have a big crush on the Groix islander of Elba?" she whispers. "Did she never get over him? Can you imagine what it will be like for them to come face to face after all these years?"

Suddenly Nolan leaps onto the kitchen stool. Standing on tiptoes, he reaches for the bowl of marshmallow bears that Didier thought he had put well out of reach. He grabs it, but his hand slips and the glass bowl crashes to the floor, frightening the life out of the dog who runs off.

"You little horrors!" shouts Urielle, grabbing the twins. "Get out of there, you'll cut yourselves! Chiara grab Belle and keep him out of the way; chocolate is poisonous for dogs!"

I hold the cocker spaniel back by his collar. We sweep up the broken glass and marshmallow bears, emptying the dustpan into the bin. The pitiful twins are keeping their heads down.

Urielle's remark has unnerved me. This is my story. It's my right to seek out my father, but I have overlooked the fact that Livia is number one in the pecking order. If I find this Mr Thunder will he want to reconnect with her? How will she react?

Nanterre, eight years earlier

You're eighteen now, your hair is scruffy and you've grown a beard to make you look older than you are. On the rare occasions you think of the father you never knew, you imagine him to have a beard. Do you look like him? How would you know? You are now a head taller than your brother. You've just started studying medicine in Paris. Your heart pounds in your chest with every beat. You don't have a stethoscope yet, nor do you know anything about cardiology, but you figure out that this rhythmic dance has its own set of rules and melody. You park your old moped amongst the brand-new shiny motorcycles and fancy bikes. You're going to work non-stop and pass your first-year exams because this is your dream. In the lecture hall, you are delighted to see Vincent, a former pupil from Perceval. Vincent asks you to flat share with him. Vincent's father is the director of a hypermarket, and Vincent works as a salesman on weekends in the video game department to earn some extra cash. He recommends you to the books department who give you a part time job. Reading gets you through bad days and boosts you on good days. This money will enable you to pay for your studies and your share of the rent; you'll finally earn your freedom.

The day you leave Nanterre for good, you don't tell anyone. You're alone in the flat. It's raining outside. You stuff your clothes and books into a scuffed leather suitcase that still smells of your mother's perfume. You haven't used it since you and Paul moved out of Chatou. You sit down, feeling giddy. You close your eyes and picture your mother buying it at the flea market: "Boys, look at all the labels stuck on this suitcase. It's seen so many countries and must have many fantastic stories to tell."

You never went on holiday; none of you felt the need. And after Alice's death, you couldn't afford it anyway. But now you want to spread your wings, cut Patty out of your life, travel the globe and experience the adventures promised by those labels.

You dig out the chamber pot from the bottom of the cupboard that you stopped using when Patty went into labour at the maternity unit. Those few days alone with Paul could have been happy, but they turned out to be grim. That brotherhood bond had gone, swept away over the years by Paul's state of exhaustion. The day Patty came home with her baby daughter, you cradled the baby, scanning her face desperately for signs of Alice. Then, in front of your brother, you handed Patty the chamber pot saying: "Luna-Alice is going to need this more than me." Paul didn't know what you were on about. Patty snatched the baby back.

"Her name is Luna! What kind of weird baby gift is this?"

You gave your niece a vintage edition of *Alice in Wonderland*.

On your last day in Nanterre, you set the kitchen table for three, but you put the chamber pot in your place instead of a plate and throw the keys to the flat inside it. You open the window above the television, unplug it to avoid starting a fire and let the rain in. You take the remote control and drop it into the rubbish chute. Then you leave, slamming the door behind you.

You stop off at the bakery where Paul is surprised to see you.

"Is the baby okay?" he asks, concerned.

"I've just come to say goodbye. I'm moving in with friends."

"Oh! So, I won't see you again?" asks Paul sadly, as he kneads the croissant dough.

"We hardly spend any time together anyway, so it's no big deal. We could have lunch one day when you're not working, just the two of us?"

Paul sighs. "You know what Patty's like. We don't see much of each other as it is so it'll just cause a row. She blames me for not doing enough for Luna, but I'll drop down dead if I don't get any sleep."

You don't insist.

Paris, eight years earlier

You quickly found your feet at the hypermarket where you work part time. The manager of the book department is good at making sure that the customers all leave with an inspiring book in their trolleys, even though they had actually come to buy washing powder or toilet paper.

On rainy days, you prefer the metro to your moped. It's the 24th of December. You are sat in the train opposite a brunette who has different coloured eyes, and it's unsettling you. You have just studied this particular feature in genetics class, it's called heterochromia. The young woman, used to being stared at, looks the other way. She is reading a large spiral-bound manuscript, tearing out the pages as she turns them. Her actions attract your attention. She laughs, touched by the text she is reading. Her eyes cloud over, her breathing quickens, her hands grip the cover. She must work in publishing. She looks up at the next station, stuffs the manuscript into her satchel which is the same blue as her left eye, and gets up, clutching the pages she has read. Normally you would stay on that line all the way home, but you get off behind her and follow her. On the platform she looks for a bin and throws the torn manuscript into it, before dashing down a passageway to change lines. You recover the pages from the bin, stuff them inside your jacket and run to catch up with her.

You stick with her during two line changes and past three bins, without her even noticing you. She walks gracefully, she must have taken dance classes, she unfurls her foot in a particular way. Nobody is waiting for you tonight. Vincent is in the mountains with his family, and your other roommates have gone to visit their parents. None of them imagine for a second that you'll be spending Christmas alone. You haven't heard from your brother. Patty must be giving him a hard time and she won't have forgiven you for the wet TV stunt. You are alone in the world. It's strangely liberating—no constraints, no Sunday lunches, no family gatherings!

You follow the young woman all the way to her front door. She threw the last pages in the bin on the corner of her street. Her hands are empty. You have salvaged everything. You go home, spread out your paper haul, take a roll of tape and reconstruct the pages one by one. Then, you dive into the story. You don't know who the author is, you only have their initials and the title of the book. It is an addictive psychological thriller, whose detective hero falls in love with his boss's wife. You devour it in one sitting that night to forget you're alone.

Since leaving Nanterre you delight in taking a long shower every morning, even if your roommates complain about having to wait their turn. You then have a massive breakfast that sets you up for the day. You look back at the four years of hell Patty subjected you to and ask yourself why you put up with it. Your mother's death had crushed your spirit. You'll never let anyone treat you like that again.

It's the 25th of December. You get up early. You take a long hot shower emptying the hot water tank in the process, then devour a soft-boiled egg with soldiers before dashing off with the manuscript under your arm.

You lie in wait for the young woman at the bottom of her building. She is probably going out for Christmas lunch. And shortly before noon, she opens the door. You follow her stealthily, just like the detective stalking the woman in the novel. She is bearing gifts and a bottle of wine. She is alone, no husband or children. Yesterday her feet danced as she walked, but today she is shuffling them. She obviously isn't thrilled at the prospect of a family get together.

She gets on the train; you sit down right opposite her. You avoid catching her eye, open the manuscript and pretend to be reading.

She leans forward. You feel her movement, but you keep your head down.

"Are you a journalist?" she asks.

If you admit that you followed her, she'll think you're a serial killer.

"This is just a manuscript, the book hasn't been published yet," I say, sidestepping the question.

"I know; I know the author."

She raises an eyebrow as she spots the tape.

"You tore each page in half? Why would you do that?"

Intrigued, your fellow passengers are now listening in to the conversation. Why does this girl care what he is reading?

"Hey, I asked you a question!" she says, raising her voice.

"It's a really gripping detective story, just can't put it down!" you reply, dodging her question again.

She reaches out to grab the manuscript, but you close it.

"Give me that, it's my copy!" she shouts. "I tore it up yesterday, before throwing it away. I don't like reading on screen. You went through the bins in the metro, didn't you!"

She seems to have trouble comprehending what is happening. Then her expression hardens.

"Did you follow me?"

You quote the hero from the novel.

"*I'm not that kind of guy, I merely followed in the footsteps of a fairy.*"

"Is this a sketch for TV, or a hidden webcam?" asks the businessman in a suit and tie sitting opposite her. "Are you two both in on it?"

"They look serious," laughs the young Rasta with dreadlocks sitting across from you, who is wearing a yellow T-shirt bearing the slogan: *Be drunk always*.

"Are you crazy?" the young woman asks you.

You have nothing to lose. The metro slows down, she'll get off and disappear from your life before she even entered it. You remember those childhood evenings, you hear your mother's voice, your body remembers the giant beanbag you used to sink into. The Rasta's yellow T-shirt is no coincidence. It cheers you up.

"*Be drunk always*," you recite to the girl. "*That is the point; nothing else matters. In order not to feel the terrible burden of time which weighs on your shoulders and makes you bend towards the ground, you need to be drunk always. But on what? Wine, poetry or virtue, as you wish. But be drunk.*"

She raises her right eyebrow. Her face relaxes. No one mistrusts a poet, you listen to them, you walk with them. The train brakes screech as it comes to a halt. It stops dead in the tunnel before reaching the station. Luck is on your side! A disembodied voice tells passengers not to disembark, reassuring them that the train will set off again shortly. God must have heard your prayer. You continue serenely:

"*And if sometimes, on the steps of a palace or the green grass of a ditch, in the mournful solitude of your room, you wake again, drunkenness already diminishing or gone, ask the wind, the wave, the star, the bird, the clock, everything that is flying, everything that is groaning, everything that is rolling, everything that is singing, everything that is speaking, ask what time it is...*"

You've played your last card. The stranger's blue eye is amused. Her brown eye remains sceptical. She finishes the poem in a subdued voice:

"*. . . and wind, wave, star, bird, clock will answer you: 'It is time to be drunk! So as not to be the martyred slaves of time, be drunk, be drunk always! On wine, on poetry or on virtue as you wish.'*"

The man in the suit smiles. He suspected that you knew each other. The young Rasta takes his leave by sweeping the air with an invisible hat.

"Charles Baudelaire, a connoisseur of the green, a man with taste."

You look at him astonished.

"Hashish," she explains. "How did you get this manuscript?"

The metro blows, sighs and shakes. The train slides slowly towards the platform before coming to a complete standstill. The doors slide open with a shudder. You hold the manuscript out to the young woman, who snatches it from you and then leaves the train. You follow her. She glares at you, forbidding you to follow her any further down the corridor towards the connecting trains. You obey, and she disappears into the crowd with her Christmas presents and wine. You collapse onto a plastic seat and admit defeat. You close your eyes, you can't win them all.

When you open them, she is standing in front of you.

"What's your name?"

"Charles. I'm not joking! My brother's called Paul, after Éluard. Our mother was a French teacher."

"Pleased to meet you, Charles. My name's Aurore, like George Sand. I'm a publicist. What do you do for a living, besides stalking women in the metro and rummaging through dustbins?"

"I'm a medical student. I want to save other people's mothers," I say spontaneously.

"We're going to be late," she replies. "Hurry."

"Late for what?" you ask, standing up obediently.

She scans the area looking for a rubbish bin and throws in the patched-up manuscript.

"I'm going to a lunch that a publisher friend is hosting for people who are on their own for Christmas. My parents are on a cruise. It will be sushi rather than turkey. Would you like to come with me?"

You nod. And so, your story begins.

Groix Island, Port-Tudy

Urielle is returning to Paris with the twins. Roz is dropping them off at the boat. Both mother and daughter have been hovering around each other for the whole weekend without speaking. Even picture-perfect families buckle under the weight of the unsaid. I'm sitting beside Roz, Urielle and the boys are in the back.

"I won't let go of their reins for the entire journey," she says. "Once was enough for me!"

"Why did you come?" asks Roz, looking at her in the rear-view mirror.

Urielle tenses up; she thought she would be able to leave without being interrogated.

"I missed you."

"I wasn't born yesterday. You look like death warmed up. Are you ill?"

"I'm fine, but I did something silly."

"Are you pregnant?"

"No chance of that."

"Are you back with that spineless scoundrel?"

"Not a chance in hell! No, moving to Paris was a mistake."

Roz breathes a sigh of relief. "I was so worried, I thought that it was a health problem or that you were taking my *korrigans* off to the Himalayas."

Urielle shakes her head. "My dream was to live in a big city, but I'm not cut out for it."

Pedestrian passengers board the boat on the right, cars drive up the ramp to the left.

"The boat will leave without you if you don't board now. Think, and follow your heart. Look on Paris as a great experience."

"More like an abysmal failure," says Urielle.

Roz turns around. "My grandchildren are not abysmal failures; they are my lucky sea fairies! Quick you'll have to run; they're removing the gangway!"

Urielle leaps out of the car holding her sons by their reins. I wheel her suitcase up to the boat and she wishes me good luck. They get on just in time.

Groix Island, village centre

We head up to the post office. Roz is clearly relieved that her daughter is in good health and is not emigrating to the other side of the world. Livia never used to worry about me. I know Roz better after three days than my own mother after twenty-five years.

"You saved my grandson, I want to take you in as my god-daughter," she says as she gets out of the car. "Do you have a real godmother?"

"Yes, Liv . . . I mean my mother's best friend. But they've fallen out."

"What, since you were born?"

"No, since the day before I arrived here."

Then I clam up. She doesn't insist.

Roz introduces me to Marielle, the main post woman, to Cory whom I'll be replacing, and to the other members of the team.

"We were waiting for you," says Cory, as she goes to a locker, grabs an envelope and hands it to me. "This just arrived."

I recognize Livia's handwriting. The address on the envelope says: "Chiara Ferrari, POST RESTANTE, 56590 Groix Island, France."

"Do you have any ID?" she asks.

I get my papers out. "What does 'post restante' mean?"

"It's a service that allows you to send a letter or parcel to any post office in the country—it's for people who are travelling or who don't have a fixed address."

I pay what's due, open the envelope and decipher my mother's scribble. *I'm sorry. Please don't blame me. I was young and desperate and made a stupid mistake. Come back. Forget about it. You should never have found out.*

Her reasoning leaves me cold. A simple *I love you* would have been enough to melt my heart. I don't want to go back or forget. I don't blame her. There is a fifty per cent chance that I am "a stupid mistake".

"Is everything okay?" asks Roz, looking worried, her maternal instinct on high alert.

I nod.

This is the first time I've left Italy. And now I'm going to be delivering letters on an island I didn't even know existed until a few days ago. Groix was swarming with visitors at the weekend, the tourists and the holiday homeowners have now gone and the little rock in the ocean will be peaceful now until the summer holidays. The shop owners are disappointed, but everyone else is overjoyed.

"My goddaughter is available," says Roz. "She's smart, sporty, responsible and trustworthy."

Her colleagues all give me a hearty welcome. They don't see me as a threat to their jobs.

I am keen and eager to get started but I slept badly. What if I get lost? What if I drop a letter on the way? I must have been mad to volunteer!

Marielle explains that for some on the island, the post office is their only link with the mainland. Many of them can't go to Lorient to do their shopping so they order online, whether it be clothes, car tyres or flowers, and then wait for the postman to deliver it.

I had been worried that I'd be thrown in at the deep end on my own, but that's not how they operate here. Post is no laughing matter. They have me sign a contract for a one-week replacement. I'm European and my Italian tax code proves that I have social security cover. I sign a confidentiality agreement whereby I agree to abide by professional secrecy.

"We're not allowed to tell a third party whether or not a neighbour has received a registered letter," says Cory. "Nor read a postcard and tell others what it says. When bailiffs come to the island, they get lost as there are no street names in the villages. If they ask us questions, we don't answer. A postman is not a snitch!"

In Rome, the postman gives me the neighbour's mail, tells me who has gone on holiday in the building, or who has received a postcard from a cousin in Venice or a niece in Puglia . . .

The Groix post office has two cars and three bicycles for five different rounds. In low season, the first boat arrives at 8:50 a.m. A car goes down to the port to collect the post and bring it back up, then the sorting begins. Large packages are delivered separately by car. Postmen and women on bicycles distribute the letters and the smaller parcels.

"I start in Locmaria and finish in Locqueltas," explains Cory. "In the summer, the sorting and the post round take longer and I'm so busy I feel like my feet don't touch the ground."

"Not surprizing on an island!" I joke.

Each letterbox has a corresponding box at the post office. Postmen and women sort the post by putting the letters in the corresponding compartments. There is an additional box for mail addressed to the village of Croix, which often gets sent to Groix by mistake. This is my first training session; I watch, I take notes, but I don't touch anything.

After the sorting phase comes the "loading up". Each delivery person takes the mail destined for the villages in his or her round and places it in their mailbag in the exact order it will be delivered. Then they stack the packs behind their bike saddles. The bicycle weighs almost five stone when empty, plus another five stone when laden.

Normally replacement postmen and women do three introductory rounds, but there is no time for that. Today, Cory will accompany me. Tomorrow, I'll be flying solo.

"Registered letters must be delivered by hand," insists Cory. "People have to sign for them on the portable terminal. Remember to take a bottle of water, some fruit or a snack with you, you'll need them."

"Roz already warned me," I say, holding up my water bottle, an apple and some Breton *galette* pancakes.

"You don't ask people to use the bathroom. The island is tiny. If you must stop, you go back home, got it? And be wary of dogs. *You* may love animals, but some of our four-legged friends don't like postmen!"

I make a mental note.

"Do you know what I like best about this job?" she asks then. "Playing Father Christmas all year long! I feel like I'm handing out presents from my sack."

They give me an electric bike. The last person who used it was taller than me, so my feet barely reach the floor. When I try it out in front of the post office, the bike starts moving by itself. I don't have the reflex to brake, the bike accelerates and I stand there like a fool on tiptoes while it falls over.

My colleagues help me lower the saddle and I get back on warily. I now know that this particular bike has a temperamental nature.

Groix Island, the Locmaria round

Once Cory's bike is loaded, we leave the post office. We pass in front of the covered market and turn left onto the road to Port-Mélite. Then we cycle past the graveyard—the dead don't receive mail, so no need to stop. The electric bike is heavier than I expected, even when empty. But I'm euphoric. In Rome, I wear a helmet, the city is noisy, my moped backfires, drivers sound their cars horns all day long, and endless traffic lights prevent you from getting any speed up. In Groix I cycle bare-headed, I blend in with the landscape, there are no large junctions and only the occasional stop sign, and no noise except for the boat's horn when it enters the harbour. Cory teaches me how to gauge the other road-users. Tourists in rental cars don't know where they are going, they accelerate or turn back without warning. If someone honks, it can only be a rental car. Holidaymakers on bikes don't respect the highway code, children ride ahead without supervision and swerve dangerously.

We turn right just before Port-Mélite and stop in a small hamlet to deliver the mail. You have to get off the bike, lean it on its stand, slip the mail in the letterboxes, push up the stand and away you go again. You don't turn around on a loaded bike, you back up and manoeuvre.

Now we head for "Aperitif junction". Back in the day, when the local men went on their weekly pub crawl on Sundays, they would meet up at the end of the afternoon on this crossroads at a bar that no longer exists. Today, the police still use this spot to breathalyze potential drink drivers.

We cycle between two fields. I feel overwhelmed by my independence and the wide open spaces around me. The obvious word that comes to mind is *liberté*, freedom. A French poem of the same name I learned at school emerges from the depths of my memory: *On my school exercise books. On my desk and the trees. On the sand on the snow. I write your name.* Alessio, you would love this island and Paul Éluard's poem.

I peddle furiously behind my mentor, my hair blowing in the wind. Before we left I had put on my sunglasses and official post office jacket. By tonight my stiff shoulders, aching back and bruised buttocks will remind me that this is not a game.

Cory scoops the mail out from the bicycle basket, slips it into someone's letterbox, and leaves. Then she stops again, uses her strong arms to expertly prop the bike against its stand and retrieves more letters. I study the plastic binder containing a map of the island to follow where we are; the map shows the rounds, as well as drawings of the villages and various landmarks such as a well, a tree or a wash house. Many houses are closed up out of season.

"How many miles is your round?" I ask.

"Twelve and a half."

I'll never look at postmen and women the same way again.

"Do you deliver to anyone called Thunder?"

"Of course."

"How many Thunder boxes are there in the post office for the whole island?"

"Forty-eight."

"And on your round?"

"Twelve."

I sigh. "So there are twelve people called Thunder on this part of the island?"

"No. We don't calculate in terms of people, but in terms of boxes," she replies. "There could be several generations living in the same house."

"Do people ever tell you about their lives? And their travels?"

She shakes her head as she pedals ahead of me. "I get offered hot coffee in the winter or a cold drink in the summer, but I don't have time to stop and chat; I have to finish my round."

There are a variety of letterboxes on display. The square, standard-issue letterboxes are often personalized with hand-painted, marine-themed decorations. I also recognize the boat-shaped letterboxes made by the carpenter, Rouquin Marteau. One craftsman has made a letterbox that looks like a blue rudder. And there are also letterboxes holding small figures like a Christmas creche.

"*Mèrh eur lihérièw ow!*" sings out a woman as Cory approaches.

"She just said, 'It's the postwoman'," explains Cory. "*Meum ès lihérièw udoh.* That means, 'I have some post for you'."

Cory rides through a pretty garden, taking care not to damage the flowers.

"Is this a shortcut?" I ask.

"No, this is the normal path through the village, it's an old right of way."

Just as I'm hoping that the round is nearly finished, we stop in the square behind the Notre-Dame-de-Plasmanec church, near a yellow postbox.

"This is a relay box. The post office car stopped by to replenish our stocks as we were running low on post," she says, opening it with a special key. Then it's back to business.

She reloads her bike. We nibble our snacks and then set off again, riding down the long lanes. Cory slips the letters in the boxes, good news, bad news, small bills, big bills. People smile at us, birds fly overhead, a small, squashed rabbit makes me momentarily sad, a majestic cat stares at me defiantly. In Loc-maria, the village is wrapped around the church like a warm scarf around someone's neck. In Kermarec, the houses tease the sand. In Locqueltas, they dance with the moor. In Lome-ner, the homes are packed together tightly but the islanders still accelerate, barely leaving a centimetre between their cars' paintwork and the walls on each side. Tourists panic at the thought of getting stuck at the narrowest point.

All these houses and all these letterboxes make me dizzy. An almond-green boat box juts out of a pink wall, a white box with a blue door is fixed to a house, a bright blue one sits at the end of a fence of the same colour, a burgundy one with a green door is perched on a dry-stone wall. According to the speedometer, we are going 7.5 miles per hour on the flat, and 15.5 on the downhill slopes.

At the end of the morning, Cory smiles at me encourag-ingly. "You're doing very well. I'll give you Marielle's number, as I'll be in surgery while you're on the road."

I don't dare ask her what she is suffering from. She scrib-bles the number on a piece of paper and I stuff it in my pocket. I go home, exhausted but happy. The round took two and a half hours.

"Well?" asks Roz when I get back.

"I loved it."

"You're lucky, the weather's nice today."

"I thought the island was flat, but it isn't at all! It's a series of uphill and downhill stretches," I laugh, massaging my calves.

I plunge my hand into my pocket and pull out the paper that Cory gave me. I unfold it. The head postwoman's name is Marielle Thunder. Perig's words come back to me. Accord-ing to him, her husband is a descendant of Jan Tonnerch.

Groix Island, The Family Cinema

I ask Didier, Roz and Danielle if they would like to go to the cinema with me, but they refuse. Since Danielle's accident they haven't had a television in the house, fearing that an image might traumatize her. She is fragile, easily panics and sometimes has epileptic seizures. They compensate with music, books, nature, the outdoors, claiming that they can live without TV. And Didier tires out his daughter by taking her on long walks. When she is physically exhausted, she is calmer.

The cinema's official name is Le Korrigan, but everyone calls it The Family Cinema. Tonight, the cinema club is showing the original Italian version of Rossellini's *Stromboli*. It will do me good to hear my native language, so I take my place in the sixth row. There are about twenty of us in the cinema. I sink into my chair.

Gabin comes in just as the lights go down. He sees me and sits in the row in front of me.

I lean forward. "I don't bite."

He moves back a row to sit next to me. The Italian production logo fills the screen. After that dinner we had with fourteen of us at the table, he and Urielle went to sit at the end of the Port-Lay dike, their legs dangling over the black water. They talked for hours, both gazing at the lights of the mainland in the distance.

We watch the film in silence. The *Greks* in the audience watch as an island is devastated by a volcano. Ingrid Bergman's performance is overwhelming. I get a lump in my throat. When we leave the cinema, I don't feel like going home to bed.

"Shall we have a drink at Beudeff's?" suggests Gabin.

We head to the port and the mythical bar, well known all over Brittany and beyond. A merry bunch are already downing beers while singing. We sit down at a free table as they bellow: "Let us drink one, let us drink two, let us drink to the lovers and to the King of France!"

"That's a privateers' song in honour of their leader, Surcouf," Gabin explains enthusiastically. "I love Groix. I met Perig, he's fascinating. He introduced me to his friend Kerwan, a former sea captain who wants me to write his memoirs. Are you ready for your job at the post office?"

"Depends what you mean by ready," I reply.

He buys the first round; I smile because it's the same word as the Locmaria "round". I'm thirsty and gulp it down. He leans towards me.

"What are you hiding, Chiara?"

"Excuse me?"

"Stop giving us the run around. What are you, exactly? An investigator? A lawyer? A journalist?"

"I work in a bookshop."

"You ask too many questions. Tell me the truth. Maybe I can help you?"

"We don't know each other."

"We're more similar than you think."

"Are we?" I ask doubtfully.

"Yes, we're two strangers who have been seduced by the charms of this island. It has cast a spell on us. It chose us. Do you not feel bewitched?"

I shrug and order a second round to make sure I pay him back for the first. Livia didn't hug me, but she raised me right. It's hot, the beer is nice and cool.

"Who is this Thunder you're looking for? Your lover?" insists Gabin.

"Of course not!"

"A friend then?"

"My only friend is called Alessio, he stayed in Rome."

I take two long sips. I'm trying to work out how to get rid of him yet at the same time I'm tempted to pour my heart out to him. My secret is weighing heavily on me, it's becoming hard to bear. What am I risking by confiding in Gabin? He's not from round here, and he'll soon be out of my life. I'm now not so sure I did the right thing in coming.

"He may be my father," I whisper, so quietly that he asks me to repeat myself. "Please don't tell anyone."

He gets in a third round and raises his glass ceremoniously.

"A father serves no purpose, trust me," he says. "From what little I know, it's just someone you have pissing contests with."

"I don't have a willy."

"And I don't have a father."

"Good evening, young'uns!"

We turn around. Perig is leaning against the bar, drinking by himself, and is well tanked up already.

"A nice drink is good for the health," he roars. "One glass is too much, three glasses is not enough. To life, to Brittany!"

"Gabin says that a father serves no purpose," I say politely to draw him into the conversation.

Perig sobers up so suddenly I can almost see the alcohol evaporating out of his veins.

"A father's role is to protect his children," he says solemnly. "Or it should be."

I remember too late what Urielle told me about his son. I search for something to say but no words can alleviate such grief. Perig reaches into his pocket, pulls out his wallet, and shows me a grainy photo of a child fishing with two tall men on a small boat. Perig is the hulk on the left.

"I failed to stop Ankou taking my son. I failed in my mission."

"Ankou?"

"The Breton servitor of the dead. He comes with his creaking cart to fetch the dead. If a living person hears his cart, he dies within the year. My son told us he had heard strange noises. I thought it was a joke, but it was that damn Ankou! The last dead person of the year in the parish becomes the Ankou the following year. The year before, it was one of my childhood friends—I was relaxed, I was confident!"

I think of Viola. Childhood friends can't always be trusted. Perig gets in a fourth round. I still haven't touched my third. I raise my palms in surrender. That's enough for me tonight. I'm on the post round tomorrow morning.

Groix Island, Port-Lay

That night I dream that all this is a mirage, that I'm taking the boat back to Lorient and that when I turn around Groix Island has vanished. I'm worried and question the other passengers who look surprised: "Groix, you say? Never heard of it. There has never been an island here. You must be hallucinating." I wake up in a sweat. I go outside to check that there really is soil under my feet. I touch the hydrangeas. I look at the little harbour with the fishing boats, the ocean beyond the dike, the mainland on the other side of the water. The dolphin has gone to dance elsewhere. I'm startled by a noise. I see Danielle walking bare foot in the wet grass. She doesn't see me and starts to whirl around like a dervish. I count twenty whirls. Then she goes back to bed.

It takes me ages to get back to sleep. I recite the end of the poem to myself. *On every breath of dawn. On the sea, on the boats. On the ragged mountain. I write your name. Freedom.*

Paris, six years earlier

You are twenty years old now and as nervous as hell. The results of the entrance exam for your second year of medical school have just been put up. If you pass you will be someone, my son, you will save other people's mothers, your existence will have meaning.

Aurore is waiting for you at the Café de Flore. You're going to order champagne to celebrate! You've acquired a liking for champagne from all the literary cocktail parties you've attended with her. You moved in with her in the heart of the Latin Quarter just a week after you met. A library is a cellar of books, a cellar is a library of wines, your bed is a raft on which you drink and read texts out loud.

You failed the exam last year and have been working like crazy ever since. Aurore has been saying you've become too serious, too stressed out, less available. Maybe, but it's non-negotiable. If you fail a second time, you can kiss your dream goodbye. Of course, there is more to life than medicine. You could become a French teacher. A baker. A publicist, yeah, why not. Or a bookseller. But no, you want to be a doctor.

You head towards the crowded lobby where the students are gathering. You see Vincent shouting with joy. And a friend sobbing, mascara running down her face. Your phone vibrates in your pocket. It's a text from Aurore: *I'm waiting for you Charlie, thinking of you.* She's afraid you'll do something stupid if you fail. Yesterday, you talked about suicide, mentioning a writer who wanted to end it all. You swore to her that you would never do such a thing. She seemed reassured.

You like life too much to end it that way. Your mother would kill you again when you got up there if you tried such a thing.

Groix Island, the Locmaria round

The first boat has brought the post, the sorting can begin. The letters slide into the pigeonholes, I slow down so as not to make a mistake. I smile stupidly, my palms are sweaty, and I have a splitting headache from last night's beer. The names sound musical and pleasant to the ear, they ebb and flow like the tide: Yvon, Stéphan, Pouzoulic, Bihan, Calloch and those blasted Thunders that I can't get out of my head.

Marielle helps me load my bike by stacking the mail in the right order. Nothing for anyone by the name of Thunder this morning in the twelve boxes comprising Cory's round. I swallow my disappointment.

The electric bike is difficult to manoeuvre under the weight of the letters and parcels. I have trouble keeping my balance for the first few yards. I grit my teeth and squeeze the handlebars. I christen my mount Pegasus. I could do with the winged horse of Greek mythology right now. Pegasus is my partner in crime, I will take good care of him.

I head out onto the deserted road, proud not to have fallen flat on my face. Yesterday evening on the way home from Beudeff's, little rabbits scampered into the hedgerows, leaping over the tall grass at the side of the road and flashing their white tails in the glow of the headlights. They must be having a lie-in today.

The round goes smoothly to begin with, even if it's not easy. The weather is beautiful, windows are open, the locals are out weeding, pruning, tinkering, repainting and walking their dogs. I ask for help; they are eager to explain, to assist me.

When I open one letterbox to deliver an envelope, I find two sweets inside. I inform the gentleman who lives there that a child has played a joke on him.

He smiles. "They're for you!"

"For me?" I ask, bewildered.

"To help you on your rounds, my dear! Don't you like sweets?"

"Yes of course I do!" I say, smiling.

Groix is a haven of peace amid the chaos. Yesterday, I stopped off at Damien the glassmaker's to buy Roz a gift to thank her for having me to stay. I noticed the picture of an old man near the blowtorch.

"Is that your grandfather?" I asked.

"No, he's a friend, an elderly gentleman who lived across the street and loved to watch me work. The photo remains, even though my friend has gone. This island may be surrounded by violent waters, but its people are extremely sensitive and kind."

Further on, I stop in a cul-de-sac. A man grumbles at me because I propped my bicycle up against his chipped painted fence. Cory did warn me that this particular Parisian is grouchy. I reassure a lady that her parcel will most probably arrive tomorrow. I ride past happy dogs, suspicious cats, screaming gulls. I am slowly getting used to the sensation of the electric bike.

My heart races at the first Thunder letterbox I see, even though I've got no mail to put in it. The lady, who is the same age as *nonna* Ornella, is surprised to see me instead of Cory. I reassure her that it's only temporary. I search in vain for a physical resemblance. I don't dare ask her if she has a son who went to Tuscany twenty-six years ago.

I could be the granddaughter of any elderly person, the daughter of any man, the aunt of any child here. But I don't see any teenagers.

Perig explained to me that in the past there was no secondary school on Groix. From the age of eleven, the school children had to go to Lorient. Today, there are two secondary schools on the island, you only have to go further afield if you want to go to upper-level secondary. But above gale force seven, the company that owns the boat doesn't compensate damages. So, if the weather is bad on Friday evening, upper-secondary students stay in Lorient all weekend. In the past, when his son Gurvan was still alive, the boat always sailed. A captain would never have left the children stranded on the mainland after boarding there all week. They were sea captains, former fishermen. Nothing daunted them and the boat held the waves. Water would splash over into the boat, and the teenagers would disembark drenched and have to dry themselves off by the fire. Gurvan loved it.

Locals suggest coffee, but I refuse, no time. They offer me some brioche, *gwastell*, a regional speciality, and that bucks me up. I arrive at the relay box behind the church and panic at the thought of losing the key. Phew, I find it and reload my bike.

I stop and grab my bundle of letters. Everyone I meet smiles at me, but without my yellow jacket they probably wouldn't notice me. I connect them to the outside world, I bring them news, I add sparkle to their lives. In Locmaria, the village still wraps itself around the church. In Kermarec, the houses still tease the sand. In Locqueltas, they relentlessly pirouette with the moor. And in Lomener, I grit my teeth as I navigate the narrow, windy streets. Hurray, I've finished, I've delivered everything, I did it!

Back in Port-Lay, I need to lie down for a quarter of an hour. But I'm so exhausted that I fall asleep as soon as my head touches the pillow. I dream that I am pedalling up a steep hill and my mystery father is waiting for me at the top. But every time I reach the summit, an evil force pulls me back down and I have to start all over again. I vaguely hear the door open. Roz whispers that my lunch is in the fridge, I'm too tired to answer her. The next time the postman brings me a letter, I'll appreciate just how much effort it took.

Groix Island, the Post Bike

After finishing the Locmaria round, the Bike has a rest every afternoon while it recharges. It doesn't understand why postwoman B insists on calling it Pegasus. It already has a name: the serial number located on its frame near the pedals.

The Bike calls Chiara "postwoman B" because the word "replacement" doesn't mean anything to it. But it *is* familiar with the notion of 20A, 20B etc. in postal addresses.

It knows that postwoman B won't stay long, which makes it sad as she is the only one who gives it any attention. Cory never speaks to it, whereas Chiara asks its opinion about things. She flatters, praises and appreciates it.

But it does wonder why she has named it after a horse. It knows the horses at the Kerbus riding school and wonders why she mistakes it for one of them. The Bike is electronic, it's sturdy, it doesn't whinny, it doesn't throw its riders off, and it doesn't leave all that smelly mess behind it which Cory unfortunately once rode through. What a nasty memory! So, she thinks it's a nag does she? It's not a nag, it is a state-of-the-art piece of technology!

The Bike can even pick up on its rider's emotions through its armature. It senses that Chiara is a nervous wreck, as charged up as its battery in the morning. It has saved her from falling off on numerous occasions. It wouldn't want to lose her.

The Bike isn't a post office employee, it's merely linked to it. The post office maintains and houses it. The post office needs it. It is a good worker, and it contributes to life on the island.

It doesn't understand why postwoman B insists on calling it Pegasus. But if that's what floats her boat, then the Bike has nothing against it.

Paris, four years earlier

Your name is Louis. You've never been to Italy or Brittany. You don't know Chiara Ferrari. Statistically there is little chance that your paths will ever cross.

Today is the first day of your externship in the intensive care unit. Your heart is pounding. You take a deep breath before you push open the door that is out of bounds for most people. The nurses see a tall lad with blue-green eyes enter. He's wearing jeans and a T-shirt under his white scrubs and bright green Nike trainers.

"So you're Florian's friend? Welcome to the unit! You're replacing Sophie who is on maternity leave. What year are you in?"

"Fourth."

"The locker room is over there. Have you ever worked in ICU before?"

"Not yet, I've mainly been doing consultations."

"Our sanitation rules are draconian. We're fighting a battle against death and hospital-acquired infections. Rule number one: disinfect your hands upon arrival, after each patient and before you leave."

You take a notebook and a ballpoint pen out of your breast pocket. A blue stethoscope tube the same colour as your eyes protrudes from your side pocket. You note the rules carefully. Then you thank her.

"Florian already explained everything to me, but better to be safe than sorry. I don't know what you guys like, so I bought some doughnuts. Are you more savoury or sweet?"

The blonde nurse with a red birth mark on her cheek turns to the redhead with a bun.

"Florian briefed him well."

Then she turns her attention back to you. "You'll make regular rounds, check vitals and monitors, and suction the patients on ventilators. No charging in like a bull in a china shop. Suctioning is a frightening procedure. You must warn the patient first, proceed gently but not too gently either, because he isn't breathing while you disconnect him, got it?"

"You mustn't fold the patient," you say, quoting Florian.

The first time Florian used this expression, you didn't understand. You thought he meant folding a patient in half, like putting sheets in a cupboard. Your friend burst out laughing. No, folding means killing. A doctor who commits medical negligence kills a patient inadvertently. In effect he destroys two lives: his own and that of the patient who put his total trust in him.

"If you have the slightest problem, don't hesitate to call us," insists the blonde nurse.

Her name is Mona, according to her badge.

"You're on an externship, you're not an intern or a department head," she adds. "We'll never hold it against you if you ask for advice. But we won't accept you making a stupid mistake because you're too proud to ask. I've worked here for ten years. I've seen stupid medical students who thought they were smart, and great medical students who wanted to learn. The choice is yours."

You promise not to do anything foolish. Then you follow Mona as she shows you around the ward. The patient in the first cubicle is a grey-faced old man whose chest heaves in sync with the ventilator as it blows oxygen-enriched air into his lungs. He is skinny and clutches the bedsheets; his life now moves in tempo with the machine. Without it, he's a fish out of water. You smile at him, hoping to imbue him with some of your youthful energy. Mona puts on gloves and shows you how to suction the phlegm.

"Good evening, Mr Martin. I'm explaining to our new student how we do things on the ward. He knows it all, but every ICU has its own ways. Before you suction an intubated patient or patient with a tracheal tube, you have to examine them, check their colour, pulse, respiratory rate, check that they're neither sweating nor cyanotic, test the pressure of the suction equipment, and the tubing connections of the suction catheter and the suction system. Wash your hands. Put on gloves. Fit the suction catheter to the vacuum stop, remove the catheter from its packaging without touching it and hold it with a sterile compress. Are you with me? You do this after disabling the alarms, of course."

You nod as you try to memorize her movements.

"Open the suction port that goes from the breathing tube to the catheter, and slide the catheter into the hole, without pushing it in too far. You mustn't suction as the catheter moves down, and you mustn't make back and forth movements. Suction at intervals and slowly move upwards. Then close the suction port and reactivate the alarms. Throw away the catheter and the compress. Wash the suction system with the rinsing solution. Wash your hands again."

She proceeds slowly and confidently; she has obviously been doing this for a long time. The patient suffocates and the oxygen relieves him. The incredible machine keeps him alive. You catch the patient's eye; he looks relieved and grateful.

"I'll be back later, Mr Martin," she says. "Louis is a friend of Florian, the man with the moustache and the blue spectacles. Louis used to work in a different ICU unit, but he was so good that we poached him, and now he works for us!"

The patient raises his hand to show that he has understood.

Once in the corridor, Mona whispers to Louis, "Never tell a patient that they are your guinea pig, that you have never done it before. They would panic and start breathing faster, out of sync with the machine, and you'd be in deep shit. If you don't know something pretend you do and ask us discreetly. Okay?"

You nod. "Will the patient make it?"

"He's alive," replies Mona simply. "He'll be given analgesics so that he won't suffer. He holds his wife's hand when she comes to visit him, and she hides her tears from him. His children gather around his bedside, he writes them loving messages on a magic slate. Sometimes he laughs and sometimes he cries. He was a heavy smoker. He tells his son that if he continues to smoke like a chimney, he'll end up the same way. But his son doesn't believe him. He didn't believe his father either."

"No one smokes in this unit?"

"Not more than half a pack a day."

"Can I suction the next patient with you, to check I've understood it right?"

"Don't worry, I'm not going to drop you in at the deep end."

You enter the second cubicle. You flinch when you see a beautiful young black woman connected to the ventilator. You were expecting an elderly person.

"Hello, Ms Fatou," says Mona cheerfully. "Louis is our new medical student. His eyes are a cross between ocean blue and the bright green of his trainers. He's going to suction you to help you breathe better."

"She can't hear you, she's asleep," you murmur, surprised.

"You never know what a patient can hear. When in doubt, we act as if they are conscious. Ms Fatou was admitted to the ward with postpartum cardiomyopathy or heart failure, two months after giving birth. We put her in an artificial coma, so she doesn't fight the ventilator. Right, now show me what you can do."

You go over the steps in your mind, put on some gloves and get to work. Your heart skips a beat as you turn the ventilator back on, your hands are shaking and you're sweating. The beautiful young woman shudders as the machine once again becomes her lungs. You're breathing better too now.

"Nearly right," says Mona.

"Did I forget something?" you ask, frantically rereading your notes. "I don't see . . ."

"You didn't turn the alarms back on."

"Shit, you're right!"

You rush to correct your mistake.

"You did a good job. And you'll never forget the alarms again. Now let me introduce you to the rest of the team," says Mona.

You feel so happy at being able to help these strangers who have placed total faith in you. There's no better feeling than seeing sick people get well again and saving lives. It gives you such a high, more than any drug could. This is the most noble profession in the world.

Groix Island, Pointe des Chats

I woke up with a jump around five. I haven't napped in the afternoon since I was a child, but that first post round really wore me out. I gratefully tucked into the cold meat lunch Roz left me, and then got this sudden urge to go and visit Perig. Luckily Urielle had said I could use her bike. I push it up the Port-Lay hill and then pedal to Kermarec, wishing I had my Pegasus.

I knock. The door opens. I scarcely recognize Aziliz. Her eyes are sunken and empty, her mouth is wrinkled, and she has a deep furrow right across her forehead. She stands on the doorstep and doesn't ask me in. I panic. I should have checked that Perig got back home last night.

"Is this a bad time?"

"Perig is on the beach near Les Chats lighthouse. He's with Gurvan."

She points to the mantelpiece, at the photo of the teenager standing in front of the ocean. I get it. I also grew up surrounded by photo frames filled with smiles and tears.

I spot the red top of the small lighthouse which belongs to the national Coastal Protection Agency. The campsite next door is deserted after the weekend and Gabin has moved to Port-Mélite to stay with Captain Kerwan. There are no swimmers to disturb the grey surface of the ocean. Then I see Perig. He is shivering on a rock, still as a statue, his eyes riveted on the water, so focused that he doesn't hear me approach and jumps when I sit down beside him.

"Aziliz told me where to find you."

He nods without taking his gaze off the waves that are breaking at regular intervals only to crash on the silver rocks. I give myself ten minutes. If my presence bothers him and he refuses to speak, I'll leave. We sit there without moving. After nine minutes and fifty seconds, I start to get to my feet. At nine minutes fifty-nine seconds, he opens his mouth: "You got your timing right, Chiara. I didn't want to be alone today."

I don't move.

"Aziliz hates it when I talk to her about Gurvan. Our friends feel helpless in the face of our pain and are embarrassed when I bring up the subject. They wish I would move on, but I can't. I need to believe that he will come back. They think I'm crazy because I won't give up hope. You asked what a father is for? Well, his role is to protect. And wait. And not listen to the voice of reason, not turn the page, and not give up. On the contrary, he should always be ready with open arms."

I don't take my eyes off the ocean. I don't look in his direction. I breathe as quietly as possible.

"The last time I saw Gurvan, we had a fight. Whereas I should have told him how much I loved him, to give him strength and courage for his journey over the sea. I was so proud of our boy but I never told him so . . . He thought I was disappointed in him. I was trying to educate him, toughen him up, offer him the world! Our ancestors were great sailors. But it was books that kept me afloat, and helped me cut through the waves and navigate through words and emotions. Aziliz is an avid reader too. When she is immersed in a novel, we live off bread and cold sausage or fish pâté. But our son didn't care for reading, he was a talented athlete. A handsome, broad-shouldered kid, a champion windsurfer, who would spend hours gazing at the sea, figuring out the wind direction. He never opened a book. It drove me crazy; I didn't understand him. That fateful day, the very last time I saw him, I said to him: 'You're completely missing the point; sporting achievements only last for so long, any fool can sprint or ride a surfboard, there's nothing heroic in that, it's banal.' He took it in his stride. I can still hear his reply: 'You're wrong, Dad, you live challenges on paper and adventures by proxy. While I feel the adrenalin of competition racing through my body, my muscles, my breath. Windsurfing makes me come alive. I experience real life sensations in real time. What you do is fake, it's an act, imitation!' Humiliated, I retaliated: 'I'm not going to take lessons on life from some tacky little windsurfer! You think you're a big shot, but you're just a loser, a nothing; wake up! You can't even read or write properly.' Clearly shaken, he retorted: 'I've read three books in my life, one of them was yours, and all three were a waste of my time.' We were over there, in that exact spot. Aziliz had prepared the same picnic for us."

On the silvery granite rock, which diffracts the sun's rays, I notice two cups, two sandwiches, a can of beer and an energy drink.

"I was offended and very upset. He was just a brash teenager, I should have known better, and taken a step back. He was dyslexic; school was torture for him. As soon as he put a winning foot on his board, he came alive. There, he was on top of the world! School friends who mocked his bad school marks were in awe of him once he got his trophy. He fast became a young idol. But I, a stupid writer set in my ways, and weighed down by the books I dreamt of writing, wanted to mould him to my image. In trying to do so, I suffocated him."

He trembles, tightens his fists and shakes his head. His face is tense.

"He knew that attacking my book was the worst thing he could do to me. An eye for an eye, a tooth for a tooth. But I got him in his Achilles heel. And that's what drowned him."

I flinch.

"He mocked my writing skills," he went on. "So I ridiculed him. I thought I was being smart, but I was merely being cruel and childish. I told him that he read like a baby. I told him he was wasting my time and my money."

I don't move, transfixed.

"Gurvan clenched his jaw and burst out laughing. Money was a touchy subject between us. At the time, I was having financial problems because a storm had brought a tree down on the roof. I may be good at words, but I'm rubbish at DIY and incapable of changing tiles. The repairs cost me an arm and a leg. Gurvan didn't cost me a penny; he had won several championships and his sponsors gave him technical equipment and clothing. He had signed a big contract, but the money was being held in a bank account until he came of age. And I, who spent all my time nobly reading, couldn't understand that my lad could earn more than me by larking around in swimming trunks in front of illiterate groupies. I felt humiliated by my son's success. I hurt him to get even."

His voice breaks.

"He swallowed his peanut butter sandwich without answering me. He drank his damn sports drink. Then he walked towards the water taking long, slow strides. He had to test a new high-tech board, which was supposedly indestructible. He jumped on, a few feet from the edge, pulled the mast back towards him and slipped his feet into the foot straps. He threw back his ridiculously long hair, arched his back and set sail. He never returned."

I look at him wide-eyed.

"Nothing was ever found, neither his surfboard nor his body. The ocean swallowed them up. I often dream that he sailed to America, changed his name, and started a new life. I keep hoping that one day he will get off the boat with his wife and children. He'll have grown up, but I'll recognize him.

And sometimes I persuade myself that he will land right here, on his surfboard, laughing at the prank he played on us. He'll be hungry and thirsty. So every year, on this date, I come down here with this God forsaken peanut butter sandwich and wait for him."

He doesn't take his eyes off the horizon.

"Chiara, I'm not senile or stupid, I know it's not going to happen, but it makes me feel better. The first few years Aziliz came with me, then she stopped. We all have our own way of coping."

He tears his gaze away from the ocean and stares at me with his bloodshot eyes.

"That's a father, in answer to your question. A man who thinks he's doing the right thing and then messes up. A grown man who reacts like a kid. A conceited arsehole who takes revenge on a child by stabbing them in the back. You're looking for your father, aren't you?"

I freeze.

"You're not here on behalf of your godmother, you're here for yourself. Aren't you?"

"Did Gabin say something?"

"No. I can tell from your voice. When you say the name 'Thunder' your voice goes all weak and quivery."

Now is no time for lies. We are alone on the beach and only Gurvan's ghost can hear us.

"What makes you think he is on this island?" he insists.

"My mother lost her husband just after they got married twenty-six years ago. She went to the island of Elba, drowned her sorrows and spent the night with a Groix islander, whose name had something to do with the weather. When she got pregnant, she didn't know which of the two was the father. I only found this out last week. That's why I came here."

"At the bar I could tell from your eyes how important it was for you. You thought you had a young Italian father.

Would it make you feel better to find out you have an old French father?"

"I need to know."

"Even if he's a bastard or an idiot like me? Are you sure it's worth it?"

"You're going to help me find him."

"I'll do all I can. I promise."

I smile at him.

"I'm going to tell you the story of a fisherman boss of my father's generation who beat the hell out of his cabin boy; he was a thirteen-year-old kid who scrubbed the deck, peeled potatoes, and fed seven hungry men in all weathers, the wind, the sea, the salt, the rain. The kid vowed that when he turned twenty he would come back and seek his revenge. The boy became a sailor, and eventually a fishing boat owner. One day, he returned to Groix and said to the old fisherman: 'You were cruel to me.' And he replied: 'Yes, but I made you into a man and a good boss.' The former cabin boy departed. He had come to thank him, because the only time he had been happy in his life was during that fishing expedition. He hanged himself the next day. The old man put a piece of the noose in his wallet, out of respect. His son kept the wallet, the rope is still there."

"That's sad!"

"They had forged a bond. I never hit Gurvan, I just wore him down mentally with my books, and disparaged his love of sport, his choices, and his success. My son didn't hang himself, he left me no rope to remember him by. He didn't thank me afterwards. I'm the one who comes to the beach every year to thank him for all the years he gave us. They don't fit in my wallet . . . Thank you for coming, Chiara. If your father is still on the island, I'll find him."

Paris, three years earlier

Your name is Louis. One day you may go to Italy or Brittany, you have your whole life ahead of you.

You enter the ICU, you walk to your locker, you get changed. You like being on night duty, you get on well with the team, the intern, and the other nurses. The patients trust you as you're gentle and take your time, no brusque movements.

"Louis will be a compassionate and caring doctor," Mona always says. She's the blonde nurse with a red birth mark on her cheek. When a patient walks out of the ICU, you are high as a kite. When they leave in a wooden box, you nosedive.

"Hi, everyone!" you say, as you enter the nurses' station.

There is no one there, how odd! Where did they all go? You frown. Even if a patient's condition worsens, there is always someone here to monitor the screens and alarms.

"Hey guys! Where are you?"

"Louis, we need you here, quick!" shouts Mona from the end of the corridor.

You start sprinting in your green trainers, preparing yourself mentally to deal with a cardiac arrest. The resuscitation unit is most likely already in place. You push open the door. The bed is empty. The alarms are off, the monitor is off, the artificial ventilator isn't assisting anyone's breathing.

"Surpriiiiiiiiiiiiiiiiiiiise!!" shout out the rest of the team in fits of laughter.

You stop dead in your tracks. You resist the temptation to glance over your shoulder to see if the party is for someone else. Their giggles fizzle out, their eyes no longer sparkle, and a quiet uneasiness sets in. Florian steps forward. It's thanks to him that you can work here four nights a week.

"You look like death warmed up!" he says. "Did we get the wrong day?"

You hesitate. What are they celebrating? Everyone has stopped smiling now, you have spoiled the surprise. You'd almost prefer them to be angry with you.

"I wasn't expecting this," you say, to give yourself time to think.

"We can see that," comments your colleague Christine. She's a Tintin fan and you recently gave her a watch with Snowy on the dial.

A table has been pushed against the wall, and you can see a bottle of white wine, a bottle of blackcurrant liqueur, some glasses and a gift package.

"It's your birthday old boy," says Florian, giving you a friendly pat on the back. "You're twenty-three years old today. Last year, you weren't on duty but this time we've managed to corner you!"

"Are you not a fan of parties?" asks Mona, surprised.

"Surely you've got time for one drink with us?" says the new medical student, Claire, in her sweet Belgian accent.

You are on duty, but one glass won't hurt.

"I . . . err, I'd forgotten," you stammer.

That's a poor excuse. You can't get out of it. You don't forget your own birthday.

"Let's make a toast to the young Alzheimer's patient who completely forgot which day it is!" jokes Florian, trying to get everyone to relax.

You decide to improvise. "We don't celebrate birthdays in my family. But thanks for thinking of me. What's in the package?"

"It's known as a gift," says Serfaty, the good-looking lanky intern. "Normally, you untie the ribbon, rip off the paper, open it and say you like it, even if you don't. Are you from outer space? What do you celebrate on your planet? The day you escaped in Daddy's flying saucer?"

You continue the banter. "*Damn.* You found out. You discovered my secret! In my world we are not born, we all pop out of the same artificial womb, and we all die on the same expiry date. No need for hospitals or ICU's as we have a predetermined functioning span."

"What's your real name?"

"I have a serial number."

"You're weird," says Mona, raising her glass.

Everyone follows suit. The atmosphere is less tense now.

"Open your gift!" she teases.

You tear off the paper. It's a book, *Alors voilà*, written by a fellow doctor, Baptiste Beaulieu.

"I loved it," said Mona. "If you already have it, don't exchange it, pass it on!"

You bow ceremoniously to her and offer her your right hand. "Will you have this waltz with me, my dear?"

You pull her along and twirl with her in the cramped little room. Everyone claps. They have almost forgotten what just happened.

But you haven't. It was a close shave. You'll be more careful in future.

Groix Island, the Triskell

Perig talked nonstop about Italy as he queued up to buy his paper at the newsagents, but got no reaction. Then he interrogated Jo Le Port, Guy Thunder, Joseph Gallo and Gilbert Nexer. He looked through photo albums. Everywhere he went he mentioned the island of Elba: at the butchers, the fishmongers, the post office, Le Menach hardware store, The 50 restaurant, and the covered market. He hung around the port as the boats arrived and departed, talking all the while about Tuscany. Next, he targeted the island's most strategic bistros, starting with those in the port and continuing with those in town.

Now he struts over to the small square behind the town hall where the bank's ATM is taken over by the tourists in summer, before lumbering back to the Triskell. Aziliz is waiting for him at home, but he's on a mission. And when he's on a mission, he loses all notion of time.

"One Spritz, please."

Cathy the barmaid drops the cup she's holding. She picks up the pieces. She has known Perig for years and this is the first time he has ordered anything other than white wine or coffee.

"Are you joking?" she asks.

"No. I've been commissioned to write an article on this aperitif which is apparently all the rage among Parisian yuppies. I need to taste it myself. Don't you have it?"

"I'll get it in if you order it often enough."

"Are you sure you're okay, mate?" asks one of his old friends, coming over. "My wife started to say strange things and we didn't pick up on it at the time, but it was the beginning of a stoke."

"I think you mean a 'stroke'," Perig points out. "No, I'm in great shape, ready for duty."

"White wine no longer good enough for you then?"

"Monsieur prefers Asti Spumante," hollers a second drinking buddy, proud to show off his knowledge.

"You don't know anything," retorts Perig. "Spritz is made with Prosecco, not Asti. I happen to rather like Italian wines."

"And Italian ladies!" shouts the first man again. "We saw you at the beach with that new post girl."

"She's just the replacement," chips in the second, "while Cory's out of action."

"Did the nosey so and so that saw me also explain that I was with Gurvan?" roars Perig.

Silence falls. You don't joke about those lost at sea, their memories are sacred.

"I have a liking for Italy *and* my wife," Perig goes on. "Besides, Aziliz is more beautiful than all your wives put together! When I retire, I'm taking her to Tuscany, to the island of Elba. Any of you been there?"

"Napoleon has, but it didn't end well!" sneers the first man.

"You're wrong!" says his neighbour. "He wasn't taken prisoner; he chose to exile himself there. He had brains, he ruled on the island for almost a year, he was their emperor, it was the good life!"

"Yeah right! He popped his clogs there."

"Not on the island of Elba, it was Saint Helena!"

A third man sitting at the counter is listening in now. "My cousins worked on Elba as sailors when they were youngsters."

"Cheers!" cries Perig, raising his glass. "Which cousins are those then?"

"Brendan and Kilian Thunder."

Groix Island, Port-Lay

I wake with a start, it's mid-afternoon. I collapsed on my bed after my second post round, just like the day before. In the doorway, I glimpse a figure leaning against the door frame.

"What's going on?" I ask myself, trying to cling on to a blissful dream that's already fading.

"When Pierre gets home, I must tell him that the shed roof is leaking. He needs to bring in some wood, it's getting cold in here!"

It's Danielle imitating a low, sultry female voice. I think she's trying to tell me something. Pierre. She said Pierre. *Pietro.* Perig?

I dash into the living room, my hair a mess, desperately pulling on my sweater.

"Is there any news?"

"Yes," says Perig. "Are you alone?"

"I am. Roz is at the post office and Didier is in the garden. The coast is clear."

My heart is racing. I'm trembling, but this is not the time to falter.

"I've found them," he adds simply.

"Them?" I ask, bewildered. "Why the plural? I already have two fathers; I don't need a third one."

"Two Thunder brothers worked for six months on the island of Elba."

I sit down, my knees go weak, and my legs shake. I think back to what Viola told me after the row. "Some French fisherman" had helped change her cousin's tyre.

"Men have always found solace in drinking," Perig says, "wherever they are, wherever they come from, to warm up, to toughen up, to give themselves Dutch courage or to talk about love. I asked around in the bistros. I came across their cousin in the Triskell."

I raise my eyebrows, confused.

"One of the brothers wanted to contact an Italian woman he had met there. He wrote to her when he returned, but she never replied. The cousin no longer remembers which one it was."

"Do you know their names?" I ask, breathlessly.

"Brendan and Kilian Thunder."

My father may be from this island. On the one hand, I feel blessed, wanted and safe from harm. On the other hand, panic grips me as reality sets in. This is all becoming scarily concrete. Until today, this was a wild goose chase based on nothing more than speculation. But anything is possible now.

"Do you know them?"

"Everyone knows everyone on Groix. They went to school with Gurvan."

Brendan Thunder. Kilian Thunder. I say their names over and over again in my head. My name may not be Chiara Ferrari, but Chiara *Thunder.* I try it the James Bond way: *My name is Thunder, Chiara Thunder. Mi chiamo Chiara Thunder, mio padre é francese.*

"Are they on the island? Have I met them?" I ask now.

"We all meet up at some point or other, on this island. One of them lives in the village. The other comes to Locmaria on holiday; he's working on his house at the moment so he's here. They fell out over an inheritance, a jointly owned threshing floor and a piece of land with a right of way, you know, the usual story. They don't speak to each other anymore, even on All Saints' Day when they put flowers on their parents' graves."

"Will you take me to see them?"

"No."

"I was hoping you would come with me. I can't just turn up saying that I may be their daughter."

"You have to do this yourself."

"How do I even broach the subject?"

Up to now, I hadn't given it a second's thought. All I had wanted was to find my father and I had assumed the rest would just fall into place.

"Can you at least tell me a bit more about them?" I plead.

"Kilian, the eldest, was a sailor. He broke his leg while out at sea. They were on a fishing trip with their nets out, so they lost too much time getting back before he could be operated on. Since then, he lives on disability benefits and drags his bad leg around, his dog by his side, mumbling into his beard. He's become a recluse, no one goes into his house—not even the nurse. The windows are so dirty that you can't even see through them."

I have a one in three chance of being the daughter of an invalid recluse whose only redeeming feature is that he loves animals. Nothing like the picture-perfect bridegroom with the Hollywood smile in the photo frame back in Rome. I've been searching for a living, protective, reassuring, loving father. Rich or poor doesn't matter, but I don't want to be related to a savage!

"Is the other one even worse?" I ask, cynically.

"Brendan is a company executive who has just doubled the fares of the ferry that runs between the island and the mainland. It makes no difference to him as *he* takes a private taxi boat. The islanders who have found jobs on the mainland can no longer visit their relatives on the island as often because the crossing is more expensive. Grandkids don't come here as much for their holidays, shopkeepers pass on the price of deliveries to the customers, and the tourists spend less . . ."

"Brendan doesn't really care about Groix at all then?"

Perig scowls. "He's holed up in his hideous hi-tech mansion where everything is remote controlled: the shutters, the garage, the alarm, the boiler, the water system, the vacuum cleaner, and the lawnmower. He monitors it all from his phone. But the moron has forgotten that we're on an island. The Wi-Fi is a law unto itself here, so when the humidity seeps in, the systems go haywire and set off the alarms. Every time he comes, he calls out the electrician and makes a laughing stock of himself. He's divorced, no one could stand his wife, she's the one who encouraged him to knock down his parents' home and build that soulless modern monstrosity."

"Do the two brothers have children?"

"Kilian only has his dog. Brendan no longer brings his son here since the divorce. Nowadays he comes to Groix with a young blonde on his arm, dressed like a hooker in a see-through blouse, tight shorts, and Jimmy Chow thigh boots with six-inch spiked heels. Aziliz showed me the same boots in a magazine."

"Jimmy Choo," I correct him without thinking.

"Jiminy Cricket or Davy Crockett, whatever, she's just a kid. In the States, she'd be asked for her ID to buy alcohol. She thinks she's in Saint-Tropez! When they arrived a few days ago, the captain of the taxi boat lent her his coat. Apparently, she's so jaw droppingly gorgeous that he had trouble steering."

He laughs and I notice he has a cheery side when he's not talking about Gurvan.

"At their mother's funeral, Kilian and Brendan were forced to see each other. In the village church Brendan was on the left side of the centre aisle, Kilian on the right. His dog, which he had left outside, howled during the service. The locals all sat behind Kilian. Nobody wanted to be on the traitor's side. Nobody except Mylane, a friend of mine who always sits on the left side, in her family's pew, and who refused to change her habits just because of a fickle so and so. The rector gave a sermon on reconciliation. Kilian left via the main door facing the town hall. Brendan slipped out the side door without thanking anyone for coming."

"Are they related to Didier and Urielle? Or Guy and Erwan? Or Marielle's husband?"

"No, they come from a branch of the family with Irish roots."

"Do you think they would make good fathers?"

"No worse than me."

I curse Viola. I was quite happy with my dead father. He approved of my choices. He gave me a nostalgic, romantic childhood. He agreed with me, we never argued, and we were both proud of each other. I need to confide in someone my own age. You're too far away, Alessio. Urielle is in Paris. Danielle is in her own little world. I only have one person to fall back on.

Groix Island, Port-Mélite

I find Gabin in the captain's garden. He's leaning against the blue fence, taking a break in front of the ocean.

"How's it going, Sherlock Holmes?" he asks, grinning.

"It's complicated," I say. "I just got two dads for the price of one."

"What?"

"I've got three potential fathers now. One Italian and two Groix islander brothers."

"Can I borrow one? You never know, I may need him one day."

"How's your writing going?" I ask.

"Only did one chapter this morning. I'm doing an event at the L'Écume bookshop tonight. Do you want to come?"

"I have to work early tomorrow. And I don't know where I fit in with these two brothers."

"You knew the risks. You opened a can of worms. And you can still cut your losses and settle for your official father, just like I've settled for my unknown father."

"You can invent any father you want in your novels."

"We all have the freedom to reinvent our lives. Think about it, Chiara."

He touches my arm with his warm hand and I shiver. My heart is pounding. My body appears to think I'm sprinting when all I'm doing is leaning against a blue fence chatting to a guy from Corsica who thinks we have a lot in common and that the island has cast a spell over us.

"You've only got one solution left," he says.

"What's that?"

"Sneak into their homes on a false pretext during your post round and steal some of their DNA."

I stare at him, stunned. I had had it all worked out, I was going to get the man Perig found to take a DNA test willingly, *not* behind his back.

"You don't need their approval," insists Gabin. "Unless you want their money?"

"Of course I don't!"

"Then do what it takes to find out."

"Gabin, is your break over?" calls the captain through the window.

I leave, shaken by Gabin's strange advice.

I walk home past the house where Kilian Thunder lives. Perig wasn't exaggerating when he said the windows were black with grime. I stop off at Quentin's, the new butcher's, to buy some pâté for Roz. Two elderly local women are happily chatting away in the local dialect, which sounds like a foreign language to me. I listen carefully, then give up trying to fathom what they are saying.

"You're Roz's goddaughter, aren't you?" asks one of them turning to me and looking sure of herself.

I nod. You can't keep anything secret on an island. They'll talk about me after I've gone, I'm juicy gossip for them. I may be a foreigner, but I feel more at home here than in Rome, my birthplace. I wonder why?

Groix Island, L'Écume bookshop and café

The blue Bookshop is delighted to be staying open late tonight. It faces the merry-go-round on the church square, right next to the Bleu Thé gift shop. People come here all year round to read, chat, drink coffee or tea on the outside terrace or at the small round tables, and attend the bookshop's various events.

A poster on the door announces that Gabin Aragon will be here tonight. Readers who research him on the Internet will come across his author bio set against a screenshot of ocean waves: *Gabin Aragon has published ten novels, including several bestsellers, as a ghost writer. You have probably already read and enjoyed his works unknowingly. He loves books, travelling, meeting people, and any form of water, be it oceans, seas, rivers, lakes, showers or the eau de vie from his native Corsica.*

Some people like his tongue-in-cheek humour, others don't understand it or think he is conceited. The blue Bookshop knows this because it has overheard customers saying so to Anne, the bookseller.

"He can't sign books because he's not allowed to say which authors he writes for," she explains. "But you can ask him any questions you like."

"Perhaps he'll make an exception for us?" says one of the gossipy ladies. "If we promise to keep it a secret?"

"You're dreaming! If he's sworn to secrecy, he won't tell a soul," retorts another.

"I saw him with Didier and Roz's daughter."

"I saw him with Perig."

"I saw him with the new postwoman."

"She's only Cory's replacement until she's back!"

"He's writing for Kerwan, he'll have to sign his name on that one!"

The blue Bookshop is not surprised to see people arriving at the last minute; it's quite used to it. Here on the island people leave home five minutes before the start of anything, whether it's a church service, a concert, a film, or a meeting. The Bookshop watches the islanders as they sink into its comfortable chairs; it's delighted to have so many visitors.

Gabin smiles at the audience. They are bowled over by this charming lad with the wild hair they would love to run a comb through. He introduces himself, explaining that he too is an islander, that islanders are more passionate and more melancholic than mainlanders.

"Words are my oars and my skiff. I'd be lost without them. They heal, they soothe, they pulse with anger, they suffer, they taunt me, they are my constant companions. Please forgive me for talking about my words rather than giving you the titles of my books. I am always hungry for writing and emotion, not to mention Roz's delicious *tchumpôt*!"

The blue Bookshop buzzes with laughter, the audience is captivated by the simple authenticity of this young man.

"I chose to devour as much as I could, and earn a living from my pen. My ego comes second to filling my stomach. I write for authors that you see on television. They have an idea for a project, the general outline, and the raw material. But they don't have the time to perfect and fine-tune the sentences, to play with an image from all angles like a painter plays with shadows. We work as a team."

"Do you earn as much as them?" asks a tourist.

"We're not going to talk money tonight," replies Gabin smoothly.

"You're skirting the issue, lad, get to the point!"

"Have you told your parents? Do they like your books?"

"I don't know my father," says Gabin, characteristically relaxed.

Throats clear, feet and chairs scrape the floor. The person who asked the question apologizes.

"The main thing is the sheer joy I get from plunging into a new story each time," Gabin goes on. "I am never reassured, never complacent, everything has to be reworked, the magic can stop working anytime. A novelist is like an actor who plays one role after another."

"Do you ever get writer's block?"

"My laptop wallpaper is a picture of the sea. That helps."

"Do you write during the day or at night?"

"During the day. The night is for love."

"Can you really not sign your books for us? We won't tell a soul, promise!"

"I didn't bring any with me."

The blue Bookshop no longer hears the speaker, it is already imagining the audience rummaging through its shelves and can hear the rustling of pages turning. The Bookshop recognizes Chiara, the stand-in postwoman, who dropped by recently to buy a guide to the island. She is sitting on the edge of her chair, tense and stressed. And she keeps glancing at a large, overweight man accompanied by a young blonde girl, who looks like a Scandinavian model, after Perig, the journalist, a fan of Jean Failler's Breton thrillers, pointed him out to her.

The Bookshop can see that the audience is mesmerized. Gabin is sincere and laid-back, and speaks with intensity.

"Doesn't it bother your wife and children not to see your name on your books?"

"I am a father to my characters, but my nomadic lifestyle is incompatible with a wife and children."

The blue Bookshop has difficulty grasping the notion of a father, even though it is full of stories in which parents play a central role.

"How long does it take you to write a book?"

"Anywhere between six months and two years of non-stop writing."

"Why are you never on TV?"

"I'm a ghost writer, readers don't know me. Why would they invite me? Television helps to sell books, as do radio and newspapers, but word of mouth is essential too."

"Did you try to publish under your own name at the beginning?" asks a teenager.

"I was too young. I've moved on since then. I've realized that just wanting to be a writer is not enough. I need to really live life before I can claim to write about it."

"Would you ever give up your financial security and try your luck in the limelight? What would you risk?"

The blue Bookshop feels sorry for Gabin. Groix islanders are proud and brave. They are bold and daring; they're not shrinking violets. And they are not motivated by money, otherwise they would have long since left the island. They simply don't understand the young writer's choice. It's incomprehensible to them.

"Writing is a risk," says Gabin. "You should read Patrick Modiano's speech when he received the Nobel Prize in Sweden. He said that writing 'is a little like driving a car at night, in winter, on ice, with zero visibility'."

"Like being at sea when the swell rises, and the sea spins you and wrings you out like a washing machine," adds a sailor.

"Like being in Lorient and having to take the boat that has become ridiculously expensive," says another local, provoking the big, overweight man that Chiara is secretly watching.

"Sometimes you have to do things you don't want to do," the portly character says defensively. "Only children believe that grown-ups are in charge. You can't have it both ways."

His rant is followed by a deathly silence. The blue Bookshop shudders inwardly.

"Money makes the world go round," the man adds. "You lot look out for each other, you fight to stay here, you have chosen this quality of life and this unique setting. I left the island to earn a living, and I know I'm losing touch with my roots as I get richer. You think I sold out to the enemy, but it's actually the opposite. I'm doing my utmost to maintain the same number of ferry crossings. I was born here. You think I've forgotten that, but you're wrong. The boat is too expensive. The timetables have changed, there are fewer boats, they put on more for the tourists but not for you guys, yet you're the ones sustaining the island. Trust me, I'm trying to keep an eye on things behind the scenes."

A hubbub fills the bookshop then seeps out through the window and wakes up the tuna fish at the top of the church's bell tower. *Brendan Thunder is not a sell-out. Brendan Thunder is biding his time. Brendan Thunder is looking out for the island.* Some believe him, others don't. The young stand-in postwoman looks relieved.

"To answer your question," continues Gabin to the teenager, "if I were to write under my own name, I would be risking my own neck, my self-confidence, my own wrath and my own reputation. But your island is bewitching, it casts a spell on you. No one leaves unscathed. You guys are not cynical or defeated. You set a great example—you make me want to get out there and fight for what's mine. Groix makes me want to shake everything up."

The public are mesmerized. The blue Bookshop and the stand-in postwoman are the only ones who notice that Brendan Thunder has stood up and walked out with his girl-friend, after first taking off his jacket and putting it over her bare shoulders. He has said what he has to say. There will be a lot of banter in the cafés and shops tomorrow. In days gone by, it would have been the hot topic of conversation in wash houses and in the streets, but washing machines and television have changed all that. People wash their clothes at home now, and no longer spend the evening on their doorstep chatting with the neighbours. Yet the bond between islanders remains indestructible. Mainlanders will never understand.

The evening was a success. The blue Bookshop likes being at the centre of things.

Groix Island, the Locmaria round

"Tomorrow will be stormy and blustery, you'll need to wrap up warm," said Perig to me yesterday, handing me a red sailing jacket smelling of mothballs. "You can wear your yellow post office safety vest over the top."

The jacket is too small to be his, and too big for Aziliz's tiny frame. I didn't dare ask if it belonged to Gurvan. I accepted it gratefully.

This morning there was an envelope for Brendan Thunder. I put it at the front of my basket, sticking out of the pile.

I stop for a few minutes at the cemetery and have a quick look among the graves for Brendan and Kilian's parents. My supposed Italian father rests in peace in the Verano Cemetery in Rome. The Groix cemetery is miniscule in comparison. I greet each Thunder gravestone with respect and humility. *I could be related to you, you know. I would be honoured to be one of your relatives. Or distraught, shaken up, who knows ... Alessio, you would advise me to see this through to the end, wouldn't you?*

I divide the cemetery into squares and examine them one after the other. I place wildflowers on each Thunder grave I find. An elderly woman with a watering can in her hand notices what I'm doing and approaches me, her eyebrows raised. I explain that I don't know which one I'm looking for, so I'm laying flowers on all of them. She tells me she comes every day to visit her daughter and understands. She then leaves without a word, not caring that her watering can is leaking.

A car stops out on the road and a door slams. It's Perig. His body droops as he passes through the cemetery gate, despite his son not being buried here. He has a peculiar gait: he propels his torso energetically forward, and his legs reluctantly follow on.

"How did you know I was here?" I ask.

"We saw you go in, but we didn't see you come out. Everything is public knowledge here. You stick out too. There are very few tourists right now."

"I'm not a tourist."

"That's right, you're Roz Thunder's goddaughter, forgive me."

"I'm looking for Brendan and Kilian's parents if you must know."

"Don't get on your high horse."

I picture the massive, long-haired plough horses from Didier's book on Groix in the old days.

"Their father had fallen out with his family," says Perig. "He didn't want to be buried next to them. He insisted on being cremated in Lorient. He came back on the evening boat."

"'Came back', how do you mean?"

"In his urn. He wanted to be scattered at his night-time fishing spot by a faithful friend who refused to reveal the exact spot to others. His wife insisted they do the same with her, to be near him. They are resting in the ocean, feeding the fish."

I chuckle nervously.

"Now get back to your round," says Perig. "You're on a mission."

I mount Pegasus. I turn off before Port-Mélite, checking the names in the folder. In my mind I raise a glass to the drinkers at the Triskell. Pegasus gallops along beside the fields.

When I approach Locmaria, where fishing boat owners and skippers once lived, my hands start to tremble on the handlebars. I could dump the letter in the wash house or in a bin, head to the port, board the next boat and go back to Rome. I would betray Roz's trust, abandon Perig to his sorrow, cut ties with Gabin, forget Urielle, and return to my previous life which though not great wasn't tragic either. I brace myself against the squeaky brakes. I glance at the ocean and the waves rolling in. I have been neglecting you, Alessio, yet you're my best friend.

It was spring yesterday, it's autumn today. Gurvan's red jacket keeps the wind out, the stench of mothballs scares away the drizzle and the hood protects my face from the elements. I breathe deeply as I put my bike on its kickstand in front of Brendan Thunder's house. We say that a post woman "delivers" the mail. But who or what are the captured letters waiting to be delivered from? What danger? What predator?

If the weather had been fine, Brendan would be outside in his garden, but in this weather only snails, stray dogs and birds are outside. I have cooked up a plan. I'll graze my knuckles on his metal letterbox and ask him for some surgical spirit to disinfect the wound. I look up at the sky and smile at *nonna* Ornella who spent my whole childhood chasing after me with cotton wool and surgical spirit.

I grab the envelope, slide it into the box, forcing my hand in and deliberately scraping my knuckles. Then I knock on the kitchen door. No answer. Yet the light is on. I knock again. A huge grey dog jumps at the door and barks, and I back away frightened. A figure appears. It's the big portly man I saw at the bookshop. He opens the door, the giant dog jumps up on me, puts his paws on my shoulders and starts licking my face.

"Shoot! Get down! Right now!"

I like his voice, but not how he's looking at me. He has the velvety tone of an orator, full of charm and the face of a seductive fifty-year-old. But he has piercing blue eyes and a hard expression. Thin lips. His figure is starting to fill out, he is letting himself go. Wild bushy eyebrows. My Italian father is the same age as me, Brendan is twice that. He notices my post office jacket.

"Is Cory sick?"

He is concerned about the postwoman's health, that's a point in his favour.

"I'm just standing in for her for one week."

"That's annoying," he says. "I'm waiting for an important letter. Cory was hardly the sharpest knife in the drawer and you seem to be even slower, have you seen the time? Do you have the registered letter I'm waiting for?"

I shake my head, unable to utter a sound. If he's my father, he's an arsehole.

"So what are you bothering me for then? What do you want?"

I want for you not to exist. For you not to be Brendan Thunder. For you not to be my father.

"I cut myself on your letterbox."

I expect him to say that he's sorry, and that he will fetch something to put on it. Instead, he walks around me, opens his letterbox, grabs the envelope, goes back into his kitchen and closes his door without so much as a glance at my grazed hand. I stand outside, frozen to the spot, my knuckles burning. The rain is tap dancing on Gurvan's sailing jacket. On the other side of the glass door, Shoot stares at me with his big, sad eyes.

I hand a young woman her post further down the same street. She sees my bleeding hand and kindly attends to it.

"Your neighbour is not a very nice man," I say trembling as she dabs the surgical spirit on my wounds.

She nods and grabs a box of children's plasters. "He treats us like foreigners because we arrived here three years ago to open up a shop. We contribute more to the local economy than he does. Rumour has it that his son sells drugs. They say he's in prison. In any case, he no longer comes here. And he left that great big dog with his father. Do you prefer a footballer or a princess plaster?"

"Footballer."

My potential half-brother christened his dog "Shoot". But he is neither a footballer nor a photographer. He's a dealer.

Paris, two years earlier

Your name is Louis and you have been working in this ICU for two years now. You get changed and place your packet of strawberry-flavour jellies in front of Elsa, the new nurse. You can't invite her to your place, she'd discover the truth. She still lives with her parents. She'd like you to move in together, but that's impossible. You are taking her to Honfleur this coming weekend.

"How old are you Louis, five?" says Elsa, frowning at the jelly sweets he knows she can't resist.

"I'm old enough to appreciate how beautiful you are," you fire straight back.

You hug her, pick her up off the ground and kiss her. She bursts out laughing and it feels so good, a moment of pure happiness amidst all the pain and suffering in this place.

"We're waiting for you to do the handover. Are you ready?" she asks you.

You go over each case, the duty doctor is briefed, everything is calm. Night falls. You love this timeless hour when you enter each cubicle and introduce yourself to the patients whose breathing is assisted by ventilators. You put your hand on their arm, even if they are unconscious; you need to feel them. Plus, you are transmitting your vitality and strength to them. You tell them your first name and explain what you're going to do to them. *I'm going to suction you, it's not pleasant I know, but we're going to do it together, gently, okay?* Their bodies relax, even those in a coma understand that you are helping them. Your warm hand and your soothing soft voice puts them at ease. On the ECG, their heartbeat slows down. You imagine how they used to be, with their loved one. You picture them young, crazy, impatient and cheerful, like in those bank advertisements where a good-looking young couple meet, get married, have children, grow old together and invest. You wince at the thought that one day you will be just like them, in an ICU bed, at the mercy of some clumsy medical student. You wonder who will come to see you then, a wife, children, friends; or maybe no one at all?

You go through the motions with the precision of a Swiss watch. You have it off pat. The nurses hold you up as an example to the new externs, as you do it so well. Back in the day, they used to record the vitals by hand on a chart hanging at the bottom of the bed and took patients' blood pressure manually. You find that unbelievable. Now a parametric monitor keeps track of everything: ECG, oxygen saturation, heart rate, blood pressure. You congratulate yourself. Because you're not really a medical student. You have mastered the techniques, but you don't know the theory. You lack the basics, the ins, and outs. But you're intelligent enough to conceal it. No one is even suspicious.

In the chilly early morning, you suction the intubated patients and calm them down. No one died in the night.

"I want you," whispers Elsa as you suction Mr Dupré, a patient with emphysema. The tissues around his lung alveoli have lost their elasticity: they can no longer inflate and deflate, which reduces the amount of oxygen in his blood. He has never smoked but was exposed to chemical fumes in the factory where he worked. In those days, workers thought it was manly not to protect themselves, their attitude was that helmets and masks were for sissies ...

"I . . . want . . . you!" mouth the young woman's crimson lips. You slow down your movements, Mr Dupré hiccups and turns blue, Elsa looks on wide eyed, and you quickly turn on the ventilator again.

"I'm sorry," you whisper, leaning towards Mr Dupré. "Your nurse is hitting on me and she's hot!"

Mr Dupre is unconscious, but you could have sworn he smiled at you from behind his tube.

You return to the nurses' station. Elsa is dying to rip off your gown, and all you can think about is undressing her. You smile at Mona, who is going through a divorce. Her husband got tired of sleeping alone while she was on nights, so he found himself a replacement.

"Elsa, can you swap with me on Saturday?" she asks. "I have an appointment with my lawyer."

Elsa gives you a furtive look and shakes her head. "Sorry, I'm going to Honfleur."

"Lucky you!" you chip in.

"I'm going with my grandmother," explains Elsa, keeping up the act.

An alarm goes off. You rush over. Mr Malik is sweating, his electrodes have come off, you replace them, you sit down beside him, you talk to him and wait for everything to return to normal. You left your mobile phone at the nurses' station so it wouldn't interfere with the machines.

"Your phone rang, Louis," says Elsa when you get back. "I looked to see who it was. You called yourself!"

You immediately figure out what happened. Damn! She saw the name on the screen. Louis Lambert called Louis Lambert.

"You left yourself a message," continues Elsa, laughing.

"That's my father," you improvise.

"Oh, so you have the same first name?"

"It's a family tradition."

"So you save your father under his first name in your phone? I save my parents as 'Mum and Dad'."

"The night of the Bataclan attack I was with the paramedics," begins Tom, the bald nurse.

Smiles fade. Fear and pain erupt into the overheated room where the sun never shines, summer or winter. In this room, you either get better or you die, either way it takes weeks. At the Bataclan they weren't patients, but healthy young people who had gathered to enjoy the music. But the incessant, jerky notes of those Kalashnikovs shattered their dreams forever.

"I remember hearing phones ringing in the dead peoples' pockets and seeing 'Mum' or 'Dad' on their screens. It was unbearable," Tom goes on.

He talks about it all the time, reliving the 13th of November 2015 every day, recounting it endlessly, the phone screens with the smiling faces of parents worried for their bullet-riddled children. He is having therapy and has returned to work. He was a normal, efficient human being, but he is screwed up now. The team huddles around him to keep him warm. Since that day he is permanently cold. He threw his phone into the river Seine. His wife stood by him, did everything to help him, and then she couldn't take it any longer. She asked him if they could take a break and left with the children. He was left to deal with his nightmares alone.

"If you have a son, will you also call him Louis Lambert?" asks Mona.

"Of course," I say.

"Do you have the same name on your cheque book and your tax returns? That's convenient," says Elsa. "Listen to his message, there may be a problem."

You look at her, surprized by her foresight. You sense impending disaster, as the real Louis never calls you when you are on duty. You leave the room, go down the corridor, through the airlock door and out into the hospital's dark courtyard. A stranger in a white coat is sitting on the steps of the orthopaedic ward smoking, her cigarette glowing in the dark. The sky is a dark blue canvas dotted with stars. You listen to the message.

"Hey, it's Louis. I'm going to have to take my name back, mate. I'm leaving Paris and moving to Marseilles with my girlfriend. I've found an internship at the hospital there, I start in a week's time. Sorry I haven't given you much notice. They know you now, you've proved yourself. It's time to tell them who you are. I'm glad I could help out. Go for it, drop the mask! This is your big moment! You can take on your father!"

Devastated, your body droops. Just when you finally felt at home, wanted, loved, normal . . .

You walk slowly back to the ward, looking dejected. All eyes are on you.

"Bad news?" asks Mona.

"Not really."

Elsa, so affectionate and caring, comes up to you. "Can I help?"

You long to tell her the truth, but you cannot. You'll have to disappear, start all over again. You have no choice.

"Louis, trust me," she insists gently.

You smile and tell her that it's nothing serious, just a family issue, it'll work out. She falls for it.

"Do you look alike?" she asks.

"Sorry?"

"Do you look like your father? Does Louis Lambert look like Louis Lambert?"

You nod, and this time you're not lying. You do indeed look like Louis Lambert, which is why you chose this particular fourth-year medical student. You are both big and sturdily built, with curly hair and a round face. Louis has blue-green eyes, you don't, so you have to wear coloured contact lenses. You set your sights on this guy, observing and studying him before making your move. He was a mere stranger who had his coffee and croissant at the café in front of the hospital every morning at the same time. You chatted and became friends. You told him your real name was Charles and you pretended to be a medical student in the year below him. It took you months to coax him, to give you the best possible chance of success, to weave your web of lies.

The real Louis Lambert doesn't know his father, it's a gaping wound. You seized this weakness and exploited it. You came up with the most impressive and convincing story ever. You pretended that your father was the new head of the ICU clinic. That your parents had divorced when you were young. That you hadn't seen the rat in twenty years. And that that was why you wanted to work in his department, but under a different name, to see what kind of person he was. The bigger the lie, the more it will be believed. If it touches an Achilles heel, even better. The real Louis was sympathetic to your situation and agreed to let you use his name. He assumed it was temporary, a good deed, helping another fatherless lad, plus it was a nice little earner. For two years, you have been impersonating him at the hospital and giving him half of your salary. He gets money to pay his rent without having to work nights, what more could he want! Then he had to go and fall madly in love with this girl from Marseilles with her hypnotic Mediterranean accent, and that really put a spanner in the works.

You can no longer pretend that you are Louis Lambert. You wince, you have heartburn from the stress. It runs in your family; you suffer from chronic gastritis although it's not as bad as the ulcer that killed your mother when it ruptured. You pop a pill to calm the burning sensation. It took you months to get to know the real Louis at the local café, not to mention the time it took you to befriend Florian, the blue spectacled guy with the moustache in the ICU, so that he could get you onto the ward. All for nothing.

You leave the nurses' station and start your round, down in the dumps. You hold the hands of the sleeping and the tired, the comatose and the conscious. You gently squeeze their fingers, something you couldn't do for your own mother. All those years while Patty was being cruel to you, you wished you could have joined your mum in that place you go after death instead of staying with that crazy bitch who treated you like a piece of unwanted baggage. France wasn't on terrorist alert at that time. Abandoned baggage didn't attract people's attention. So no one noticed this piece of human baggage left on the platform of a desolate station, a dumbstruck little boy with a hollow look in his eyes and a broken heart.

You jump. You were lost in your memories and squeezed the fingers of the patient in cubicle 6 too hard. Mr Bulle is about your age and a backpacker. He caught some nasty virus while globetrotting. He has been in the ICU for a week. It wasn't just weed he was smoking out there. His mother comes to see him every evening after work, talks to him, plays his favourite music on headphones, and reads him his Australian girlfriend's emails. Mr Bulle's eyes are open now, and panic stricken; he is distressed. He has regained consciousness but can't breathe. The tube in his trachea makes him cough on his catheter and he panics. He is fighting against the artificial ventilator and tries to grab the catheter. The balloon of the catheter is inflated to stay in place. If he pulls it out, he'll blow out his vocal cords. You seize his hand to stop him, you tell him that everything is fine, that he is in hospital, and to calm down as the machine is helping him breathe. The patient doesn't know where he is. He was travelling in Myanmar when his girlfriend called their insurance to say that he was delirious and no longer recognized her.

"You are in Paris, Mr Bulle. Your mother will be here in a little while and your girlfriend has sent you some videos from Sydney. You have contracted a nasty bug, but we are treating you and you will get better."

But the patient isn't listening to you, he is trying to escape your clutches. You make a split-second decision. You are not supposed to remove the tube without the consent of the whole team, without checking the patient's lung capacity or the oxygen and carbon dioxide measurements in his blood. If you extubate him and he relapses, you will have to ventilate him with a mask and then reintubate him, with all the risks that entails. You think you can hear Mona's voice whispering to you: *Medicine is often a matter of experience and intuition. You can't learn everything from books, sometimes you have to follow your instinct rather than the rules.* The cubicle is right at the end of the corridor. If you call for help, they won't hear. If you let go of the patient, he will pull out his catheter. If you restrain him, he will struggle and injure himself. So you grab a syringe and connect it to the catheter in order to quickly deflate the balloon.

"Cough, Mr Bulle, I'm going to remove the tube that is bothering you, cough!"

With a wild look in his eyes, the patient obeys, and you gently remove the catheter from his throat. Mr Bulle sits up. Phew, he's awake, he is out of his coma. You smile encouragingly. He catches his breath, then asks in a low, hoarse voice:

"Pa . . . ris? Not . . . Yan . . . gon? Have I missed . . . my . . . meeting . . . with Aung San . . . Suu Kyi?"

You smile. "I don't know, sir. But I do know you're alive!"

They give you a good dressing down—an extern isn't supposed to extubate a patient! Though the on-call nurse congratulated you on your quick thinking. In this case, it was appropriate. He instructs you to inform Mrs Bulle, the mother of the young man, who is now sitting on his bed, bewildered, and full of questions. A part of his life has disappeared, a black hole has swallowed up part of his timeline. You lend him your mobile phone so that he can send a message to his girlfriend. She replies that she loves him with a selfie of her hands drawing a heart. You are convinced that if you hadn't intervened Mr Bulle would have been stuck in limbo forever.

This is your last shift. You won't see Elsa again. You're desperate to tell her everything, but you decide against it. She loves who she *thinks* you are, a fourth-year medical student. Not a liar who has flunked his exams twice, who lives in a pokey studio, and isn't even a real member of the medical staff. Later on, when the day shift arrive, you'll do the hand-over, you'll breathe in the distinctive odour of the ICU one last time, and then you'll go and say farewell to Mr Bulle and his unconscious bedfellows. You will have a last coffee with the nurses and Elsa, whom you will not be taking to Honfleur after all. Tomorrow, you will tell them all that you are moving to Marseilles, that you are taking a job at the hospital there. They will soon forget you. Louis Lambert will disappear from their world. On these wards patients are remembered far more than their carers.

It had all been so easy. Investigating, convincing Louis Lambert to let you use his name, playing pool with Florian, gaining his trust. People are far too trusting. You were asked for your name and address, you said Louis Lambert, they noted your social security number and your previous externships, the administration did its job well. But no one checked whether you were actually the real Louis Lambert.

You will have to invent another life for yourself. No one has called you Charles for years, you wouldn't be able to handle it. You can still hear your mother's voice when she says your name, it's like music to your ears. You won't give anyone else that privilege. You repainted her room in blue and orange to make her feel more comfortable and surprise her the day she came out of the ICU. She never even saw it or even knew. When that slumlord reclaimed your house, he hollered when he saw the bright colours. *What the hell is this?* If you had been older, if you had squeezed Alice's fingers like you squeezed Mr Bulle's, you would have saved her life. Then all three of you could have danced along the river Seine in your brightly coloured trainers.

You will have to reinvent yourself once more, change your eye colour, repaint your life in a different shade. Why just be one person when you can reinvent yourself every morning?

Groix Island, the Locmaria round

This time, I'll get it right. If that nasty, ill-mannered man is my father, I'd rather know. I need proof. I'm not going to leave him a choice.

I set off for Locmaria. A tiny rabbit runs straight across in front of me at the last moment and I swerve, narrowly avoiding a nasty fall. Pegasus rears then gallops on. My calves feel like concrete, my shoulders ache. I pull up in front of Brendan and Shoot's house. I'm going to force his hand. Even if it means my first time inside my potential father's home won't be the dream scenario I had imagined.

The kitchen light is on. I knock. Shoot charges at the door. Brendan opens up, looking as hostile as ever. He grabs the dog by its collar silently and holds out his hand for the registered letter he is expecting. *Nonna* Ornella always used to say: "There are two types of people in the world: those who have been raised, and those who have merely been fed." Brendan is clearly one of the latter, and obviously too much judging by his waistline. He waits for me to hand him his letter. Here goes.

"Can I use your bathroom, please? I live in Port-Lay, it's too far away."

His eyes glaze over, he wants to refuse but doesn't dare. He depends on the post office; he'd better not get on the wrong side of Cory's replacement. He reluctantly steps back, still holding Shoot.

"There's a toilet on the ground floor," he growls.

A door opens. The gorgeous blonde enters. My one-in-three-chance of a father is shagging a kid!

"I'd prefer the bathroom," I say, counting on female solidarity.

The blonde steps aside to let me through. "It's on the first floor on the left."

Without further ado, I charge ahead through the living room, which is full of cold, futuristic furniture, up the stairs and lock the bathroom door behind me. Damn! The young woman has short blonde hair. Brendan has thinning blond hair. So whose comb is whose? Same for the toothbrush. Which one is his? I don't know what to do, so I take out the little plastic bags I brought with me, put on my gloves, take hair from each comb and carefully label the bags "hair 1" and "hair 2". I do the same with the toothbrushes; I cut a few bristles from each and label them "brush 1", and "brush 2". I open the bin and steal two cotton buds smeared with yellow ear wax. Yuck! I also take some chewing gum I find which is more likely to be from the girl, but you never know. Plus some razor blades. Then I flush the toilet, stuff the little bags into Gurvan's large-pocketed jacket and run back downstairs smiling.

I thank Brendan politely, as my mum taught me to. "Sorry for bothering you. I'm Italian, I'm from Tuscany. Do you know the island of Elba?"

I hope to God that Perig was mistaken, and that some other nice, warm, cheerful Groix islander is my father. But to my horror, the miserable grump replies.

"I know it," he grunts.

Then he turns around and slips a capsule into the coffee machine, as if I have already gone. The message is clear.

"Pleased to meet you," I say.

I hit the road again with my stolen evidence.

Groix Island, village centre

Kilian is out walking his dog; the coast is clear. Groix islanders rarely lock their doors, they trust each other. I mean, who would risk taking the boat with goods stolen from an island where everyone knows each other? Tourists double lock their houses and their cars. According to Urielle, some Parisians even padlock their hearts at night.

Two elderly islanders are chatting in front of Kilian's house. I try to decipher what they are saying. It's all gobbledygook to me. What are they talking about? I lean Pegasus against the house wall and knock loudly on the door. The men go quiet.

"You won't find him in at this time of day," they tell me.

I feign annoyance. "I've got an important letter for him."

Thank God they don't know that their village isn't on my post round.

"He doesn't lock his door, like his father and his father's father. When he was at sea, the house was open for months on end. Not like the idiot down there, barricading himself in even when he's just in his kitchen. Does he think we're going to steal his rolling pin or what!"

They guffaw. "You can go in and drop off your letter."

"Are you sure?" I ask.

"Absolutely!"

I turn the handle and go inside. It's just as I expected. The filthy kitchen reeks of cigarettes. It hasn't been cleaned since Napoleon was exiled to Elba. The furniture is grey with dust, the plate and cutlery on the table are coated in grime. An ashtray overflows with stinking cigarette butts. I feel sick and want to run out the door. But I'm on a mission.

I place the letter on the table, causing the dust to fly up in swirls. I hold my breath. Outside, the two men continue their conversation where they left off. On my guard, I open a door and discover a surprisingly clean toilet. Another door leads into a bedroom containing minimal furniture: a bed, a bedside table and a chair. No ceiling light or bedside lamp. Kilian obviously doesn't read before going to sleep, besides I don't see a single book. But this room is abnormally clean too. The third door thrusts me into another dimension. I enter a bright artist's studio with a glass roof overlooking a walled garden. No one outside would ever imagine this room existed. The light-coloured wooden floor is sanded and varnished, and water-colour equipment is laid out on the long trestle table that serves as a work surface. There are brushes, tubes of paint, notebooks, paint pallets, metal boxes, sketch pads, large sheets of paper, along with a jumble of water containers, daisy-shaped mixing pallets, their petals all different colours, and pieces of white Plexiglas speckled with pigments. *Nonna* Ornella used to paint with watercolours too. I used to watch her with admiration. I am rubbish at painting. I used to pass her the tubes of cadmium yellow, cadmium red and carmine red, cobalt blue and ultramarine blue, yellow ochre, burnt sienna and burnt amber.

I carefully turn the pages of a sketch pad. Kilian Thunder is very talented. He has sketched the port at various times of day. Sailors hoisting their sails, fishermen raising their nets, passengers boarding the boat, Urielle and her kids hurrying towards the gangway. Another sketchpad transports me to the Pointe des Chats. At the foot of the lighthouse topped with its red cap, Perig looks out to sea as he talks to me. The ex-fisherman with the limp has captured the island in fine detail.

Kilian can no longer set sail and leave the house, so his brush travels in his place. The locals never see him paint, but he notices everything before locking himself away in his studio. He is not a recluse; he is just a quiet solitary soul. The brilliant staging of his filthy kitchen ensures that he is left alone. There is a hotplate in his studio along with a fridge, a stove, a saucepan, crockery, and a large basket for his dog beside a bowl of water. If I am his daughter, I haven't inherited his artistic talent.

Time is running out. I reluctantly leave the room. The last door leads to a bathroom where I find exactly what I'm looking for. A clean, white sink, a toothbrush with flattened bristles, a hairbrush, a razor, and a bin. Terrified that Kilian might return home any minute, I take out my plastic bags, put on my gloves and steal some hair from the brush. I also take used dental floss, toothpicks, and nail clippings. Plus mucus-covered used tissues. It's disgusting. I shove the labelled bags into my pockets, take three cigarette butts from the kitchen and reach for the door handle. But just then the door creaks open, like in a horror film. My whole body tenses up. I've been caught red handed.

Kilian is shocked to find me standing in his kitchen. He doesn't look like his brother at all. His blond beard is so long it touches his yellow oilskin. His nose looks like a potato.

"What the hell are you doing in here?" he roars.

I point to my yellow post office jacket and the letter on the table. "Your neighbours outside said I could come in and drop off your post."

"There's no one out there. Where's Marielle?"

"I'm Cory's replacement. I'm Roz Thunder's goddaughter."

He calms down when he hears her name.

"My neighbours were messing with you. I don't let anyone inside my home!"

"I'm sorry . . . I didn't know . . ."

He steps aside. His dog walks in, sniffs me and growls, showing its teeth.

"Quiet, Aristotle!"

The dog immediately falls silent.

"Where is your accent from?" snarls Kilian.

"I'm Italian," I say. "From the island of Elba. Do you know it?"

His face freezes. "Yes, I do. Now get out of my house."

"Why did you call your dog Aristotle? Is he a philosopher?"

"Because he's a *Grek*," he mumbles.

At least he has a sense of humour. I leave and clamber onto Pegasus. Kilian opens the door again, brandishing the envelope addressed to his brother—the letter I used as an excuse to enter his house.

"This letter isn't for me!" he scowls.

"Your name is Thunder isn't it?"

My voice goes all weak when I pronounce that name.

"I'm not the only Thunder here, ask around!"

"Do you know this Brendan Thunder?"

"Never heard of him."

"Nice to meet you," I say, as I cycle off. I notice the two old men drinking in the L'Ancre de Marine pub nearby, and I wonder whether Kilian will notice that his used tissues have disappeared from his bathroom bin.

Groix Island, Port-Lay

When I walk into the living room, Danielle is looking at Didier and singing: "You may not be the strongest, son, but between us we'll be millionaires, whether I'm rich or poor, you'll always be blessed with a father."

Now it's my turn. I scrupulously follow the advice on the website. I wash my hands, I don't drink coffee, I don't brush my teeth. I have prepared an envelope with my name and date of birth, and signed the consent form. I've also bought some cotton buds and cut the ends off to make the saliva swabs that the labs are so fond of calling "paternity kits". I rub the first stick inside my mouth and against the inside of my cheek as I count to twenty. This is to collect saliva and epithelial cells. I then let it air dry in a clean glass. I repeat the operation with three other sticks, without letting anything come into contact with the tip of the swab. I wait an hour, then I place the sticks in the envelope.

Our DNA is the same in all our cells, skin, mucous membranes, blood, or hair. Each parent passes on half of their genes to their children. My genetic code consists of forty-six chromosomes, of which twenty-three come from Livia and twenty-three from my father. Paternity testing out of sheer curiosity is banned in France where it has no legal value, but I'm not French and I want to find out. I don't want the results sent to Roz's house though, so I asked Gabin if I could give his name instead of mine. He agreed but pointed out that it would set tongues wagging if anyone saw the address of the English genetics lab and could start the rumour that he is Kerwan's son.

My envelope will leave by boat, sail to Lorient, then cross the Channel and head for London. I signed the three consent forms using different fake initials and making up three names and dates of birth. Brendan Thunder became Mr Shoot, and Kilian Thunder became Mr Aristotle. I ticked the box "test without mother" even though Livia is the only person I *am* sure of! I paid extra to speed things up. Gabin will receive the results at his post restante address.

Groix Island,
main postbox, village centre

The Big Yellow Postbox sits at the back of the post office, proud and haughty, snubbing the smaller postboxes scattered around the island. It is the most important postbox on Groix, the one the locals make a beeline for. They know that if they miss that day's collection, their mail won't leave the island until the next day.

The Postbox overlooks the bakery, adjacent to the covered market and the newsagents, and observes the tourists in summer and the locals all year round. It is the hub from which all sorts of administrative documents are dispatched, be it retirement papers, tax returns, adult education applications, medical files, disability benefits, social security, maritime documents and so on. It also sends greetings cards and birthday cards. Everyone uses it, young or old. People squint trying to read the collection times. Some people tap the lid after entrusting it with an important letter, like stroking the head of a faithful dog.

The Postbox recognizes the new postwoman who is replacing Cory on the Locmaria round. It is glad that she doesn't lean her bike against it—that can chip its paintwork, and besides, it's very annoying. The postwoman slips a large envelope into the right-hand slot, above the words "Other districts" and "Abroad". The Big Yellow Postbox knows it's destined for England, where the postboxes are red. The envelope lands on top of the others with a thud. The Postbox guesses the weight of its contents. Hmmm. Let's see. Hair. Cotton buds. Dental floss. Cigarette butts. Chewing gum. Toothpicks. Nail clippings. Razor blades. Used tissues. In plastic bags or paper envelopes.

The Postbox has never heard of genetic markers or DNA ancestry. Those words mean nothing to it, like hearing someone speak a foreign language. It feels the postwoman's hand tremble as she posts the envelope. Then, like an idiot, the young woman puts her hand in the slot to check that her envelope hasn't got stuck, and that no one else can take it out, as if there are gangs of letter thieves on this peaceful island. She takes a deep breath, inhales the delicious aroma of warm bread from the bakery opposite and smiles gratefully at the Postbox.

Groix Island, the Locmaria round

It's the last day of my job; the last piece of tiramisu, or the last square of chocolate. I distribute the mail. Pegasus trots along happily. I bounce through the early morning sunlight and fragrances, watched avidly by sea birds who mistake me for a fishing boat. My bike rears up, neighs, snorts, nostrils flared, ears vibrating. The sun looks so close I feel like I could grab it by standing on my pedals and reaching up. The ocean is so beautiful that I long to ride on its surface and play leapfrog with the waves.

Children are at school, secondary school pupils are in Lorient, shopkeepers are looking after their customers, sailors are at sea, and I'm out here all alone. Where I come from, adults speak loudly, dogs bark, Fiat 500s honk, the smell of pizza fills the streets, the Pope reaches out to the buzzing crowds in front of the Vatican, tourists rant in a mixture of languages, and football fans go crazy when a goal is scored. The very air is vibrant, it pulsates, fizzing up like Prosecco, a constant *crescendo*. Here I'm isolated; even my guardian angel hasn't made the trip, maybe he gets seasick. I ride alone through the villages, in my red jacket and yellow safety vest. I'm a mad dog, a flying fish, a playful dolphin, a quiet pheasant after the hunting season, a laughing gull.

And then, suddenly, it starts to drizzle, and I discover that the rain in Groix doesn't fall to the same beat as the rain in Rome. It doesn't have the same rhythm, the same smell, or the same taste on the tongue. The rain that washes the streets of Rome causes umbrellas to burst open and Vespas to skid, while the rain in Groix teases the hydrangeas and tinkles on the boats' oilskins and decks. I take down the hood of Gurvan's jacket, I breathe in the scent of the moist air, the smell of freedom. At last I approach the Bay of Locmaria.

Groix seafarers have travelled the seas, their wives have toiled the earth and raised their children, and now here I am, turning up with my questions. I'm just a pen, a shadow, a stranger, my feet don't leave any prints on the sand, I leave no trace.

"You have a short memory, Chiara!" Pegasus protests.

I've offended him. I apologize to my wet bike; I stroke its frame and pat its handlebars. If only I could feed it a sugar cube or an apple on my stretched-out palm.

"Even if you're not from here, even if this soil isn't yours, even if the DNA results you're waiting for are negative, you're part of Groix now, you belong here," he whispers. "You've travelled all over the island delivering the mail. Not everyone has that privilege. It's an honour."

"Stop talking rubbish, Pegasus. I'm taking you back to the post office later and you'll forget all about me."

"Yes, of course, because bicycles don't have a memory, do they? And so what? The island has cast its spell on you, whether you like it or not."

Then Pegasus goes silent. All I can hear is the murmur of his battery. I'm not hallucinating, of course bikes don't talk. Alessio, I swear to you that I'm not dreaming.

I continue on my round. The rain stops, the raindrops perched on the clothes lines glisten in the sun, the silvery mica schist rocks sparkle, the puddles on the cracked tarmac road dry up. I take one last look at the personalized letterboxes: the blue lighthouse, the green fish, the sailing boats, the seagulls, the dolphin, the good luck trinkets, the lobster, the ladybird, the rudder and the famous Rouquin Marteau series of boats. Each one is like a link in a chain, creating a harmonious island.

"I don't wish to bother you dear letterboxes, I just have a few letters to slip into your fat bellies, if I may?"

They look amused to see me doubting myself and talking to Pegasus. At the bottom of a garden overlooking the ocean, a small dog runs up to me. The door of the house at the top of the field opens.

"Not in the box, give them to the dog!"

I frown.

"Give him the letters!"

The dog opens his jaws and snarls. I hold two letters out to him. He takes them between his teeth and obediently runs off to the house where his master bends down to retrieve them.

I arrive in Brendan's street. The young blonde woman is dressed in jogging bottoms and black wellington boots, and is playing outside with the grey dog. I can't help but notice the famous monogram on her boots.

"Hey, Shoot!" I call out, braking.

"Hey!" replies my potential father's girlfriend. "If you need to use the bathroom, feel free."

"I'm fine, thank you. I didn't know they made wellington boots?"

"They're not mine, they belong to my boyfriend's mother. She doesn't wear them anymore."

Brendan's mother, who is now fish fodder in her husband's secret fishing spot, wore Louis Vuitton boots?

"She left her stuff here after her divorce. We're the same shoe size."

If Brendan and Kilian's parents were divorced, then why did their mother insist on having her ashes scattered next to her ex-husband?

"She took her husband to the cleaners, took everything he had, hung him out to dry! He loved her and put up with her whims because she was the mother of his son."

"Of his two sons, you mean?"

The blonde in the designer wellies stares at me with raised eyebrows. "Efflam is an only child."

"Efflam?"

"My boyfriend. We've been together for two years."

I'm lost. "You're not Brendan Thunder's girlfriend then?"

"Are you crazy? I'm sixteen years old. He's even older than my father! I'm his son Efflam's girlfriend."

She bursts out laughing, leaving me feeling stupid.

"Everyone on the island thinks you're together," I say.

"He's just being kind to me, because we're having a rough time. I miss Efflam terribly. They won't let me see him; they even monitor our emails. He's fragile, I worry about him."

"Are you not allowed to visit him?

In Italy, you can meet prisoners in the visiting room.

She shakes her head. "His doctor won't let him see anyone."

"What, is he sick as well?"

She furrows her eyebrows, which are practically white. "As well as what?"

"Being in prison."

"What prison?"

This conversation is surreal.

"Let's rewind. So, you are not Brendan Thunder's girlfriend?"

"Are you dumb or what? I'm his son's girlfriend."

"His son the junkie."

"His son who suffers from an addiction."

"And is locked up."

"He gets authorized leave."

"What, you mean with an electronic tag around his ankle?"

"No, silly, a psychiatric hospital isn't a prison!"

"What?"

She looks at me pityingly. "A PSYCHIATRIC HOSPITAL. You know, for psychiatric problems. Efflam is in rehab. Because of the baby."

"What baby?"

"Our baby," she replies. "That's why he decided to go to rehab, to be a good father. Brendan promised him he would look after me and he's kept his word. My parents threw me out when I discovered I was pregnant. They wanted me to get an abortion, but we want to keep this baby. Brendan took me in. When Efflam gets out, we'll go to Ireland with Shoot. The baby will be born there, we'll be fine."

So Brendan is not a sell-out cradle-snatcher after all, he's a father who is doing his best to protect his son and his future grandchild.

"Your neighbours all think that Efflam is in prison for drug trafficking."

"What rubbish! Brendan is discreet and secretive; he doesn't care what people say. Just don't tell anyone any of this, promise? Postmen and women are like doctors, they're bound by professional secrecy, aren't they?"

"I won't breathe a word," I say.

When she turns to the side, I notice her tiny bump.

"That's why Brendan was upset when I suggested you use the bathroom, he was afraid you'd notice my pregnancy vitamins. He's superstitious and there was so much mud-slinging during his divorce. The first time you came he was afraid because we were waiting for a registered letter with my test results, but everything is fine."

So I'm not the only one waiting for test results.

"Why does he not introduce you as his daughter-in-law? That would clarify the situation."

"He doesn't imagine for one second that people would assume otherwise!" exclaims the teenage mother-to-be.

I can still see Brendan's face at the bookshop the other night. He knows what people are saying about him, he finds it amusing. And the rumours make the other men green with envy, so he goes along with them, gloating, pretending to be Casanova. The two brothers are alike. Kilian hides his talent from the locals. And Brendan lets them think he's a ladies man. Well, I've got a secret too . . .

Groix Island, village centre

I catch my breath as I reach the church square after the harsh climb up from the port on Urielle's bike. I miss Pegasus already. Then I hear a voice calling out to me:

"Chiara, *cara*!"

Startled, I brake. I could have sworn that was Viola's voice, but that's impossible. My eyes soon prove me right, however. My godmother is standing right in front of me, warmly wrapped up in a candyfloss pink Puffa jacket. It's much colder in Brittany than in Rome. I never see her with no makeup, even at the beach in the summer. Her face looks very different without it. Her features are drawn and her hair is dull. She resembles an aging little girl. She sticks out like a sore thumb here, incongruous, out of place, irrelevant.

"What are you doing here?" I ask.

"I've come to ask for your forgiveness."

"My forgiveness?"

It wasn't me she betrayed. I get off my bike. "You should apologize to Livia not me. How did you find me?"

"I explained to the first ten people I met that I was looking for my Italian goddaughter and I showed them your photo."

She hands me her phone, on the screen I see my massive grin. The handsome absent one didn't have a gap in his front teeth like me. But neither do Brendan or Kilian. Or Livia. It had to be me, didn't it.

"There was even some nutter who thought you were the postwoman; can you believe it?"

Viola gave me a warm and happy childhood. And ruined Livia's fiftieth birthday. Without her, I would have pined away from sadness. Without her I wouldn't even know Groix existed.

"Which hotel are you staying in?" I ask.

"I'm taking the last boat back. I booked a room in Lorient, an early train tomorrow, then a plane back to Rome. I have a job to go to, plus my mother needs me."

Viola is fifty years old and still can't cut the umbilical cord.

She scrutinizes me. "You've changed, Chiara. You've matured."

"And gained weight, of course, with Roz's cooking."

"I loved the man you thought was your father," she bursts out.

"Everyone loved him, according to you."

"No, I was *in* love with him. I wanted him all for myself. Your mother stole him from me."

My mother and her best friend have gone mad. They're fighting over the remains of a man whose bones have slowly been turning to dust in Verano for the last twenty-six years.

"I don't want to know, it's none of my business," I say with a shrug.

"Your mother seduced the man I introduced her to and with whom I had fallen in love. I blamed them both. I became a secret widow, mourning my lost love for him. Then Livia got drunk one night and consoled herself in the arms of the Breton sailor."

She stops for breath.

"I spent the night dancing with his friend, the other Frenchie. He was a wonderful dancer. I was wearing a brand-new yellow dress and looked radiant. For the first time I outshone Livia, who was dressed all in black. That evening, she had no colour in her face at all. I was hoping to see my Frenchman again. I gave him my address, but he never wrote to me. They were just passing through, Chiara. It was of no consequence."

"Maybe I'm the consequence."

"You should have been my daughter, not my goddaughter. I would have taken better care of you."

"But Livia is my mother!" I retort instinctively. I automatically defend her. I owe her my life.

"I heard that one of them wrote to her and she didn't reply?" I say, remembering what the cousin of the Thunder brothers told Perig in the Triskell.

"The letter never arrived."

"His name was something to do with the weather, it was 'Thunder', wasn't it?"

Her face lights up, and she nods.

"And his first name? Brendan? Or Kilian?"

"I never knew. I danced with one, your mother slept with the other."

She makes no bones about it.

"Did you tell Livia that you were in love with her husband?" I ask.

"Yes, the day after she turned fifty. I couldn't do it before."

"Do you feel better now?"

"No, I haven't slept since. I want to repair the damage I've done, put things right. You are my family."

"It's too late."

Her eyes plead with me, but I'm far away, elsewhere. On an island in the Tuscan archipelago where Napoleon left his mark, in an unfamiliar room where a man and a woman are locked in an embrace eight months before I enter the world. I forget all the kindness and attention Viola gave me, the cinema trips, the tea parties, the walks at the Villa Borghese. I'm unappreciative and ungrateful, like my mother. The apple doesn't fall far from the tree.

"Don't miss the last boat," I say.

Her lips quiver. "When are you coming back to Rome, Chiara?"

"That's none of your business."

She takes it in her stride. "Did you find them? The two brothers? Are they here? Did they mention me?"

Kilian has his dog and his watercolours, Brendan has his son and the unborn child, there's no room for Viola in their lives. At least not right now. I don't want to rush anything until I get the test results.

"Did you come here for them?" I ask. "They've forgotten all about it."

"I've brought you the letter in which your mother wrote to me that it was better for everyone if you were her husband's daughter."

I step back without taking it. A car comes up from the harbour, Brendan is behind the wheel. He turns in front of the merry-go-round, oblivious to this woman who looks nothing like the girl who once danced in a yellow dress in Tuscany. Viola pays no attention to the bald-headed driver. Did he dance with her? Or did he sleep with Livia?

"This letter isn't addressed to me," I say.

"Come home with me, *cara*."

"I'm staying here."

She looks pitiful.

"I need time and space."

"Marco has been looking everywhere for you. He went to his brother's wedding alone. He met a woman there who was less complicated than you."

"And now he's stopped looking for me," I finish for her. "You're getting good at this, throwing out home truths all for the sake of honesty."

"You were well suited," she says. "He's a decent, kind young man, not a married liar like Mattia. Maybe you can still patch things up?"

"Marco didn't take long to replace me," I say quietly. "He deserves to be with someone who makes him happy. What you did was a blessing in disguise. I like it here."

"You're not the same person."

"About time too."

I watch Viola head towards the port in her pink Puffa jacket. I turn around and look at the granite monument behind me. I read the inscription: "The municipality of Groix honours its children who died for their country, 1914–18, 1939–45, 1953–1962." The same names crop up each time. I count eight Thunders.

When I was little, I liked it when I got a temperature and sweated and had to stay in bed. I especially liked it when I had a cough. Because when my chest was painful, Livia would rub it with an ointment from a blue box. It stung my eyes, helped me breathe and forced my mother to touch me. I would feel her fingers on my skin. She didn't caress me fondly, she would slap the ointment on my chest with gusto. But in that moment we were like a real mother and daughter. The absent hero would smile at us from his frame. No chance he would catch it. All three of us were in my bedroom. Whenever a child at school had the flu, a sore throat or earache, I would beg them to cough in my face. Livia would despair, as she always had to take time off work to look after me. But I was never happier than when I was in bed with my mother, a box of Vicks and my father's memory.

Groix Island, village centre

Bethy, with her huge smile and red glasses, an avid reader who likes discussing literature with Gabin, has invited some friends over for dinner. Her neighbours Pat and Mimi will be there, plus Loïc the ex-butcher, Perig and Aziliz, Françoise, Gabin and me.

Roz suggests I make a savoury rosemary cake for the aperitif. We prepare it together, something I have never ever done with my mother. We weigh the ingredients, soften the butter and preheat the oven, then mix, whisk and pour the mixture into the mould before baking it. This is all so new to me, it's a delightful moment and a short break from reality, given that I don't live on this island and that Roz is not my mother. I am forging memories, which will give me the strength to confront the humdrum existence I'll return to in Rome. I thought all cakes are stodgy, but Roz's is light and fluffy and it only took ten minutes to make. She got the recipe from a friend in Lomener. Next time, she will teach me how to make her friend Martine's magical chocolate cake.

Loïc's friends Santu and Saveria join us after the aperitif. They speak French with the same accent as Gabin, and they are wearing the same Corsican pendant as him.

"Where are you from?" he asks, flashing his charming smile.

"From Cap Corse, in the north. There's no place on earth more beautiful."

"I'm from the south, where there's no sea more breathtaking anywhere."

They size each other up. Loïc thought he was doing them a favour by introducing them, but instead we're witnessing a cockfight. Northern Corsicans and Southern Corsicans don't like each other.

"Back in the day, it was the same here, between the west at Pen-Men and the east around Locmaria. We didn't marry people from the other side of the island, we didn't associate with them," says Perig.

"We may not live in the same districts, but we are all Corsicans. Even those in the south are better than the *pinzuti*, the mainlanders," explains Santu with a contagious laugh.

The starter is delicious, and the wine is rich.

"We've known each other for years, haven't we, Loïc?" says Santu, affectionately.

"Your father used to come to Grands Sables beach to fish for dab or sea bass."

"It was his cousin, *poor* Sampieru, who introduced him to Groix. Do you remember?"

His "do you remember" floats up and down like a radio wave. His accent is less jerky and more melodic than Gabin's.

"Who are you talking about?" asks Bethy as she emerges from the kitchen with a roasted leg of lamb with herb crust, accompanied by green beans and mushrooms.

"A cousin of Santu's father," replies Gabin politely, trying to include her in the conversation. "Does he live here?"

Saveria just looks at him. Santu turns to Pat.

"I brought you the I Muvrini CD I told you about, the one with 'Barbara Furtuna'."

He then turns back to Gabin. "Do you sing?"

"Completely out of tune but I love Corsican polyphonies. Who is this Barbara? A special guest on the disc?"

Santu coughs. Bethy asks me for the rosemary cake recipe.

"By the way, Saveria is the queen of *fiadone*," announces Santu to Gabin. "Did your grandmother make it for you when you were little too?"

"Of course."

"I mean the real one, without *brocciu*?"

"Yep, without *brocciu*."

"With chocolate and nuts?" checks Saveria.

"Yes, the lot."

"You are about as Corsican as I am from Groix!" says Santu slowly. "Why are you lying?"

There's a deathly silence.

"Is this a joke?" asks Gabin, white as a sheet.

"You claim to be Corsican and you're wearing the pendant, but you know Corsica about as well as I know Timbuktu!"

"The *fiadone* is a Corsican specialty, a cake made with *brocciu*, which is its principal ingredient!" adds Saveria. "I set a trap for you and you fell right into it! And no grandmother would put chocolate in it."

"Why the trap?" I ask, coming to Gabin's rescue.

"Because even a *pinzutu* from the mainland knows that 'Barbara Furtuna' is either the title of a song or the name of a polyphonic group. It's not a woman, it's a Corsican expression meaning 'bad luck'."

The atmosphere is fast becoming hostile.

"Okay, so I don't speak Corsican and I don't cook," says Gabin. "Is that a crime?"

"If you were really Corsican," continues Santu, "you'd know that if I say 'poor' before Sampieru's name, it means that Sampieru is dead. It's a mark of respect. Therefore, he no longer lives here. So, you're lying to us."

Gabin moves his chair back and stands up, calm and dignified.

"I'll leave you real islanders to it," he says. "I'm Corsican on my father's side, but he didn't do the decent thing in legally recognizing me. I know nothing of your traditions. My grand-mother never deigned to meet me. Yes, I lied, it's true, to feel like one of you."

"I'm sorry," says Santu. "I had a feeling something wasn't right. I apologize. Stay, let's have a toast. I was wrong."

"No, *I* was wrong," replies Gabin. "Corsica has never wanted me. I hoped Brittany would be more welcoming."

He leaves the room. The friendly get-together is a wash-out. The excellent leg of lamb makes up for it. Bethy decorated the dish with pastry leaves and flowers. She and Mimi go for a smoke in the garden. My week standing in for Cory is up. Now I just have to wait for the results of the DNA tests. I can lie in until noon tomorrow if I want.

I think about Gabin in that great big house in Port-Mélite, wearing his heart on his sleeve and the Corsican pendant around his neck. Santu has brought some blue-berry liqueur, he sings "Barbara Furtuna". Saveria whispers to me that the song tells of exile, lost freedom and the heartbreak of leaving one's homeland. Pat plays "Dirty Old Town" on the harmonica. Loïc starts singing with Françoise, Perig and Aziliz: "The elderly speak of times gone by, in Locmaria and Port-Tudy, if you don't follow, that's too bad, half French, Breton half, they claim you see your joy there, they claim you find your cross there, I'm talking of Groix Island." The evening ends on a good note, but I can't get Gabin out of my head.

Aziliz signals to Perig that it's time to go home. Pat and Mimi cross the garden, Loïc sets off in his car, and Françoise gets on her bike. I set off down the road on foot with Perig and Aziliz. He's had too much to drink, but he knows where the police lie in wait for drunk drivers so he'll take the side roads to avoid them.

"I'll go and see how Gabin is doing," I say.

"I have to talk to you, Chiara," replies Perig.

He sits down on the low wall in front of the small, white-washed town hall.

"I didn't want to tell you, but it's better that you know."

"Have you spoken to the Thunder brothers about me?" My heart pounds.

"This isn't about the Thunder brothers, it's about Gabin."

"So he lied, he's not Corsican. Who cares, right? I believe in him. When the earth crumbles beneath your feet you need a strong anchor. Gabin and I are two outsiders under the spell of this island. We're alike, we have to pull together."

"He's been lying about everything," says Perig.

"What?"

Mattia, Viola's lover, springs to mind. Is Gabin married with a family? Or has he escaped from a psychiatric ward, like the one Efflam is doing rehab in?

"He's not a writer," Perig bursts out.

"Of course, he is!" I exclaim. "He publishes his books under other people's names."

"That's what he told us. But it's not true."

"So you're going to lay into him too?" I say jokingly.

A pair of young lovers stagger across the square. We wait till they pass before continuing the conversation.

"I've only written one book, which didn't sell. But I know the drill and he obviously doesn't," says Perig.

"Go on."

"He thinks that authors take their books to bookshops to sell them to readers."

"Well yes, they don't give them away, they have to earn a living!"

"That's not how it works. It's the booksellers who sell the books. If the authors want any, they have to buy them."

"What, their own books?"

"Yes."

"Are you sure?"

"Absolutely sure! But Gabin doesn't know this. The other evening, at the bookshop, he said he hadn't brought any books with him. That made me suspicious."

A dog who appears to be an insomniac wanders by with its nose to the wind and stops to sniff us. Then it continues its solo rambling. Perig shakes his head.

"Everything he claims is fake. That lad's an imposter."

"Or a pathological liar?" suggests Aziliz.

The dog happily ambles back to us. He sniffs us again, recognizes us and walks off disappointed.

Groix Island, Port-Mélite

The shutters are closed, there are no lights on, the house is in darkness. It is past midnight. I lean against the wall opposite and text Gabin: "I'm out front. Can we talk?" He replies instantly: "I'm asleep." I type: "Wake up." He replies: "I'm snoring." Suddenly the door opens.

I can't help but find him sexy, that big lying mouth of his, his wild curly hair, his red New Balance trainers and his outrageous stories. He doesn't look like he's crazy, just sad. I walk behind him up to his room which has a view out the back. Kerwan is not in danger of hearing us as he sleeps in the front bedroom.

"So you were asleep were you?" I say.

"Snoring away happily."

"Sorry about earlier."

"I felt trapped, like a wild boar in a Corsican net."

"Don't worry about Santu and Saveria, they'll leave, they don't matter, they're not from here," I reassure him.

"Neither am I. Neither are you. It takes four gravestones to be considered a genuine Groix islander, four generations of the same family buried here on the island. We're outsiders."

"We are those we love and those we miss," I say. "All the rest, where we come from, what we do, is insignificant."

He frowns. "I disagree. A baker from Rueil-Malmaison has nothing in common with a Parisian doctor or a Corsican writer. Our choices define us and lead the way by reducing our possibilities."

Captain Kerwan doesn't feel the cold, he has turned off the heating. His house is damp and I shiver. Gabin rubs my back to warm me up, then pulls me against him. I put my head on his shoulder. The blow he was dealt tonight struck a chord with me that is still resonating.

"My father's absence has actually had a more positive effect on me than my mother's presence," I say to him.

"I didn't know my father either. One day I asked my mother why he wasn't there. She replied: 'You and your brother are the best things that ever happened to me. He doesn't know what he's missing, I feel sorry for him.' I never asked her again after that. *He doesn't know what he's missing* became a joke between us. I have no family left. Everything I possess is in this bag: my clothes and the last book my mother ever read to me. That's all I need."

His smile lights up the room. This guy is fascinating and broken.

"Santu and Saveria were right, I've never been to Corsica. My father could be Corsican or Breton, or he could be from Normandy or God knows where. I don't know his name, his origins or what his mother used to cook. But I do know this island."

He rolls on his side, pulls up my jumper and strokes me. I feel electricity run through me where he places his warm hand.

"*Enez Groe*, Groix Island, is a mere pebble in the midst of the ocean, three leagues from the mainland."

He traces the outline of the island on my body with his fingertips. "There you have Grands Sables beach, the only convex beach in Europe."

He carries on and I close my eyes in ecstasy at the tsunami of sensations under my skin.

"It used to be there, but since then it has moved around the cape due to the currents, and now it's here."

I reach out and caress this mysterious, pale-eyed mythomaniac. I explore his body and join in his game.

"I live in Rome, in the historic town centre dominated by the seven hills, the Aventine, the Capitoline, the Pal . . ."

Gabin-like-the-actor doesn't let me finish. He embraces me, I wrap my body around him. I don't even know if I put on a thong or a pair of knickers this morning. We rip off our clothes. He smells of leather, pepper, and vetiver. He says I smell of fresh, pungent mint. Our first kiss is fiery, blissful and easy. I was eager to taste his lips and the aroma of his skin. His warm breath carries the fragrance of summer sand on Fregene beach. Our bodies find each other and pulse with desire. For the first time in my life, I let myself drift towards a shore I cannot see. The passion we feel for each other is unbearable and overwhelming. We lock eyes, anchor ourselves to one another and set sail. I used to be afraid of losing control. Now I'm afraid of losing myself.

After we make love, we are famished. Gabin left in the middle of dinner and the row made me lose my appetite, so we are both starving. He puts his jeans back on and walks down to Kerwan's kitchen shirtless. I follow him, pulling on his big cable knit sweater. There is nothing to eat in the captain's fridge, only beer and cider. He eats all his meals at the Café de la Jetée at the harbour. Gabin opens a cupboard and finds some whisky—not the common touristy kind but a special malt for real connoisseurs. I find some dark chocolate with sea salt in a drawer. Kerwan does his shopping on Groix, we'll replace his supplies. Gabin describes to me a taste he doesn't know and likes to imagine: a special bottle of champagne that he will probably never open. His mother gave him a bottle from his birth year, which he sacrificed when he cut all ties with his brother and sister-in-law. I take a sip of whisky and pass it to him through my kiss. We go back upstairs. Our stomachs are satisfied, but our bodies are still hungry for each other.

By sunrise, we have been around the world together. We slept with our bodies entwined, blotting out sad days and dark thoughts. I'm no longer the girl without a father, I am no longer my mother's daughter, I am *this* woman with *this* man. Just the two of us. Gabin, his cheeks shadowed with copper stubble, climbs out of bed. I stare at his muscular buttocks as he opens the window. And as the fresh morning air fills the room, I tell him that he is crazy, to which he replies, "crazy about you." He comes back to lie beside me.

"Are you disappointed that I'm not Corsican?" he whispers.

"I couldn't care less."

"Would you be disappointed if I told you that I'm not a writer?"

"Same."

He smells of warm bread, life, laughter and music.

"That's lucky," he says, "because I was born in Chatou, a town west of Paris. And I have never written a book either under my own name or as a ghost writer."

"Neither have I."

"Would it disappoint you if I said my name isn't Gabin?"

"Even that's not true? Are you some character out of a book?"

"No. We're real," he says.

And then he proves it to me. A long while later I ask him his real name.

"Charles. After Baudelaire."

So Gabin-like-the-actor is actually Charles-like-the-poet.

"And for the last two years I have called myself Louis, as in Louis Aragon."

He plunges his gaze into mine. "I have nothing to hide, Chiara. I was just dreaming."

"And if I told you that my childhood friend Alessio isn't really my childhood friend, would you be disappointed?" I ask.

He leans on his elbow, facing me, and teases my skin with his fingers. Charles' hand feels even better than Gabin's.

"You can't disappoint me, Chiara. Did you invent an imaginary friend because you were lonely?"

"No, Alessio was my father. He helped give me a normal childhood, like other kids my age. He didn't come here with me. He stayed in Rome. I don't need him anymore."

I don't need you anymore, Dad. The word "Dad" seems to burn inside my mouth. But I prefer it to Alessio. I'm going to stop calling you by your first name. You're not my best friend, you never have been, we never even knew each other. *Nonna* Ornella always said how audacious you were, well she's right, you had the audacity to die on me. You're my age, you left us at twenty-five years old, you will still be twenty-five when I am fifty or eighty. Goodbye, Alessio.

"Charles suits you better than Gabin or Louis," I say.

"My mother adored Baudelaire. *But the real travellers are those alone who leave, For leaving's sake; hearts as light as balloons, They never step back from their destiny, And, without knowing why, always say: Let's go!* I followed Baudelaire's advice and took a trip."

"*A voyage is like a shipwreck, and those whose boat has never sunk will never know anything about the sea.* Do you know Nicolas Bouvier?" I ask him.

"*The Way of the World* is one of my favourite books."

"It's getting a bit crowded in here."

"They are about to leave."

"We were delighted to see you Italians and Corsicans, poets and writers. But we would like a little privacy now."

"Exactly. See you soon, come back whenever you like."

"We won't see you out."

Our bodies set sail for a deserted island where we are the sole castaways.

"They don't know what they're missing," says Charles in a hoarse voice.

"We're the only ones left," I say, tangling my legs with his and riding the waves with him.

I find his hungry mouth irresistible. I want him to discover novels, red wines from Barolo in Piedmont, the songs of Fiorella Mannoia, Bach's fugues and the little triangular sandwiches you get in Rome's bars. The ones filled with prawns, not tuna.

Groix Island, Kermarec

Your name is Charles, you have never been to Italy, you met Chiara Ferrari on the boat heading for the Breton island of Groix. You find her and her luscious lips drop dead gorgeous. You want her to discover poetry, Burgundy wines, the songs of Barbara, the Requiem de Mozart and cream puffs. The ones filled with whipped cream, not custard.

You have come to set the record straight with Perig. The journalist asks you to sit down. He pours you a coffee from a large Breton coffee pot. Standfirst the cat jumps into your lap without asking your permission and starts digging his claws into your thighs as if he's kneading dough.

"I'm glad to see you," says Perig. "Even if you are neither Corsican nor a writer. You're a hollow shell tossed about by the waves. You had us all fooled."

Straight to the point as always.

"As a child, I dreamt of becoming a writer. But I'm too conceited and not generous enough, no doubt."

"What do you do for a living when you're not lying?"

You pour your heart out to him. You want to cross your legs but Standfirst won't let you.

"My mother died of a perforated stomach ulcer. I went into medicine to save other people's mothers. But I flunked the exams twice in a row. If I couldn't become the person I wanted to be, I couldn't be myself. All I had to do was to take on a new role, to slip into someone else's skin."

"The Corsican writer?"

"I first worked for two years in an intensive care unit under a false identity. I loved it."

"Fishermen fish, Gabin tells lies. Is that how you see life?"

"It makes it better. I was a good doctor, competent and compassionate, but my alias went to live in Marseilles and wanted his identity back. I didn't want to turn up here as a Parisian. It sounded better to say I was from an island. I lived with a publicist from Porto-Vecchio for a while, I thought I had learned enough about Corsica from her to sound credible."

"A good liar has to do his homework. Do you not read spy novels? You should have prepared yourself instead of just showing up. Santu and Saveria were shocked by your deceit and trickery. Word gets around fast here. The rumour will blow up and sweep away everything in its path."

"I can't just steal away like a criminal," you say, holding his gaze. "I wasn't expecting to fall for Chiara. I've told her everything."

"Are you cheating on her too?"

"No!"

"If you hurt her in any way whatsoever, I will find you wherever you are and you'll wish you'd never been born," roars Perig.

"I often regretted being born. But now I'm glad. I will go wherever Chiara goes. My arms will always be there to hold her."

"I'll create some kind of distraction, put them on a false trail," decides Perig. "It's the best strategy. I'll say that you pretended to be Corsican, like the hero of your next novel, for a character study. But you'll owe me one."

He leans towards you. "Kerwan is my friend. You're going to write his memoirs."

"I'll keep my promise."

"You'd better!" he replies. "Plus, you're going to write a novel. Take the plunge, be bold, spend time wrestling with words, toil like a sailor on a fishing expedition, then offer your text to publishers. If you've got talent, they'll recognize it. For once in your life, prove that your lies are true. Anticipate, surpass yourself, imagine, share, create!"

You stay silent. Chapters line up in your head, a paper jigsaw puzzle whose pieces slide smoothly into place where they fit perfectly.

"The locals won't give a monkey's that you're not Corsican. But they'll never forgive you for lying to them about your profession."

"I'm not sure I can do it . . ."

"Are you that bad?"

You balk, offended. "I don't know, I've never tried."

"Well, what are you waiting for?"

You don't like his authoritative tone, you're not a kid anymore.

"Thanks for your advice," you say, cutting the conversation short.

"I didn't give you any!" protests Perig. "I tried that with my son, I shan't do it again. Become what you're pretending to be. Hit back, stop hiding behind other people. Children talk about what they want to "be". Adults know what they "are". It's no small feat, it takes a lifetime."

If you'd had a father like Perig, you would have clashed, challenged each other, loved each other. There's no way Alice could have loved an idiot. Why didn't she live with your father? Was he married to someone else? Did he live on the other side of the world? Was he ill? Violent? Mad as a hatter? Dead? And that's just a few scenarios, anything is possible. You don't even know if you had the same father as Paul. Two fatherless brothers, two illegitimate children. Alice didn't want a man in the house. She slept alone, with just her heart-beat for company.

You want to find out to what extent Chiara has confided in Perig. "Do you know why Chiara is looking for this Mr Thunder?"

"Because she is looking for herself. Just like you are. And you found each other."

He gets up, walks to the sideboard, comes back with a bottle of brandy and fills two glasses.

"I don't like drinking alone, and Aziliz can't drink with me anymore. When Gurvan didn't return to shore, we alerted the emergency services and the local coastguard. They sent out the helicopter and the rescue boat. I spent three days and three nights on the water. On the fourth evening, I got completely plastered. Aziliz vowed never to drink again until our son returned. Every time a drowned man is found on the beach, I hide the bottles. If he does return one day, dead or alive, she'll be passed out before I've had my first sip. Start writing, Gabin!"

"I didn't tell you everything. My real name is Charles."

Perig's eyes go round like saucers.

"Why did you choose Groix?" he asks.

"Because of Wilhelm Albert Włodzimierz Apollinaris de Kostrowitzki: *Under Mirabeau Bridge the river slips away, And lovers, Must I be reminded, Joy came always after pain.*"

"I know Apollinaire. What does this have to do with the island?"

"*Joy came always after pain.* Joy. And also this Breton saying: *He who sees Ushant sees his blood. He who sees Molène sees his sorrow. He who sees Sein sees his end. He who sees Groix sees his joy.* I needed joy."

"Go share your joy with Chiara."

As you walk away, you hear him mumble the end of the poem.

"*The night is a clock chiming, The days go by not I.*"

Groix Island, village centre

You were lost before you met Chiara, now you're lost when she's not by your side. When you walk, your fingers lock, like two magnets clinging lovingly to each other. You stroll along at the same pace, a spring in your step, gracefully, confidently, in tune with one other. She is the encounter you were hoping for, the cyclone, the whirlwind, the unleashed swell, the arched wave, the poem, the woman who gives meaning to your life without you having to lie. You would put down your anchor, take back your name, and be yourself for her, like you used to be when Alice was alive. Before Patty came along.

Perig explained what the saying *He who sees Groix sees his joy* means. Sailors returning from fishing expeditions risked being shipwrecked on the islands of Ushant, Sein or Molène. But when they got to the stony shallows of Groix, they knew they were out of danger. You know you're safe here with her.

You walk into the post office and greet Roz behind the counter. A large white envelope labelled "Post restante" is waiting for you, a big white gull exhausted from its journey from England. You are dying to open it and find out. You resist temptation. Chiara must learn the truth first.

Roz, busy with a backpacker, doesn't see you leave. Lost in your thoughts, you bump into Jo Le Port, a friend of Perig's, at the bottom of the steps.

"Look where you're going, mate!" he says with a smile.

You apologize. You know where you're going: to the northwest of the island, near the big lighthouse. To Pen-Men, where Chiara has gone with Didier and Danielle.

Groix Island, Pen-Men

Didier has made twin kites for Nolan and Evan. He asked me to help him test them out this morning on the cliffs.

He misses Urielle. Danielle spins around, arms stretched out horizontally, singing: "*Me zo ganet é kreiz er mor, e bro Arvor.*"

Didier translates for me. *I was born in the middle of the sea, in the land of Armor.* It's a poem by Yann-Ber Kalloc'h, the Groix poet who lost his life in the Somme in 1917.

We are in the nature reserve where colonies of protected seabirds nest. Didier takes us to a place where we won't disturb them.

"The wind is up, the weather's perfect, the landscape clear. We won't get caught up in trees or power lines here," he says.

The kites are in the shape of gulls with a round eye, a yellow beak marked with a red dot, and white feathers. I have never flown a kite before.

"We each take a kite, you face the wind, then hold it up and give it slack by pulling on the line. Like this, look!"

The wind inflates the canvas of his bird, which starts to glide impeccably. Mine flies away, swirls and nose dives towards the ground. I'm no good at this.

"Try again!" he yells.

Didier takes my arm to show me, which doesn't bother me anymore. Physical contact with Charles and snuggling up in his arms has changed my physical interaction with others.

I'm no longer held captive by my fears. I make another attempt, running, my canvas gull hesitates, then joins its twin in the sky. Danielle looks up at them, speechless and amazed. We play in the wind under the watchful eye of the lighthouse which prevents the boats from crashing onto the rocks.

"I'm worried about Urielle," says Didier. "She used to confide in me, before she took up with that spineless jerk."

"The *korrigans*' father?"

He nods. "She's unhappy, I wish I could help her, but I feel powerless."

As I move nearer to him to listen, our kites get caught up, he releases his, and mine swoops down. I run along and it takes off again.

"Hey!"

I turn around. Charles is striding towards us holding a large white envelope. *My* envelope. In a second, my whole life could change. I run towards him, followed by the canvas gull. Didier, oblivious to what is happening, makes his kite loop the loop under the distracted gaze of his eldest daughter, who is as fragile as a sandcastle.

"Is it postmarked England?" I ask, panting.

Charles hands it to me. I cling to it like a castaway to a lifeline. He takes the kite from me. My fingers are trembling.

"Aren't you going to open it?"

I shake my head; my eyes go all misty. He pulls me against him. Didier smiles, he prefers Charles to the spineless jerk.

"I'll go on alone, I don't need you anymore," he says recovering the second kite.

We walk hand in hand to a rocky ledge jutting out over the ocean, dotted with wild flowers and bird droppings. I sit on the stone. Charles goes quiet.

"It's right here," I say. "Inside. Three possibilities: Alessio, Kilian or Brendan."

"Precisely. Just open it," he urges.

"You're right."

A bird circles above us, it has no string attached to its foot, the horizon is its hunting ground. Suddenly I am struck by the realization that I don't have the right to open it without Livia. After all, this is all about her. I'm just collateral damage. A happy consequence or a stupid mistake, depending on your viewpoint.

"I have to leave for Rome."

Charles puts his arm around my shoulders. I don't know how I'll cope away from him.

"I'm coming with you," he says.

Everything seems so natural.

Didier's phone rings as we join him. He picks it up, wedges it between his cheek and shoulder, and mumbles "Yes?" while pulling on the strings of his kite. He suddenly lets go of the canvas bird which nosedives towards the grass.

"I'll be right there."

He is a member of the island's fire brigade. He treats, cares for and comforts people. He sees babies being born, he gives bad news, but most of all he saves lives. He leaves us in charge of Danielle and the gull kites and runs towards his car.

Groix Island, Locqueltas, small yellow postbox

The shy Small Yellow Postbox stands up straight at the crossroads opposite the La Malicette restaurant. It's hardly used out of season, and lives in fear of being removed. People send far less post now that they use computers and mobile phones. In the old days, the village was populated all year round, there was a grocery shop, and people went out into the square in the evening to gather with friends and neighbours. Now the island goes into hibernation till the school holidays come around again. The grocer's shop has closed, and cars whizz by without stopping.

Sometimes you get tourists on foot or on bikes who stop at the Small Yellow Postbox to unfold their map of the island and work out where this dead-end road leads. The Small Postbox waits, hoping desperately that they will have a card or letter to post. It knows that the Saint-Gunthiern Association, which maintains the island's fountains and wash-houses, publishes a calendar every year with beautiful photos. The Small Postbox is disappointed that no one has come up with the idea of publishing a calendar of the island's postboxes. It imagines itself on the cover, standing proudly at the entrance to Locqueltas.

A local resident approaches with his dog. The Postbox recognizes him, he isn't a Sunday hiker with big boots. No, he is walking normally and blends into the landscape. As he passes in front of the Small Postbox, his mouth twists as he slows down, staggering. His dog, off the leash, has run ahead of him. The man almost falls, and grabs the Small Postbox with both hands. He is having difficulty breathing. He winces, before collapsing in a heap at the foot of it.

The dog runs back, walks around its master, puzzled at first, then worried. It scratches at the bag his master is carrying on his shoulder and sniffs his face. Then it sits and howls frantically like the mournful sound of a ship's siren.

Groix Island, village centre

I am a paternal orphan as my Italian father died before I was born. This morning, I had a one in three chance of remaining so. Tonight, however, the odds have increased to two in three, as one of my potential fathers has just died. The nurse who came to Locqueltas to visit a patient found his body sprawled in front of the postbox. She took his pulse, put her index and middle fingers on his carotid artery and confirmed his death. This is sad for us both, as we perhaps missed each other a few metres before the finishing line, as he knew Livia and Viola when they were young.

When Didier broke the news to the surviving brother that his brother, whom he no longer spoke to, was dead, he burst into tears. He came to pay his respects, said he would carry the coffin, and insisted on paying for the funeral and taking in his dog.

"A pulmonary embolism," Charles explains to me, "is a clot that circulates in the blood and blocks the pulmonary artery or one of its branches. I flunked my medical exams but I did spend two years in intensive care."

He stops and fiddles with his black pearl bracelet. "A patient gave it to me on my last shift. His name was Mr Bulle; he had caught some horrible virus in Myanmar. The guy was in a coma, everyone thought he was a goner. He woke up when I touched his hand, I swear to you. He believed that garnets ward off nightmares and bring love. He was right. Here, it's yours."

He removes the bracelet, puts it around my wrist and tightens the drawstring. I can feel the heat of the envelope in my pocket, like a ticking bomb about to explode.

I put off Rome for a few days; it can wait. The parish vicar no longer lives on the island, he is here for forty-eight hours only. The funeral is tomorrow. Why wait. No one will come from the mainland.

Danielle looks at her parents and starts chanting in Breton: "*Sodade, sodade, sodade dessa minha terra.*"

Didier puts on the CD of the Cape Verdian singer Cesaria Evora. Danielle imitates her to perfection; I can't distinguish between the two performers. Roz says the word "*saudade*" is a longing, the sorrow you get from absence, nostalgia, the desire to be elsewhere. Danielle can see that we are sad.

The coffin enters the church through the main door. The pews are all full, unlike the day of their deceased mother's funeral. The funeral ritual is the same as in Italy. The mass ends with communion, then the faithful march in front of the coffin to sprinkle the deceased with holy water as he sails away to the afterlife.

In the front row, his brother has shrunk several centimetres. He is alone in his pew, next to the man lying in the dark box. Nobody dared sit near him. Odd to think there is a two in three chance that I should have been seated there next to him.

At the end of the service, Brendan walks up to the lectern with a heavy gait, adjusts the microphone, and turns towards the congregation.

"Kilian, my brother. We were at loggerheads for a long time over some stupid inheritance. Ankou came to get you and prevented us from reconciling. Today I publicly beg for your forgiveness. You are on your way to paradise. You saved my son's life. Efflam is not in prison, as some of you may think, he is in rehab for his addiction. He regularly took drugs at parties hosted by young, stupid bastards, sorry vicar, but that is an accurate description."

The poker-faced vicar pretends not to have heard. A deaf local leans in towards her neighbour. "Can you understand what he is saying?"

"One evening, he felt ill. He called you, his godfather. He told you where he was before he lost consciousness. You alerted the emergency services who saved him at the last minute. If it weren't for you, I'd have lost him."

His voice breaks, as he continues.

"I was eternally grateful to you, yet at the same time I was mad at you, because *I* was his father. *I* should have been the one calling for help. *I* should have been the one alerting the emergency services. *I* should have protected him and told him that he was destroying himself taking that crap, sorry vicar, but there's no other word."

The vicar looks up at the heavens like Don Camillo in his village of Brescello.

"You saved Efflam. You watched over me when we went fishing as kids. You took the rap for my misdemeanours more than once. I don't care about the right of way, the threshing floor. It's all bullshit, sorry vicar, but there's no better word for it. Don't worry, Kilian. I'll take care of your dog."

"Isn't he overdoing it a bit?" whispers a man in front of me.

"No, he's speaking from the heart," retorts his wife. "You don't have one, so you wouldn't understand!"

The vicar takes over and asks us all to stand.

"And for all you gossipmongers out there," cuts in Brendan, "the beautiful young blonde by my side is not my girlfriend. She's my son's fiancé, the mother of his unborn child, who will be born out of wedlock, apologies vicar, but that's how it is nowadays. You will still baptize my grandson, I hope?"

Overwhelmed, the vicar flings open his arms. The congregation, taking it to be an order, rises, causing the old pews to creak.

"We came for a funeral, and they announce a birth," whispers a man behind me.

"I *thought* she was too young for him!" whispers his neighbour triumphantly.

"And way too young for you too!" says another.

Aristotle, sick of waiting, starts barking in the square.

Nonna Ornella told me that when someone is close to death in certain villages in southern Italy, the villagers gather round and whisper messages for their dead relatives in the patient's ear, so that they can pass them on when they get to heaven. Like a registered letter you don't have to sign for. It's too late for Kilian, but on the off chance, I ask him to tell the young man who took his last breath in the Piazza del Popolo, how grateful I am to him. I don't know if I deserved to be his daughter. I just know that he has been a wonderful father to me.

The funeral procession bypasses the church and heads for the cemetery behind the coffin carried by Brendan and his cousins. Aristotle and Shoot follow solemnly in their footsteps. Kilian is laid to rest. Groix must be firmly anchored to the bottom of the ocean, otherwise it would drift away. I wonder if it has a base, like a mushroom?

The islanders file in to shake hands with Brendan. When everyone has offered their condolences, he takes the floor again:

"My son's fiancée has gone to tell him that his godfather has died. Last night I went to my brother's house to get the suit he should have worn today. Kilian didn't have one, so we put him in his jacket and a pair of everyday trousers. He had no shoes, only boots, wooden clogs and slippers. We put clogs on him, they'll last longer, the roads in paradise may be bumpy, they'll keep him steady. I'm sorry, vicar, not sure they repair the roads up there. I couldn't find his Sunday best, but I found something better. My brother had an incredible talent, he painted the island in watercolours. In fact, he painted you all, at all hours of the day. I have spoken to the mayor, and he has agreed to exhibit his work at the library. He brandishes a watercolour in which Aristotle is running along the ocean at sunset. Brendan drops it into the grave. The paper flutters, then nosedives like Didier's kite, and lands on the coffin.

"*Au revoir,*" whispers Brendan.

Leaving the cemetery, I walk Perig to his car. I show him the envelope from England in my pocket. I tell him that I will open it with my mother.

"Keep the jacket, you might need it over there. You still have the option of not finding out, Chiara."

"I've put a lot of energy into this, I'm not backing out now!"

"Only you can decide, Sklerijenn."

"What?"

"Chiara translates as Claire in French and Sklerijenn in Breton."

"If I turn out to be the daughter of one of the Thunder brothers, what will that change for you?" I ask.

He doesn't answer, plonks himself down in his car, closes the door and rolls down the window.

"Nothing. Your father, whoever he is, is a lucky man."

Groix Island, the morning boat

Roz comes with us to the port without asking any questions. She cried when I announced my departure at dinner last night. She said there would always be a room for me in Port-Lay. Danielle then began to sing "I wish I knew how it would feel to be free", and clapping along. She didn't emerge from her room this morning, she can't bear farewells. She lives in the present; the past and the future scare her. Didier kissed me, I just find that normal now.

Roz hugs me tightly. "Take care of yourself my dear."

These simple, heartfelt words warm me as much as Gurvan's jacket.

We board the boat. Some locals who recognize me as the stand-in postwoman greet me with a discreet nod. I'm no longer an outsider. I'm now navigating in a no-man's land somewhere between foreigner and islander. I borrow Charles' laptop and search the Internet for Danielle's song. Nina Simone's heart-wrenching voice takes over the upper deck of the boat. *I wish I could break all the chains holding me.*

Two young people in hoodies clap, a young girl in a pea jacket performs a dance step. Charles holds me close, and we twirl around together as the boat sails towards the mainland.

Train between Lorient and Paris Montparnasse

We're heading for Paris, before flying to Rome tomorrow. But before that, Charles has an important mission to accomplish. We talked about it last night. At first he said it was out of the question. And then he mulled it over.

I can feel the envelope from the English lab scrunching in my pocket against my heart. Or rather against my pulmonary artery, according to Charles.

"You know it all!" I say.

"I used to be a doctor, remember."

The passenger in front of us, who reeks of sweat, has no qualms about listening in to our conversation.

"What did you call yourself?"

"Louis Lambert."

"I prefer Gabin Aragon, it sounds more mysterious."

My photographic memory rewinds to a French poem I learned at school. "*My beautiful love my dear love my tearing apart.*"

"*I carry you in me like a wounded bird,*" continues Charles. "*And those without knowing watch us go by.*"

The sweaty passenger doesn't miss a crumb of our conversation.

"What's your real surname?"

"Blue."

"Charles Blue?"

"Yes."

"But you have green eyes."

"Blue when it rains, green when it's sunny, according to my mother."

"Aragon was wrong. Love can be happy," I say.

Bored with our silly, mawkish joy, the passenger leaves to find something juicier to listen to. We cry with laughter together, which is much better than spending our lives crying alone.

Nanterre

You get off the suburban train in the centre of Nanterre. You ring the doorbell of a modest, unattractive house. Chiara hangs back slightly. The door opens, and a mean-faced, thin-lipped woman appears. She has spiteful, squinty eyes and her body is leathery and wizened.

"Yes?" she groans, not recognizing you.

She hasn't seen you for eight years. You're a big, strong, broad-shouldered man now. Besides there is no reason you would be in her thoughts tonight.

"Is Paul there?"

She turns around. "Paul!"

A man comes to the door. He has a sad mouth, long unkempt hair, and the look of someone who has given up on life. His dark eyes are the colour of burnt bread. He raises an eyebrow, then his face lights up. He laughs, he is beaming, he flings his arms open, and you fall into them like a child. You hug each other. Unbelievably he is still wearing the same aftershave, laced with flour.

Patty frowns as she realizes who you are. She cranes her vulture's neck to size you up. You hold her gaze. Your eyes collide, you look daggers at each other.

"Paul, this is Chiara," you say.

Your brother has the same dimple as you in the middle of his chin. He's unhappy, he's resigned, he has let himself go, there's no fight left in him.

"Come in!" he says, inviting you both to follow him.

Patty glares at him, he doesn't seem to care. He takes you into a dull soulless living room, which contains no books or flowers just a television screen bigger than the table. Paul disappears and Patty fires off questions like a machine gun: "Where do you live? What do you do? Why haven't you been in touch? When I think of all the trouble I went to for you! How ungrateful! And that time you left, after wrecking our TV! I knew you were bonkers but not to that extent! Be careful, miss, he's not right in the head that one, he's always been weird!"

You don't answer her, you ignore her, she is invisible, you gloat and enjoy the moment. Chiara follows suit and ignores the raging woman who venomously spits out her recriminations at you. It's surreal. Patty curses, rants, and jabbers, repeating herself over and over again. You look right through her as if she doesn't exist.

Paul returns with some glasses and two dusty bottles of Mercier champagne with faded labels.

"I told you to throw away that junk," barks Patty. "Besides, they're lukewarm, it'll taste disgusting!"

Danielle would imitate her raucous croak perfectly. Paul uncorks one of the bottles. It releases a breath, a whiff of inspiration, and a discreet whisper. Your brother sniffs the cork, gently tilts the bottle and fills four glasses.

"This is a little piece of history," he says.

The wine is a golden colour, iridescent with green and yellow hues. A few sluggish bubbles escape to the top, a trail of froth appears and then quickly vanishes. The champagne takes on a sunny hue, as if Aladdin's lamp has just been rubbed. Patty snatches her glass, tastes it, scowls and places it back down.

"It's flat, it should be poured down the sink."

Paul raises his glass solemnly.

"*In order not to feel the terrible burden of time which weighs on your shoulders . . .*" he begins.

" *. . . and makes you bend towards the ground,*" you add.

"*You need to be drunk always,*" finishes Chiara.

"I can see why he loves you," says Paul.

Patty stares at you all in astonishment. You put your nose to your glass, you breathe in the scent of the past. The first notes are discreet, modest, restrained. The champagne reveals itself timidly at first, then stronger aromas take over. You can make out the sweet hints of raisins, pineapple, perhaps candied mandarins. Followed by spicy notes, nutmeg, white pepper, roasted almonds and nougat, all finally merging into subtle hints of liquorice and mocha. Aurore taught you how to distinguish them when she was in charge of the book launch of a famous wine specialist. She has since set up home with the man, you saw them in each other's arms on the cover of a magazine at the newsagents. Only vintage wines touch her lips now. You are delighted for her.

"Our mother used to say that Charles and I are vintage boys, so she gave us each a bottle from our birth year," Paul tells Chiara.

"She used to say that champagne was a stairway to the stars," you add. "We were supposed to drink them on our twenty-first birthdays."

"So let's taste mine," says Paul. "My vintage birth year has great aging potential, I'm a guy with substance."

You take your first sip. The champagne tastes intense and unusual, crisp without being acidic. The onslaught to the palate is clean and structured, handing over to warm, fruity flavours which are replaced by hints of woodland undergrowth, humus and fungi.

You make a toast. "To Alice Blue."

Paul and Chiara raise their glasses. Patty shrugs. You scan the room for evidence of a teenager.

"Where's Luna-Alice?" you ask.

Paul's face darkens as Patty explodes.

"She's called Luna! That kid's been nothing but trouble for us, she's at a sports college in the South of France. We couldn't cope with her, and it costs us an arm and a leg. Good riddance I say!"

"She's passionate about swimming. It's normal to make sacrifices for your children," Paul snaps. "You made her life impossible, you two were at each other's throats all the time, she begged me to let her go. I miss her."

"I often think about her," you chip in. "Swimming helps you cope when life is unbearable, I know that from my own experience."

"She doesn't even know you exist," snarls Patty.

"I send her postcards regularly," you tell Paul, ignoring your sister-in-law. "It's my way of being there for her from afar."

"I throw them all in the bin before she sees them," Patty sneers.

Your body automatically stiffens, but you won't give Patty the satisfaction of seeing you react. Remember she doesn't exist, she is a nothing, a transparent, insignificant and pathetic little viper that has run out of poison.

"You had no right to do that," roars an indignant Paul. "She knows very well that Charles is my brother, and I often tell her about us."

The "us" clearly refers to you and Alice to the exclusion of Patty, which sends her into a rage.

"She's *my* daughter; she belongs to me!"

"Did you receive your birthday cards every 14th of December at the bakery?" you ask Paul.

"And I think about you every 9th of April," he replies.

"Paul wasn't born in December!" snaps Patty.

You steal a glance at Chiara. "Eugène Grindel, known as Paul Éluard, was born on the 14th of December 1895."

"Charles Baudelaire was born on the 9th of April 1821," adds Paul.

"Your feet stink," you say.

"You've got dog breath."

You don't hear Patty; you pretend she's not there. Your three glasses are empty, you refill them. You, your brother and Chiara slowly finish off the bottle. The blond and sweet aromas contrast with the dark taste of liquorice and mocha. This is no longer just champagne; it has turned into a noble wine that has reunited you for a few rare and fleeting minutes. The transient sensation of the last sip lingers after the aromas of blond tobacco, honey and wax have faded. You glance at your watch. You get up.

"Let's go."

"Already?" asks Paul.

You plunge your bluey-green eyes into his. The atmosphere is volatile in Patty's house.

"Come with us. There's nothing to keep you here."

"Your brother is mad, don't listen to him!" bawls Patty.

"Don't tell me you're happy here?" you insist, staring at him intently.

For a split second you wonder whether he'll ditch everything and follow you. He takes a step towards you. Patty whimpers like an abandoned dog. Then he stops. The moment has passed.

"Luna-Alice is still a child, I can't leave her alone with her mother, she'd destroy her. I have no choice but to stay until she's eighteen."

"Her name is Luna, and you owe me!" screams Patty, her face distorted with anger. "I took you in, I took your dumb brother in too, I got you a job, you were on the streets, two losers raised by a freak of a woman."

You hold back from lashing out at her with ugly words of your own. She has just insulted Alice; how dare she speak of your dead mother like that. Paul glares at her.

"Don't you mention my mother ever again!" he shouts. "Otherwise, I'm out of that door! I only stay with you out of pity, love for our daughter and to pay off my debt to you. Believe me, it's a heavy price to pay."

He hands you the vintage bottle from your birth year and pushes you towards the door.

"Go quickly before I change my mind."

"Are you sure?"

He nods. You take Chiara's hand and walk away.

Chatou

You are Charles and Chiara. You get off the suburban train in Chatou-Croissy. You stroll through the sleeping town. You pass the Italian deli, Iaconi, and Chiara reads *Amore per il gusto* out front, which makes you hungry. You cross the town square, Place Maurice-Berteaux, where the market stalls have already been set up. Tomorrow morning, it will be crowded. Your heart is pounding, right down to the tips of your fingers which are gripping hers. You stop in front of a small house on the riverside. An upstairs window is lit, a teenager is hunched over a book, pencil in hand, headphones on.

"That was my room," you say.

"He seems happy," murmurs Chiara.

"It's a happy house, I don't blame it for what happened to Alice."

Chiara tells him of the grim apartment in Rome she grew up in, black furniture, grey walls. One night, while her mother was asleep, she painted her childhood bedroom apple green. She had planned it down to the last detail. She had spent her savings on paint and brushes and hidden them in her school-bag. Livia screamed on entering the room and gave Chiara a good shaking. It was a hard won victory, but Chiara was delighted with the result: she had put some colour in her life and her mother had actually touched her. She had banished the funereal decor from her room. Alessio, ever encouraging, had congratulated her.

"Your room looks yellow," says Chiara, squinting to see better in the dark.

"When I was there it was blue."

The teenager in the window runs a hand through his hair and looks out into the night. He approaches the window and presses his forehead against it. Is he smiling? Is he crying? Is he dreaming? He can't see you. You don't know who he is, and why he is working late. You are a stranger in your childhood home. You don't belong here anymore. You and Chiara start walking again.

"Are we going back to Paris?" she asks.

"We still have one important thing to do."

"What?"

"Settle a score with a slimy rat."

She looks panicked.

"A rat?"

"An old acquaintance you could say. That's what Mum called him."

She looks at you, tilting her head. You reassure her with a kiss on the tip of her nose. When you think about her, your heartbeat accelerates; you checked it by taking your pulse.

When you worked at the hospital, you learned that the heart contracts to circulate the blood through the body. If it beats very hard, it pushes the blood around faster and brings more oxygen to the muscles. Thinking about Chiara takes your breath away, you gasp for oxygen at the thought of her leaving. Your heart knows this and speeds up accordingly.

Le Vésinet

You walk faster than usual. Chiara is struggling to keep up. You are still holding her hand. You come to a street where beautiful mansions are surrounded by large gardens. One of them stands out from the rest. It's a squat, single-storey, rectangular dwelling, devoid of charm. It resembles a shoe box.

"I'm not surprised he lives here," you mumble.

"Who?"

"The rat. He's going to have a nice surprise when he wakes up."

You take four cans of black spray paint out of your backpack.

"Top of the range, one hundred per cent acrylic, ultra-resistant, interior and exterior, recommended for decorating and customizing."

"You're worrying me. What are we going to do?"

"We're going to make sure the guy gets a good night's sleep, and isn't disturbed by the daylight."

You check left and right to make sure no one is around. You climb up and over the high front gate and disappear on the other side. Chiara just stands there petrified.

"Are you coming?" you whisper.

"No, you're crazy! This is trespassing. I'm a foreigner, I don't want to end up in a French jail!"

"Are you scared, chicken? Okay fine, I'll do it on my own."

She hesitates, imagining her mother's face if the French police arrest her for breaking and entering. She is terrified and thrilled by the idea at the same time.

"I'm coming!"

The gate isn't high, and she scrambles over easily. You walk down the gravel driveway together.

"What if there's a dog? An alarm? Cameras? Motion detectors? What if he's armed and pulls a gun on us?"

"Then we'll die without a care in the world, and with honour!"

You lean towards her in the darkness and place your lips gently on hers. You forget about the imminent danger. You kiss in the moonlight. Your breath mingles, your bodies tighten. You reluctantly pull away from each other.

"Come on," you say, locking your fingers in hers.

You head towards the shoebox mansion. There are no lights on inside. A large car is parked in front of the house, crouched there silently like a beetle. There are no vicious dogs on the prowl. A bird brushes past you.

"Why is that swallow flying so low at night?" asks Chiara.

"It's a bat."

She shudders.

You quickly change the subject. "We're going to plunge this slimy rat into the void. He's scared stiff of the dark. This'll calm him down."

"How come?"

"He'll wake up in the pitch black. He'll think he's having a nightmare. Then he'll wish it had been a nightmare," you say, pulling out some small blue tubes from your pocket.

"What's that?" asks Chiara in a concerned voice. "Poison? A hallucinogen? Superglue?"

When you get back to Paris later tonight, you'll surprise Chiara by taking her to see the Eiffel Tower glittering and shining in all its splendour. You'll be there just before one in the morning, at that magical time when it sparkles for ten full minutes. You'll kiss her and say: *This is for you.*

Le Vésinet

The slumlord wakes up, checks that the crown jewels are in
place, stretches, and sniffs the stench of his own body odour.
He hates deodorant, a man should smell like a man. He
asserts his virility, marking his territory with his scent and
yells at anyone who has a problem with it. He also yells at the
people next door who always say hello to him in an attempt
to be neighbourly. He doesn't want to be greeted; he wants
to be feared. He has a lot on his plate today. First, he needs
to raise the rent on the Chatou house where that widow lives
with her son. Second, he needs to terminate the lease of that
old dear in Montesson. Third, he needs to stick some more
immigrants in those crappy houses he owns along the ring
road. Life is a game of Monopoly; you win by buying a hotel
and a house and putting the other players out of business. He
looks up at the ceiling where his digital alarm clock shows the
time and temperature.

He can't bear to sleep in the dark. He operates the remote
control of the electric shutters from his bed. He hears the
reassuring sound of the shutters opening, but outside it's
pitch black still. Surprised, yet not worried, he opens the second curtain. He can't see the sun, or the trees in the garden,
or the familiar lamppost on the other side of the street. He
gets up, stark naked, goes into the next room and opens the
electric shutter there. It's still pitch black outside. He can't
bear it; it drives him instantly mad.

His hands tremble, he gasps for air. He doesn't even think to do the obvious and turn on the light. His first thought is to escape. He instinctively runs to the front door, grabs the key and pushes it into the lock. It won't go in, it resists. He breaks out in a cold sweat and bends down to look through the keyhole; the lock is clogged up with something. He rushes into the kitchen, tries another door lock and encounters the same problem. What's going on? His vision goes blurry. He pinches himself to make sure he's not dreaming. He is a prisoner, locked in the dark. Just like when he was a child, and his father locked him in a tiny toilet, with the light switch on the outside, to punish him. Curled up on the floor, paralyzed by fear, he would imagine he was in a coffin and lay there terrified until his father released him. His mother was too afraid of her husband to intervene.

He resists the temptation to curl up on the floor like he used to. He can't get out; the doors are all jammed. The day hasn't dawned, maybe some president somewhere has pressed the nuclear button. Maybe it's the end of the world? He will die, alone, dried out, mummified, in a four hundred square metre grave. His mother is dead, he didn't even go to the funeral. His father is languishing in a shabby retirement home, where he visits him just for the sadistic pleasure of pushing his wheelchair into the toilet and locking him in. The old man nods, not even giving him the satisfaction of being afraid. He falls asleep, oblivious to his surroundings, his mouth askew, dribble running down his clothes. He leaves him there all afternoon and departs feeling frustrated at his botched punishment.

The slumlord doesn't think to open the fridge for light, or use the torch app on his mobile phone, his brain has seized up. Instead, he howls silently to himself, in a daze, trapped in his home. In his panic, he suddenly realizes that all he has to do to free himself is open one of the windows. He would rather die outside under the stars, than be locked in here. He rushes into the living room and tries to open the window, but it's jammed. It's been so long since he opened a window he has forgotten how to release the latch. Breathless, he grabs a golf club from his brand-new bag, a top-of-the-line driver, gets into position, imagines the ball on his tee at the hole, and plays the most crucial shot of his life.

The invisible ball goes nowhere, but as he follows through the club hits the glass and he dislocates his right shoulder. The security glass doesn't break, it merely cracks. Thieves rarely use golf swings to break in. An idea springs into his mind: the skylight in the bathroom. He rushes to it, his shoulder slumped, his arm dangling against his body. It's night outside here too. In fact, it's night everywhere! The distraught man manages to open the skylight with his left hand, swings it open, climbs onto the toilet, and stands so that his upper body emerges into the night air. His terror subsides. He bursts into wild laughter, despite his pain, because the day has dawned. No atomic bombs have exploded. Night has disappeared and taken its parade of horrors with it.

He doesn't have the strength to pull himself up outside with one arm, but he shouts his relief at a man walking his dog, and a startled passer-by. With his good hand he scratches off the black substance covering the outside of the skylight. Pieces of it get stuck under his fingernails. He sniffs them and tests the blackness with his tongue. Black paint. His windows have been sprayed with black paint. Then he thinks of his clogged door locks and puts two and two together. Some bastard blocked every exit in the house. He has no friends, only enemies, so the list of possible suspects is long.

"I'll get you, you bastard, wherever you are!" he bellows. "I'll blow your face off, I'll destroy your home, I'll gouge your eyes out, you'll regret the day you were born!"

A man taking his little boy to school sees his neighbour emerging from his hideous flat rooftop, naked and yelling a barrage of insanities. He covers his son's ears and eyes and calls the police. A quarter of an hour later, the officers arrive. The man hasn't moved, he's still on the roof, shouting and repeating the same obscenities. The policemen climb up, restrain the exhibitionist, force him outside, wrap him in a blanket and ask the paramedic with them to administer a sedative to calm him down.

The pervert has gone stark raving mad, he sprayed all his windows with black paint. He should be locked up!

Paris, Montmartre

There are no more paint cannisters in Charles' backpack, just the vintage bottle of champagne carefully wrapped in a grey jumper. After admiring the illuminations at the Eiffel Tower, we spent the night in a small hotel in Montmartre, near the famous Amélie Poulain café. When I make love with Charles, I have the same sensation of freedom I had when I was flying along on Pegasus doing the Locmaria post round. I can only describe it as a feeling of total harmony, overwhelming and intense. My love for him is playful and shared, togetherness and joy, moments of complicity and surprises, adventure and upheaval.

Urielle has invited us to have breakfast with her and the kids. We buy twelve mini croissants and twelve mini pains au chocolat. She lives in a sunlit flat on the sixth floor with no lift on avenue Trudaine. It was originally several maids' rooms which have now been converted and joined together.

"The Sacré Coeur is my daymark in the sea of roofs," she says. "A daymark is a nautical term meaning a reference point on land, visible from the ocean, which allows sailors to get their bearings."

I follow her into the kitchen while Charles plays with the little rascals. "Have you taken the metro yet?"

"I tried, but I felt claustrophobic, as if my chest was being crushed. I got off as soon as I could. I switched to those rental bikes, but almost got hit by a bus. Now I walk along the Seine. It takes me longer to get to work, but at least I can breathe."

"Are you going to be okay?"

She sighs. "They won't renew my fixed term contract as I've taken too much sick leave. As soon as one of the twins comes down with something, the other gets it a week later. As a result, I have twice as much time off as the other mums. My boss jokingly said to me that if it weren't for my charming little monkeys, I would be perfect for the job!"

She shakes her head angrily. "My charming little monkeys eat me out of house and home, not to mention their clothes, medicines, food, and heating. And they need a father, too. He sends them emails and beautiful photos from Nepal they have absolutely no interest in. He writes that he will bring them presents back. Sometimes, when they hear a noise in the stair-well, they run to the door thinking it's him. It breaks my heart."

"They are happy, but I can see you're not."

"I can't admit that I made a mistake. I would lose face."

'What does it matter?"

"I would be too ashamed."

"So, you'd rather be proud and unhappy?"

"Hey, girls, do you need the help of three helpful young men?" shouts Charles from the living room.

"Hey, girls!" repeat Nolan and Evan in unison.

We go and join them. The hungry *korrigans* pounce on the pastries.

"I like this sea of rooftops," says Charles. "But it's not a patch on the view from your parents' place in Port-Lay. Do you prefer carbon monoxide to the breath-taking beauty of Brittany?"

"I longed for freedom. Cooped up on an island for twenty years felt like prison."

"I get it," replies Charles with irony. "It's true that you seem very cool and relaxed here. It's not as if you're constantly racing between the crèche, your office, the shops, the baby-sitter, and your flat."

"At least you get to enjoy Paris at the weekend," I say, coming to Urielle's rescue.

She shakes her head sadly. "The City of Light has got an amazing array of museums, clubs and activities for children. I would go if I wasn't so tired all the time, if my little ones let me sleep, if my fridge magically filled itself, if my housework was done, and if I wasn't such a lousy mother."

She lovingly watches the twins wipe their chocolatey hands on the couch.

"Give me the news from Groix. Did you find what you were looking for?"

Charles and I exchange glances.

"I think you should know, my name isn't Gabin."

The twins giggle, delighted with this new game.

"My real name is Charles. Like *Charlie and the Chocolate Factory*. Like the Prince of Wales."

Urielle looks up in astonishment.

"And I'm neither a writer nor Corsican."

"Are you an actor?" she asks, looking for a logical explanation.

"No, I'm a liar."

I place my hand on his.

"You guys are together, I thought as much," says Urielle, delighted. "And you, Chiara? What's your real name? You had us all fooled. Were you guys already together when we met on the boat?"

I set her straight. "No, I told you the truth."

"Did Perig help you?"

I nod.

"So you no longer need Groix then? You took what you came for and now you're leaving?"

She sounds aggrieved. The twins, indifferent to adult strife, chuckle as they fight over the last mini croissant.

"That's typical tourist behaviour. They get off the boat excited, enthusiastic, they soak up the summer sun, marvel at the absence of traffic lights, feast their eyes on the twilight and the raging waves. Then they leave, abandoning us for the winter, offering nothing in return."

"Pegasus told me I'm part of Groix," I say softly.

"Pegasus?"

"The post bike."

Intrigued, the twins crane their necks to hear the rest.

"We're not abandoning anyone," says Charles. "Chiara has an appointment in Rome."

"Are you coming back to Groix afterwards?"

I look at Charles. We haven't discussed it. Urielle said "coming back" as if we were coming home. Where *do* I belong? I don't have to go back to Italy. Urielle left the island in search of freedom; I went there in search of freedom.

"Chiara has finished her job at the post office, she has to hand deliver a letter to her mother. We'll see after that. Can you do me a favour?"

Charles takes the champagne out of his backpack.

"Can you keep this bottle until I return? I can't take it on the plane."

"I'll take good care of it," promises Urielle.

The boys are bickering. They've stuffed themselves with so many pastries they're going to be sick.

"You don't look like a Charles," says Urielle.

"Don't I?"

Gabin-like-the-actor hides his face in his palms, then opens them. He is no longer the same man. His gaze is different. So is his body, strangely. His figure, his demeanour and his attitude have changed.

"My name is Louis, as in Aragon," he says. "I'm a medical student. I'm going to suction you, it's not pleasant I know, but we're going to do it together, gently, okay?"

He inspires confidence, he is a medical professional. And at the same time, he is my boyfriend.

"Impressive," says Urielle under her breath.

Once again, he buries his face in his hands and then reappears. The medical student has been replaced by a fragile and endearing young stranger.

"My name is Charles as in Baudelaire. I am Alice's son and Paul's brother. I live in the Yvelines. One day I will be a writer."

He buries his face in his hands a third time, then reappears as the man I know.

"My name is Charles Blue. I am in love with Chiara. I sailed the seven seas searching for her. For her, I will drop my anchor and pick up my quill."

Urielle smiles.

"My name is Urielle Thunder," she whispers. "I am the *korrigans'* mother and Danielle's sister. My heart got caught up in my ex's fishing nets. I am a Groix islander. I tried to settle in Paris, but I'm not cut out for the speed, the stress and the violence of the city. I want to slow down, live a different life, one that is more profound, more meaningful, and more in tune with the ocean."

"My name is Chiara," I say. "I am the daughter of Livia and of a man whose name is written inside the envelope in my pocket. I am in love with Charles Blue."

Nolan tilts his head when he hears the words "in love". He laughs hesitantly when he catches my eye. Then he does something unusual for such a young boy, he comes up to me, and gently strokes my cheek with his sticky hand. Is this something he saw his father do to his mother, before he left for Nepal? Then he runs off to find his brother.

Elba Island, Tuscany,
twenty-six years earlier

Livia wishes she hadn't come but Viola had been so insistent that she had given in. She is too exhausted to resist. She has hardly eaten since Alessio died three weeks ago. Her parents, who had travelled to Rome for her wedding, came back again for their son-in-law's funeral before setting off for the Basilicata region in the south of Italy, which borders Puglia and Calabria. They wanted to take her with them, but she refused. They've never been close. Ornella, Alessio's mother, is devastated and in shock. Livia has given up alcohol. She had her last glass of Prosecco the day before the accident, when she and Alessio went to the Barberini cinema. For the rest of her life she will hate the actors who starred in that film. Just as she will always hate the delicious coffee she was drinking at Rosati's, when Alessio crossed the road to join her.

The driver of the Vespa got away with mere cuts and grazes. It's so unfair. She knows his name, she read it in the police report. She drove to his apartment block every day for ten days and lay in wait. One night, when he came out and walked down the street, she had a strong urge to press down the accelerator and avenge her husband's death. She imagined the stranger's blood on the yellow stone of the palazzo, his squashed body, his weeping wife at his side, calling for help.

Livia dreamed of doing this, but she didn't have the guts to carry it out. The very next night, she lit a match and threw it at the murderous Vespa he had just brought in from the garage. The thing burst into flames within seconds. It exploded; the tank had been full. People came out of the building, screaming, panicking, shouting at each other. Livia sat still behind the wheel, savouring the scene, until the firemen arrived. She drove home feeling pleased with herself. Dead men tell no tales.

Livia felt bad about going to this party with Viola, it was inappropriate for a widow. She put on the first black clothes that she could lay her hands on. She isn't hungry or thirsty, all she just wants is to join her husband who was snatched away from her so violently. She follows her childhood friend into the brightly lit house where people are dancing, completely oblivious to her tragedy. Suddenly, she sees him! It's as if her whole body is awakening after a long nightmare. Her wedding ring with their initials engraved inside no longer burns her skin, it sparkles.

Livia recognizes his elegant, lithe physique, his broad shoulders, his hair, his nonchalant walk, the way he holds his head. She recognizes the eau de toilette that no other lad of their age would wear. His father used to wear it, so he started wearing it too to please his mother, who had lost her husband to cancer. The mere smell of that fragrance makes her shiver. It's like Alessio is standing there, right in front of her. Her hands reach for him, her skin calls out to his, her body trembles.

She laughs out loud; it was just a bad dream. They are going to embrace, capsize, roll, they have just got married. She won't tell him that she thought he was dead, he would be upset, she will banish it from her mind. Alessio is alive. He is not lying in that horrible box with the golden handles in the

Verano Cemetery. She is not a widow. They have their whole lives ahead of them. She opens her mouth to cry out for joy and let go of her grief. Just as she is about to utter his name, he turns around. The shock is so violent that she nearly collapses in horror. It's not him! He has the same lanky figure, the same hair, the same posture, the same eau de toilette as Alessio. But his eyes are a paler blue. His nose is more rounded. His lips are thinner. He is a total stranger. She feels like the sky has just caved in. It wasn't a nightmare, she didn't dream it, her husband really is dead, and she really is a widow.

In a trance, she walks towards the buffet. She knocks back three glasses of limoncello one after the other, despite not having eaten anything for days. It burns her oesophagus, sets her blood boiling, and makes her dizzy. She leans against the wall to avoid collapsing in the middle of the party. And then she lets go, ready to fall into the chasm that is engulfing her . . .

"Are you alright, miss? Hey? *Tutto bene? Signorina?*"

A strong arm stops her from falling into the abyss. The stranger who looks so much like Alessio helps her to a chair. She breathes in his eau de toilette and closes her eyes.

"You nearly collapsed, *Signorina*. Can you hear me?"

She doesn't reply. He doesn't have the same voice as her husband, the illusion is fading. Now she wants him to go away and stop bothering her. Wants him to stop reminding her that Alessio is not coming back. She opens her eyes again.

"It's okay," she sobs. "Leave me alone."

"You have to eat something. Limoncello is deceptively easy to drink."

"Just leave me in peace."

The stranger moves away. She can breathe now. He turns his back on her. She looks around in vain for Viola. She wants to go back to Rome.

"Here, choose one."

The Alessio lookalike has returned with a plate of chicken liver *crostini* and *lardo di Colonnata*. She reaches out reluctantly and eats one, then two, then three, without saying a word. Just so that he'll stay leaning over her like that. She resents him for inflicting such torture on her, for resembling her dead husband. But she can't help staring at him. She forgets that his eyes are paler, that his nose is bigger, that his lips are thinner.

Suddenly, just as she is about to tell him to take the plate away they play Riccardo Cocciante and his winning song from the San Remo festival. Her heart shatters into a thousand pieces. "*Se stiamo insieme*". If we're together. She puts her hand on the stranger's arm, gets up and leads him to the dance floor. He wraps his arms around her. They dance, bodies locked tightly together. The closing lyrics crush her again. *Mi manchi sai.* I miss you, you know? She freezes, like a puppet whose strings have just been cut. He smiles at her. She buries her face in her young husband's neck. She presses herself against him. She takes his hand and pulls him after her.

He is not accustomed to this. On his Breton island women are not this forward. But she is very beautiful. He wants to talk to her. She silences him with a kiss. He laughs, happily. Livia smiles, reassured. They embrace. They blot out the rest of the world. The sheets smell of lavender.

Rome, twenty-six years earlier and fifteen days later

Viola walks down the stairs of her building with a spring in her step. She slides the key into the lock and opens the letterbox that usually only contains bills. Her heart still thumps when there's one addressed to her coward of a father who preferred to blow his brains out than see her grow up. She is desperate for a letter from the Frenchman she met on Elba a fortnight ago. They danced together the whole night. They are two of a kind, the kind you don't notice, the kind that slip by inconspicuously, neither so beautiful nor so ugly as to leave an impression. Insignificant, average, bland all come to mind. She gave him her address. He was surprised at first by her temerity, then slipped the paper into his jeans pocket.

As a child, she naively imagined that she and Livia had the same chance of happiness. Her illusions were soon crushed. When she met Alessio, for her it was love at first sight. But he only had eyes for Livia. Viola deduced that in the future she would have to choose a less handsome, less seductive man. Someone who matched her.

The other evening, on the island of Elba, she had set her sights on this poor fellow, who was a perfect match for her in terms of averageness. He will write to her and invite her to his island in France. She can already see herself leaving Rome and her mother, leaving the grieving Livia far behind and dancing her life away in Brittany with her fisherman. Beaming, she reaches for the envelope with the French postmark. She unseals it, cuts her index finger on the sharp edge of the paper, and sucks the bead of red blood on her fingertip. She immediately falls in love with the handwriting which slants to the right. She doesn't speak French; he doesn't speak Italian. They danced together until the early hours, he dances like a Celtic god, she's pretty good too. What's more, it's the only thing she does better than Livia.

Viola slips the letter into her pocket and walks to the street corner, so that her mother can't spy on her through the window. She leans against a tree. She sighs with happiness as she reads the first words, written in English. "Dear Viola". Then she is overcome by a wave of nausea. The letter is not from him. The letter is not for her. Once again, her best friend has beaten her to it. She cries out in rage and frustration.

Dear Viola, I am the French guy you and your friend Livia met recently on the island of Elba, in Tuscany. I don't have the address nor the full name of Livia. Can you help me, please? Give this letter to Livia, with my address and my phone number, so that she can call me? Thanks a lot. Take care. Kind regards.

She doesn't even look at the signature. She screws up the letter spluttering with rage. Her English is basic, but she gets the gist of it: the man who wrote this letter is the one who spent the night with Livia. And he wants to see her again. It then strikes her that *her* Frenchie will never write to her. And that men with pale eyes will always fall for Livia. And that she is cursed, doomed to celibacy, to loneliness, to casual affairs, to other women's husbands. That she will never have children. That she will always be second best.

She throws the letter into the bin. Three others follow. They all meet with the same fate. He'll think that Livia doesn't want to see him again. What hurts Viola the most is that her lover probably didn't lose her address. He knowingly chose not to write to her.

Groix Island, twenty-six years earlier and three months later

He closes the empty letterbox under the watchful eye of his brother. The pale-faced Italian woman dressed in black will never reply to him. He must resign himself to this and forget her.

Their father sent them fishing in Italy for six months to toughen them up. He and his brother have just returned to Brittany. He had had trouble leaving Groix. He had taken with him a silver pebble, a sprig of heather and a bottle of his father's eau de toilette, because girls don't like men who smell of fish. He sometimes wonders if that evening really did happen. Maybe the lady in black, the music, the limoncello, the white bed, the red duvet, and the lavender-scented sheets were all just a dream? He had to leave early the next morning before she woke, to pull in the nets. His brother danced the night away with a girl in a yellow dress whom he doesn't wish to see again. He prefers dancing to fishing; their father would be furious if he found out.

He has tried to contact the mysterious goddess, but she isn't interested. He won't set foot in Italy again. He'll fall in love with other women, he'll forge his own path, but he'll never forget the lady in black . . .

Rome, the Verano Cemetery, today

I hail a taxi from Fiumicino Airport. It takes us to the municipal cemetery which spans several hectares. The man who has a one-in-three chance of being my father rests here a few graves away from Marcello Mastroianni, whose daughter is also called Chiara. Alessio Ferrari smiles in the photo that adorns the white marble slab. The following inscription is engraved below: *Giusto é il Signore, perche le giuste opere ha care, X Salmo di Davide.* For the Lord is righteous, he loves righteous deeds, David, Psalm 10.

Dad, you crossed over at the age I am today. Though you weren't there, you still raised me. I was brought up on stories of your childhood, photos of you, *nonna* Ornella's anecdotes, and your love of pasta with chilli and *osso buco*. You were my best friend, my confident and my rock, and you protected me from Livia. What would I have done without you? Despite only talking to you in my head, providing both the questions and answers. Despite you never arguing with me. You protected, supported and guided me. Whatever happens next, the piece of paper in my pocket will never separate us. We're better than that. We're stronger than that.

I came here today to introduce you to the man I love. This time I didn't ask your opinion, I chose him all by myself. What's a father for anyway? To teach his chicks to fly, to push them out of the nest and show them how to flap their wings, otherwise they'll crash to the ground.

Livia didn't keep any of your belongings. Not even a few clothes. I would have loved to roll up the long sleeves of your sweaters on my skinny arms and imagine you in your cashmere. She kept saying that you were hers, and hers alone, because she had the good fortune of meeting you. I appeared after the tragedy in Piazza del Popolo, the blood, the death certificate, the tears. She touched your hands, heard your voice, laughed with you. She even said you bickered sometimes. You never scolded me. You never pronounced my name. I didn't climb on your lap. You didn't teach me how to drive. We never danced together, never had dinner in a restaurant, never enjoyed a glass of Barolo together, never talked politics. I wish I knew why you chose Livia and not Viola. And where you found the strength, after your father's illness, to take *nonna* Ornella around the world. I have never been able to console Livia. It's not my fault, I was just a baby. Someone else's baby, perhaps. An eternal mistake, a living reminder.

Alessio, is there an afterlife? Or just death after death? This is Charles, the man I love. If, by opening this envelope, I discover that you are not my father, it won't change anything between us. Alessio, I'm wearing Gurvan's jacket. Gurvan is Perig's son. I have made more friends in Groix in the space of a few days than I ever have in Rome. What's the point of death? To make room on earth for those who follow? No mathematician can calculate how many of us there would be if no one died. We would fill all the oceans and all the landmasses, squeezed in together like sardines. We would never fit on planet earth. So God makes us play musical chairs.

I climb the mobile stepladder to touch your marble slab, your eternal home, three metres above the ground. Unlimited lease, perpetual concession, no risk you'll disturb the peace. When I was a child, I was afraid of heights. I didn't climb the stepladder and stayed at the bottom looking up at you. I'm no

longer afraid of heights. I stroke your photo with my fingertips. You haven't changed, you've got no wrinkles, you haven't
aged one iota. You have a happy, carefree smile. I'll grow old,
and you'll remain forever young.

The other day Danielle sang "My Heart Belongs to
Daddy", perfectly imitating Marilyn Monroe's smooth sassy
voice. A little girl in her thirties vamping it up. Didier left the
room a little too quickly, his eyes red. "Yes, my heart belongs
to daddy, da, da, da, da, da, da, da, da, daaaady."

Rome, Centro Storico

Our taxi is now heading towards the old historic part of the city. Livia doesn't know that I'm coming, I didn't tell her. Her life is organized like clockwork. At this time of day, she is bound to be at home. I ring the intercom.

"*Chi è?*"

"*Io.*"

She buzzes me in. My stomach doesn't churn. I'm not afraid of her anymore. Now that I'm not alone.

We get out of the lift. Her arms are limp and dangling, as always. I don't offer her my cheek; my right hand is safe in Charles' left hand. She stares at him and realizes that happiness has triumphed, that love is more powerful than despair, that I have changed, and that I won't let her ruin my life anymore.

"*Grazie a dio*! You're here! They found a body on a beach on Groix, I heard on the news last night. I was so scared . . ."

I look at Charles and hope with all my might that it's not him.

"Come along in," she says, backing into the flat.

We sit on the black sofa in the grey-walled living room. I feel like a visitor, even though I grew up here. Livia goes ballistic, forgetting that we are not alone.

"Cheating on your husband is only human. Cheating on a ghost is unforgivable. Do you see, he was no longer there to defend himself, to insult me. I felt bad, I felt dirty."

I don't introduce Charles to her, we skip the niceties and go straight to the crux of the matter.

"Why didn't you ever tell me?"

"You were just a child. And I didn't want to destroy Ornella."

Nonna Ornella had regained a new lease of life when I was born. Knowing that I might not be the daughter of her beloved son would have finished her off.

"Can I get you a coffee?" offers Livia.

"Lovely," answers Charles.

"You look like your father," he whispers, leaning towards me as she leaves the room.

"How do you know?"

"Because you don't look like your mother."

I smile at him.

"I stopped by the bookshop where you're supposed to be working," announces Livia, placing three cups in front of us. "They're furious."

"Marco was too, according to Viola, but it seems that he has consoled himself since," I say.

"So you went to see her before you came here?"

"No, she came to Groix to show me the letter that you had written to her."

"But you refused to read it."

"How do you know?"

"You're my daughter."

Livia drinks her coffee and puts her cup down.

"This is Charles Arag . . . Charles Blue."

I still have trouble with his last name. Livia smiles at him, but her smile doesn't reach her eyes.

"Is this your first time in Rome?"

"We're not here to sightsee," I say softly. "I found the two Frenchmen who were on Elba Island. I got paternity tests sent over from England to find out if I am the daughter of one of them. Their surname is 'Thunder', they are brothers. Do you remember the name of the one you . . . ? Was it Kilian? Or Brendan?"

I omit to mention that the first one has just joined Alessio in heaven.

"We barely spoke. He looked a lot like Alessio."

Nowadays neither of them resembles the magnificent absent hero in the photos.

"I was exhausted, I wasn't sleeping, I wasn't eating. I drank three glasses of limoncello. He reminded me so much of him, even the same eau de toilette, same build, same hair, I thought he had come back, that his death was just a bad dream."

I remember what the drinking buddy in the Triskell had said to Perig.

"He tried to see you again, he wrote to you. Why didn't you reply?"

"I never received anything from him. The letter must have got lost."

The faces of the people I delivered the mail to flash before my eyes as I take the crumpled envelope out of my pocket.

"In any case, these are the DNA test results. I wanted to open them with you."

Livia looks at me wide-eyed. Charles holds his breath. My mother grabs the envelope, opens it, and takes out a sheet of paper folded in half. The paper is thin, almost translucent. She tries to drop the envelope and unfold the sheet of paper to read the results, but she is trembling and gets it the wrong way round. She holds onto the envelope and drops the thin sheet of paper instead.

Don't tell me you had nothing to do with that, Alessio, I won't believe you! I whisper to my father in my head. Just at that moment the wind starts to pick up, and a draught gushes into the flat. The window slams. Livia makes a clumsy attempt to swipe at the sheet of paper, but it slips out of her fingers and flies out of the grey-walled, black-furnished apartment. All three of us rush out onto the narrow balcony, clutch the railing and lean over into the street.

We watch the sheet of paper flutter up into the air, and then do a nosedive. Its journey doesn't end there. It skims the leather seat of a motorbike, and lands on the roof of a Ferrari. It hesitates as the elegant car drives off along the Tiber river. It takes off once again and lands on the upper deck of a double-decker bus full of camera-toting tourists. We watch in horror, speechless, as the bus drives off.

My biological father's identity is on the upper deck of a bus heading towards the Colosseum, speeding past the same red postboxes you see in London where the envelope was posted. The truth is running away from me surrounded by smiling American and Asian tourists who marvel at the ochre and pink buildings. Livia shakes her head in disbelief. Charles puts his arms around me. I am devastated. Even if I call the lab, they won't give me the result on the phone. We will have to write, argue, pay again, wait.

"Your father doesn't know what he's missing," says Charles.

What do I do now? Do I phone the bus company? You think you're clever, Alessio? Are you having a good laugh watching us from your cloud with its bird's eye view of the earth below? Suddenly my quest seems futile, ridiculous, grotesque. What difference will it make if Brendan Thunder is my biological father? I'll be called Chiara Thunder. I will be a full-blooded Groix islander and you can't put a price on that. I'll have a family grave in the cemetery, near the stone woman and child who pray for the lost sailors. I will have mica schist rock in my veins, garnet in my heart, sea in my eyes, and courage in my guts. I'll be able to argue with the neighbours over shared ownership of a threshing floor or a right of way. I will be an islander. I'll have a living father! A junkie half-brother in a madhouse, *not* jail. A half-sister-in-law wearing Louis Vuitton wellies. A soon to be born half-nephew or half-niece. I'll no longer be a foreigner. No longer Roz's adopted goddaughter.

Will Brendan love me? Will Efflam trust me? Will I be able to help him? Maybe he'll be jealous, or he may think I'm just after their money. I'll never be Brendan's real daughter, just a misfit, the product of a dirty secret, the indiscretion of youth, a cruel mistake. I won't necessarily gain the trust of the locals either. I'll be thrust on them, forced on them. You can't make up for lost time, I wasn't born on the island, I didn't go to the school blessed by God or the school run by the Devil. I didn't grow up among them. I'm Italian, and proud of it.

Brendan Thunder is not a sell-out, he is an observer, an informer hidden inside a Trojan horse of a company that links the island to the mainland. He doesn't need me, he has enough on his plate with his son. If I am Brendan's daughter, then Alessio Ferrari has nothing to do with me. Livia cheated on him, betrayed him, let him down. I have no right to him. My best friend risks turning his back on me. *Nonna* Ornella will turn in her grave. I will no longer be worthy of her *penne* or her *osso-buco*. Instead of gaining one father, I will lose three.

What difference will it make if Kilian Thunder turns out to be my biological father? I'll be called Chiara Thunder. I will be a full-blooded Groix islander with a family grave in the cemetery near the stone statues. I'll have watercolour in my veins, a gentle, sensitive nature, sea in my eyes, and courage in my guts. I won't even be able to argue with my new dad. I'll officially hail from the island. I'll have a newly deceased father, and a grave in the cemetery to put flowers on. I'll be an orphan for the second time. I'll inherit the legacy of a sullen recluse with a dodgy leg, a dog named after a philosopher and a filthy dirty kitchen designed to fend off intruders.

Would Kilian even have liked me? I entered his house behind his back, searched his den, uncovered his secret, and violated his trust. Would he have forgiven me? Kilian Thunder was not an outcast; he was a very subtle and sensitive artist. He didn't need me. Aristotle was enough for him. If I am Kilian's daughter, then it means Alessio and *nonna* Ornella are not related to me. Instead of gaining one father, I will lose three.

What difference will it make if Alessio Ferrari turns out to be my biological father? I will remain Chiara Ferrari. I will never be a full-blooded Groix islander. I will have pasta in my veins, grappa in my arteries, the famous Italian movie industry in my DNA, and a penchant for *canzoni d'amore*. I will have a smiling father in a photo frame. I will know for sure that we would have loved each other, and such a waste will break my heart. If I am his daughter, then the Thunders are nothing to me. I will just be like any other tourist or foreigner on the island. I will still be an orphan, that void will not be filled. Instead of gaining one father, I will lose three.

As Livia and Charles look at me aghast, I suddenly realize that the journey mattered to me more than the destination. All roads lead to Rome.

"Well, who cares about the results really?" I say.

Livia hesitates, then her lips curve up in a smile which reaches her sad eyes. Her lifeless body trembles, colour comes back into her cheeks, her ears seem to prick up and her nose wrinkles. Like Sleeping Beauty waking up after a twenty-five-year-long sleep. I don't stop there.

"You're here, I'm here. We are lucky."

"We're here," she agrees.

"*Ho sete*. I'm thirsty," I say softly.

What is a father for? Good question. Parents are not useful, they are merely a necessary part of the deal, whether you are like them or not. We adapt, we rebel, we tear each other's throats out, we love each other. Alessio was my father, my big brother, my imaginary best friend, it was both comforting and heart-wrenching to love him. I'm sick of talking to a man in a photo frame. I want something real, like my man's arms, Perig's pipe, the *korrigans'* mischief, Danielle's songs. I prefer the simplicity of Groix. Life with Charles is both unique and beautiful. I love the thought of emerging from the twisted alleyways of Locmaria and heading for the beach at low tide when the sun makes the sand sparkle. And now I want to drink. I'm thirsty. Not thirsty for limoncello, thirsty for a mother.

"*Mamma, andiamo da Rosati insieme?* Mum, shall we go to the Caffe Rosati?"

Rome, Piazza del Popolo

All the tables on the outside terrace are occupied. Young women drink espresso, Spritz or freshly squeezed orange juice. Their spring dresses expose their legs and their cleavage, they have their lives ahead of them, they are daydreaming of love. Boys with slicked-back hair, mirrored sunglasses and burgeoning beards watch them as they smoke from across the street. Like a boat making its way to a buoy in a regatta, they check that the coast is clear before approaching them. Traffic circulates more smoothly than in Alessio's time, you now have to obtain special permission to drive into the historic part of the city on weekdays.

I'm sat at a table with my mother and Charles. It feels like I've known him since the dawn of time. I now know that he sleeps without pyjamas and on the right side rather than the left. He doesn't put the toothpaste cap on properly. He prefers mustard to ketchup. Meat to fish. Mozart to Bartók. And he loves Éluard and Baudelaire.

Charles reaches over to his backpack, pulls out two packages and hands one to each of us.

"My mother used to teach French," he explains to Livia. "She said that everyone has a book that will change their life. Some find it right away; others spend their whole lives searching for it."

I recognize the logo of the Parisian bookshop he rushed into after our breakfast at Urielle's. My parcel contains

Apollinaire's *Œuvres poétiques* in Alice's favourite edition.
Charles chose the *Bilingual Anthology of Italian Poetry* for
Livia. She runs her fingertips over the bible paper, and
reads out the names of the authors: Leopardi, D'Annun-
zio, Pasolini, Pavese, Pétrarque. She's not sure why he
gave her a gift, but thanks him anyway. She hasn't been
back to this square since I was born. I don't want to traumatize her, just loosen her chains. She opens the book at
random, and stumbles upon Cesare Pavese, the author of
"Death Will Come And Have Your Eyes". Tears stream
down her face. She holds out her arms to me. Can you
hear this, Alessio? Can you see this, Charles? And the rest
of you, do you realize what's happening? My mother is
holding out her arms to me, and for the very first time we
are hugging each other. I discover her smell, the texture of
her skin, the silkiness of her hair. I know the scent of the
men I have slept against, the softness of their torsos, their
broad shoulders, their faces prickly with morning stubble.
These are the only people I have touched as my mother
refused all physical contact with me. All I knew of her was
her sadness and her rejection of happiness. Today, however, we are holding each other tightly, almost crushing
each other with warmth and tenderness. Her body vibrates
on a soft note, a melancholic and fragile soprano, nothing
like the powerful, low, deep notes of Charles' body.

And we stay like that, our hearts thumping, out of breath,
making up for lost time. We rewind, diving back into the
past. We catch up on everything, the calamitous summers
and the painful Christmases. We relive all the birthdays she
erased from the calendar, we blow out the candles of her last
twenty-five cakes on the right day and not the day after, we
swim at Fregene beach, we go to the cinema, concerts, the
opera. We eat ice cream and we visit Venice and Florence,
Pisa and Siena, Genoa and Turin, Bari and Capri, Naples and

Palermo. We sail to the Aeolian Islands together, and it's all so unbelievably tender. Making up for lost time, we fill up our senses, our lungs, our stomachs, and our souls.

We get blisters on our feet from climbing volcanoes, and wrinkles on our fingers from the sea water. We prepare tiramisu and rosemary cakes. We invite friends over for dinner. We sing. We dry our tears. We replace sadness and guilt with joy and happiness. We have found each other; we are mother and daughter once more. We hold each other tightly for ages, rekindling our love. Charles goes for a walk round the square to give us some privacy. Then, very reluctantly, I pull away from Livia.

She has spent half her life broken-hearted and distressed, convinced she was to blame. If it wasn't for her, I would never have discovered this beautiful island and I never would have met Charles. I was searching for a father, instead I found a mother. She was always there but we used to pass each other like ships in the night. It's like we've only just met.

"Will you come and visit us on Groix?" I ask.

Charles smiles. We're going back, it's a no-brainer. Livia hesitates. She has a thousand and one reasons to refuse. She's scared of flying. She gets seasick. Her one-night stand from Brittany never tried to find her again. She doesn't know whether the young, French Alessio lookalike is now fat and balding, or lying six feet under. She has been hiding behind her pain for so many years now, cocooned inside her grief which protected her from the outside world. Breaking out of that shell will be terrifying. She puts her hand on my shoulder, I feel the warmth of her fingers, and this simple gesture speaks a thousand words.

"I'll come, Chiara."

Life suddenly resembles Roz's savoury rosemary cake.

Groix Island, Kermarec

We took a plane from Italy and landed in France. We ditched the green, white and red flag for the blue, white and red one. We traded the green of Louis' trainers for the "Blue" of Charles' name.

Perig and Aziliz are sitting facing the sea at the back of their house. Standfirst is lying on the grass a few metres away from a pheasant that is craning its neck to observe him.

"It's Chiara and Gabin!" shouts Aziliz.

"Chiara and Charles, you mean," says Perig.

They are poles apart. She is tiny, dramatic, and strong, and he is like a crystal dolmen. They support and strengthen each other like buttresses. Charles gently places his backpack on the table and takes out the vintage bottle of Mercier champagne that we picked up at Urielle's before taking the train back to Lorient.

"It's the long stories that make you thirsty."

Aziliz gets up, goes into the house, and returns with four glasses. Suddenly the drowned man found washed up on the beach comes to mind. But Perig and his wife have not changed, they are just as we left them.

"Will you have a drink with us, Aziliz?"

She nods. "I had vowed to never let a drop of alcohol touch my lips until our son returned. You've made me realize that it's time to move on. Perig was convinced we would never see you again. I bet the opposite. I won the right to drink again."

"It's a vintage champagne from my birth year," announces Charles uncorking the bottle. "It has almost no bubbles, it's like wine. Forget about the lack of fizz, concentrate on its aroma, its flavour, the notes."

Aziliz toasts the sea and Gurvan, then takes a sip from her glass and closes her eyes as the alcohol seeps into her taste buds.

"They found the body of a yachtsman who fell off a boat a month ago," says Perig. "Let's drink to those he left behind."

The champagne sparkles at sunset like the Eiffel Tower at one o'clock in the morning. I recognize the sweet taste of candied fruits and the suave bitterness of coffee.

"Let's also drink to Alice Blue and Alessio Ferrari," proposes Charles.

"And Kilian Thunder," I add.

"If you've come back for good, you'll have to move Standfirst," says Perig. "Unless you want to live with him."

Aliziz's eyes are sparkling more than the wine in our glasses. "Standfirst has moved into Gurvan's studio, the old garage where our son used to sleep among his surfboards. I clean it once a month. The spiders are persistent, but I get rid of them," she says.

"You'll have to take the boards, sails, masts, wishbones and other bits of equipment to the Strouilh," Perig tells Charles. "They're open on Thursdays and Sundays."

"Take them where?" he asks.

"The Strouilh. The island's recycling shop. You give them the stuff you want to get rid of and they sell it on. *Strouilh* in local dialect refers to the waste at the bottom of a fishing net."

"Okay, we will," promises Charles.

"Are you sure you don't want to hang on to Gurvan's stuff any longer?" I ask.

"Yes, we are, unless you want to sleep on it, but that would be rather uncomfortable."

Charles comes to the rescue. "Are you offering to rent us the studio?"

"What's the point of making money if it means paying more tax?" grumbles Perig. "This place needs to be heated, maintained, and repainted, you've got your work cut out. Just don't complain about the backwash keeping you awake on stormy nights."

The studio, on the side of the house, has a large bay window through which you can see surfboards stacked on top of a large bed facing the sea.

"There's a shower room at the back and a small kitchen. It's not much to look at, but . . ."

"It's perfect for us," I say.

"We were often asked to rent it out in the summer. We couldn't."

"I'm going to make some money writing for the captain; there's no way we'd accept to live here rent free," says Charles.

"Are you trying to make me angry?" says Perig. "Buy the paint, roll up your sleeves and get to work."

Once inside, we discover a large, cosy, sunny room. It is the opposite of a mausoleum; the bright colours of sails and strapping brighten up the faded walls. You can hear the sea beating against the rocks. Our fingers are locked together.

"What colour do you imagine in here?" Charles asks me.

"Anything but grey, and no dark furniture!"

"Tomorrow we'll go and look at a colour chart at Le Menach."

"The surfboards will make someone happy, even if they're outdated."

"Do you not think it breaks their hearts to get rid of them?" I ask.

"No, it's a weight off their mind."

We join Perig and Aziliz again. We politely hide our joy from them.

"If it doesn't tempt you, we understand," says Aziliz. "Don't feel obliged to take it."

I hug her, so moved that I can't find the words. If Danielle were here, she would sing. I don't sing, I hug instead.

"I'm tired," mumbles Perig. "I'm looking for someone to take over as press correspondent. I won't be easing up just yet, but sometimes I find it hard to keep up. I need someone young who knows how to write and who can help me. The locals know you, Charles."

"It would be an honour," replies Alice Blue's son.

We make a list of everything we need to renovate the studio. We'll borrow Didier's trailer to take the surfboards to the Strouilh.

I help Aziliz carry the glasses to the kitchen.

"We don't want any rent, we owe you!" she whispers. "You've been a godsend to Perig. When you left, he was choked up for the first time since Gurvan died. He's finally coming to terms with his loss."

Perig leads us back to the white gate.

"If Gurvan ever comes back," he whispers, "it's unlikely, but not impossible, life works in strange and wondrous ways, doesn't it? He won't blame me for getting rid of the boards, he'll get new ones, his stuff is out of date."

Groix Island, Port-Lay

We're a bit tipsy as we drive back at a snail's pace around the Lomener bends, convinced that the tiny roads between the houses are too narrow for our car. Fortunately we don't bump into the local police.

Didier, Roz and Danielle have prepared dinner. Roz reads aloud to us from her tablet; it's a text written by the Groix storyteller Lucien Gourong and posted on Anita's website. To save The Family Cinema, he appeals to the "Groix islanders, the exiled Groix islanders, and the neo-Groix islanders transplanted from elsewhere, who have chosen this exceptional, singular island with their hearts, whether residents all year round or holiday homeowners, tourists for a day or a week, or perpetual travellers." I find his words moving and healing. I too belong to this cohort, exiled and haunted by the past. I think back to what Urielle said, about tourists who draw on the island's beauty and leave without giving anything in return. I'm an ingrate, a *triskell* with spirals that rotate anti-clockwise. Charles will write Kerwan's memoirs, documenting the events that take place on the island. He even mentioned writing a novel. But what about me, what is my contribution to the island going to be?

Urielle's personalized ringtone reverberates from Roz's mobile.

"Yes, sweetheart?" she answers anxiously.

Didier freezes. Roz's face relaxes, and her smile reappears. It's the smile from the photos in the living room where she is posing with Didier before Danielle's fall. What are parents for? To pick up the pieces of their injured daughter, and then act as if it were normal for her to express her emotions through song because she can't communicate any other way?

"Urielle and the *korrigans* are coming back to live on the island!" she cries out joyfully after hanging up.

Didier is beaming. Belle barks. Danielle, totally unfazed, sings: "I had finished my trip, and I put my bags down, you came to meet me."

"She is going to help out her cousin, who lets guest rooms all year round, and get involved with the international Island Film Festival which is held every August. She has got her old voice back too!" says Roz elatedly.

"Her old voice?"

"When she used to sing Reggiani, Barbara, Brel and Michel Legrand with her sister, at the island's festivals. They grew up listening to our old vinyls. They were the opening act for the local group Les Renavis."

Danielle launches into another song: "When a fish has a broken heart, it can't drown its sorrows."

"They have a repertoire of sea shanties and covers, you've just had a sneak preview," adds Didier.

Charles and Urielle are both bursting with plans. He will write, she will be in charge of the guest rooms, her sister will sing, the *korrigans* will fly their seagull kites. I am truly happy for them. But I feel like I'm left stranded in the harbour . . .

"Les Renavis will be in concert at Pop's Tavern next weekend," says Didier. "We'll take you if you like. Danielle loves it when they sing 'The island of Groix'."

"Try to get the hell out, she'll get to you, like a woman takes a lover," hums Danielle.

The witches' island has certainly got to me. It has tricked me. I wasn't a daddy's girl before, but now I've become a Franco-Italian-Groix daddy's girl.

Groix Island, Grands Sables beach

Danielle swims whatever the weather. Her father watches over his thirty-year-old daughter as if she were a child. She hasn't had a seizure in years, but she is not supposed to swim alone. I sit down next to Didier. The water is too cold for me, I'm used to the Mediterranean.

Someone is walking towards us, it's Cory.

"Roz told me I would find you here. Marielle and I were talking about you this morning."

I tense up. Did I make a mistake, have I lost or forgotten a letter? Did Kilian complain about me breaking into his house before he died? The official postwoman of the Locmaria round sits down beside me.

"I'm superstitious, Chiara. I didn't tell anyone that my medical procedure on the mainland was actually IVF. And the good news is that I'm pregnant! I don't want to take any risks, so I'm going to stop work until the baby is born. I won't come back until the end of my maternity leave. Would you like to replace me? Marielle agrees."

I stare at Cory, dumbstruck. I won't be left behind. I'll be able to ride my Pegasus again. Cory misinterprets my silence.

"If you're not interested, they can find someone else . . ."

"Yes! *Certo! Voglio!*"

I think of the Neruda poem that Alessio was so fond of. I will not die slowly, I shall live. The sound of my laughter erupts into joyful bursts that ripple across the waves. Danielle emerges from the water and hears the end of my poem. Unfazed, she sings: "For the time that I have left to live, would you stop your drunken life to be able to live with me on your mimosa island."

With the advance that Kerwan paid Charles, he was able to buy two second-hand electric bikes from Régis at Vel'o Vert. I christened mine Morvarc'h, "horse of the sea" in Breton, the black horse that can gallop on water according to local legend. My Morvarc'h is spirited, fast, somewhat scratched, dignified and proud. I scramble onto him.

The horse from the legend blew flames from its nostrils as it carried off Queen Malgven and her lover King Gradlon. My Morvarc'h gallops to my lover to tell him the news. Years ago Livia married Alessio, then met Brendan and Kilian. Today, I too have met someone. Childhood is a distant memory. I have gained an extra day to note on my calendar: my mother's birthday. A memorable day. A loving day. Unwittingly, Livia has given me Groix as her legacy, and it's only a matter of time now before we make up with Viola. Brendan has Efflam and the unborn baby. Kilian had Aristotle and his paintbrushes. The most important thing in life is not to be alone and to love.

Groix Island, village centre

Your name is Charles Blue. You have been to Italy and Brittany. You met Chiara Ferrari on the boat to Groix. There was statistically little chance your paths would ever cross.

It's high noon in the church square. Sitting on the outdoor terrace of Bleu Thé, you savour Gwenola's Far Breton while reading the book that your sweetheart gave you yesterday when you'd finished painting the Kermarec studio in ochre. At the front of Jean d'Ormesson's *Oeuvres*, she had slipped in a card on which she had copied a quote by the author from a Canadian radio show: "If there were no cracks, we wouldn't write. The crack is there. The crack is what makes you write."

You sit there reflecting that if God created the world, he spent longer creating this island than other places. You see Chiara arriving on her new bike and it feels like summer has come, even though it's the middle of spring. She loves her new Pegasus so much that you feel a little jealous of the bike. You can't bear to fall asleep, can't bear to be separated from her even when you dream. Chiara literally stole your heart.

An elderly lady sitting at the next table tells her husband that there is more rain in life than rainbows. You don't agree. Since you met Chiara, your life is one big multicoloured rainbow. You don't notice the passers-by, the merry-go-round, or the church with the life-size tuna fish. All you can see is Chiara. She fills your entire field of vision with her tousled hair, her lips as red as Gurvan's jacket, her teeth as white as sea foam on stormy days, the blue heart-shaped spot in the middle of her chocolate brown right eye.

She raises her hand to greet you and her bracelet catches the light. Mr Bulle didn't lie to you, his dark red gemstones did bring you luck. In the past, garnets were used as abrasives to pare down rough stones. The island has worn away your outer shell and polished your rough edges. The loud-mouthed islanders with their dreamy souls have accepted you. Chiara has revolutionized your life, shaken you up, torn down your barriers, rebuilt your allegiances. The happiness that you didn't believe in has finally found its way to you.

You're going to have her read the synopsis of your first novel. It will be about poems, Alice, the Chatou flea market, the second-hand La Pléiade collection, fantasy, tears, tenderness and dancing. It will also speak of anguish and ulcers, intensive care and ghost writers, revenge and love, warm fresh bread and Far Breton. It will have a stripey jacket, like a sailor.

Chiara eventually found her mother, and you avenged yours. You are now at peace. Every year you, Alice and Paul plant a new flower in the garden at Chatou. Last summer's was a pale blue wisteria. To carry on the tradition, you and Chiara will plant a passion flower in Kermarec.

A car goes past, the driver's window is open and a song by Paolo Conte floats through the air. Your lips want to break out in a smile, your hands want to touch the softness of your lover's body, you finally know that you're in the right place in your life. *It's wonderful, it's wonderful, it's wonderful, I dream of you.*

You have put down your anchor in Chiara's heart and on Groix island.

Groix Island, Rome, Montesson, Chatou, Frankfurt, Venice, 2017.

Kenavo d'an distro. Goodbye and see you soon.

No postboxes were harmed during the writing of this book, good wine was drunk, music was played, letters were posted, laughter filled the air, and rosemary cakes were eaten on the sea front.

Music

"Via con me", Paolo Conte

"Maintenant je sais", performed by Jean Gabin

"L'Italien", performed by Serge Reggiani

"Plaisir d'amour", performed by Tino Rossi

"Musiques celtiques", An Triskell

"Blue Moon", performed by Elvis Presley

"Je t'aimerai", Michel Tonnerre

"La donna é mobile", opera *Rigoletto* by Giuseppe Verdi

"La Bicyclette", performed by Yves Montand

"Le 31 du mois d'août", mariner's song

"Pierre", Barbara

"Rich", Claudio Capéo

"Barbara Furtuna", performed by I Muvrini

"Dirty Old Town", Ewan MacColl

"Me zo ganet e kreiz ar mor", traditional Breton song, music and lyrics by Yann-Ber Kalloc'h and Jef Le Penven

"Sodade", Cesaria Evora

"I Wish I Knew How It Would Feel to Be Free", Nina Simone

"Se stiamo insieme", Riccardo Cocciante

"My Heart Belongs to Daddy", performed by Marilyn Monroe

"Ma plus belle histoire d'amour", Barbara

"La Complainte de la Bernique", Les Renavis

"L'île de Groix", Gilles Servat

"L'Île aux mimosas", Barbara

Savoury rosemary cake recipe by Brigitte de Lomener

3 eggs
150 g flour
110 g sugar
125 g salted butter (this is Brittany!)
225 g raisins and candied peel
125 g hazelnuts, almonds or walnuts
One tablespoon of fresh rosemary
Vanilla extract (one capful or one sachet)
Baking powder (half a sachet)
A pinch of salt

Preheat the oven to 180°C (thermostat 6).
Soften the salted butter.

Mix the flour, sugar, yeast and salt. Add the butter in pieces, then whisk by hand or with an electric whisk.

Add the eggs, vanilla, rosemary, raisins, candied peel, hazelnuts, almonds or walnuts.

Pour into a cake tin, put in the oven and cook for 15 minutes at 180°C (thermostat 6), then 50 minutes at 110°C (thermostat 3-4).

It tastes even better if the rosemary is fresh from the garden.

Acknowledgments

My heartfelt thanks go to Héloïse d'Ormesson and Gilles Cohen-Solal for their faith in me and their friendship, to Juliette Cohen-Solal, Valentine Barbini, Rebecca Benhamou, Roxane Defer, Charlotte Nocitau, and to the very talented Anne-Marie Bourgeois, it is always a tremendous pleasure and pure joy working with you. Thank you to Véronique Cardi, Audrey Petit, Sylvie Navellou, Anne Bouissy and Bénédicte Beaujouan, as well as the entire Livre de Poche team, for embarking on this amazing adventure with me.

Thank you on *Enez Groe* to William Duviard and his Rouquin Marteau workshop, to Françoise Faraud, Marielle Tonnerre, Jo Le Port, Guy Tonnerre, Joseph Gallo, Lucien Gourong, Loïc Le Maréchal, Jean-Pierre and Monique Poupée, Pat and Mimi Sacaze, Hugues and Laurence Sidersky, and all my friends from the 7 Gang. With a thought for the young Canadian, soon to be the island's new butcher, who was neither Canadian nor a butcher after all . . .

Special thanks to the booksellers, and particularly Lydie Zannini and Nathalie Couderc, and a smile for Gilles Tranchant, Sandrine Dantard and Dominique Durand.

Thank you to the sales team who bring my words to the booksellers, to the bloggers who keep them moving on their websites, and to you, dear readers, who have embarked on this Breton journey with me.

A warm thank you to Anne Goscinny, Grégoire Delacourt, Baptiste Beaulieu and Sorj Chalandon. I'm sure you have already read their books, but if not what are you waiting for?!

Thank you to my mother, a truly fine lady.

Unconditional thanks to Vincent Rouberol, Anne de Jenlis, Renata Parisi, Yveline Kuhlmey, Sylvie Overnoy, Nausicaa Meyer, Christine Soler, Catherine Ritchie, Catherine Ferracci, Isabelle and Nadia Preuvot, François Boulet, Guy Lebeau, Mathilde Pouliot, Silvia Gatti, Didier de Haut de Sigy and Christelle Bernasconi.

And to my cocker spaniel Uriel.

Thank you to Christophe Bonnefond, head winemaker at Maison Mercier, and to my cousin Emmanuel Mercier.

Thank you to Sylvie Billot, Marie-Sophie Nielly, Christine Lemonnier, Marylou Déranlot and Didier Piquot, who helped me move house without going as mad as a hatter.

In loving memory of Gus Robins.

In loving memory of Évelyne de Jenlis.

In loving memory of Jean d'Ormesson.

Hugues Ternon, Alberte Bartoli, I miss you both dreadfully.

Papa, if your heart hadn't given up so soon, I wouldn't have gone into medicine to save other people's fathers. A colleague would have written Marguerite Duras' death certificate. You and Maman would have come to see me on Groix Island. You would have roamed the countryside with your walking stick. But you are not here. So once again, I had to give myself an imaginary papa. I am and always will be a daddy's girl.

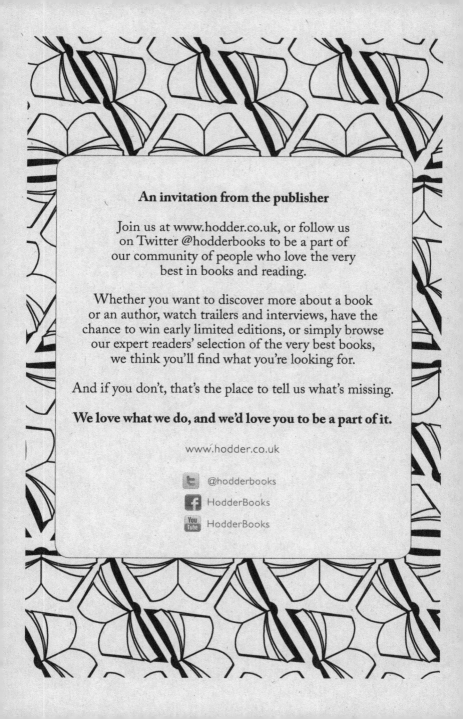